PETER

THEY NEVER SAY WHEN

REGINALD Evelyn Peter Southouse Cheyney (1896-1951) was
born in Whitechapel in the East End of London. After serving
as a lieutenant during the First World War, he worked as
a police reporter and freelance investigator until he found
success with his first Lemmy Caution novel. In his lifetime
Cheyney was a prolific and wildly successful author, selling, in
1946 alone, over 1.5 million copies of his books. His work was
also enormously popular in France, and inspired Jean-Luc
Godard's character of the same name in his dystopian sci-fi
film *Alphaville*. The master of British noir, in Lemmy Caution
Peter Cheyney created the blueprint for the tough-talking,
hard-drinking pulp fiction detective.

PETER CHEYNEY

THEY NEVER SAY WHEN

DEAN STREET PRESS

Published by Dean Street Press 2022

All Rights Reserved

First published in 1944

Cover by DSP

ISBN 978 1 915014 15 3

www.deanstreetpress.co.uk

'In this ladies differ
Essentially from men,
For they seldom say yes
And they never say when!'

CHAPTER ONE
RUSTIC INTERLUDE

THE Crescent & Star, set a quarter of a mile from the main highway, was reached by a winding leafy lane that promised adventure at each turn. The inn – an antique Manor House – small, compact; endowed with the peculiar atmospherics which some old houses possess – stood fifty yards off the lane at the end of a narrow carriage drive. At the back of the house, shrubs, bushes and gorse grew thickly. The gardens in front of it, untended through scarcity of labour, added a touch of mysterious wildness to a spot already amply endowed with beauty. Great untended rhododendron bushes flanked the driveway, many of them so overgrown that a car must push its way through their thick branches.

Not many people knew of The Crescent & Star. Those who did were the more happy. For Mrs Melander, the hostess, was a lady of a certain charm, acumen and versatility. Sometimes the inn was full, but often, as just now, it was empty except for two guests. On such occasions Mrs Melander – who, as has been suggested, was a woman of discernment – and her two daughters Suzanne and Emilienne, provided adequate if not delightful company.

It was raining. It had rained for six hours unceasingly. Dark clouds turned the August evening prematurely into something like night. The rhododendron bushes dripped. An antiquated owl, denizen of one of the trees in the wood near the inn, hooted dolorously as if he had made up his mind to contribute something to the sombre atmosphere which enshrouded him. Rivulets of rain ran from the gutterspouts and splashed into the narrow stone courtyard at the side of the hotel in miniature cascades.

Windemere Nikolls came unsteadily through the French windows at the side of the house on to the verandah. He stood swaying a little, looking with glassy eyes towards the wood. Nikolls was cockeyed. He was wondering whether he was *really* hearing the owl.

He was of middle height, broad-shouldered and big. He ran a little to stomach. He was one of those men whose trousers' waistband seems always a trifle too tight. He moved lightly but unsteadily along the verandah, round its continuation to the back, where at the centre it was bisected by ten wooden steps leading down to the lawn.

Suzanne Melander was sitting on the top step protected by the verandah awning, her shapely chin cupped in one hand. She looked at Nikolls sideways. She said:

'Well, how is he?'

Nikolls leaned against the wooden pillar that supported the verandah awning. He yawned ponderously. He said:

'Babe, I reckon you're in love with that guy.'

She looked towards the wood. She said coolly: 'Well, supposing I said I was! What then, Mr Nikolls?'

Nikolls said: 'I wouldn't say a thing. But it just gets me beat, that's all. Why everybody falls for him like they do I don't know.'

She smiled amiably. She said: 'You mean when there are fine specimens of manhood like you about?'

Nikolls hiccoughed a little. He said: 'Listen, what's the matter with me? I reckon I'm a right sorta guy.' He gazed reminiscently towards the damp woods. 'When I was a kid of sixteen,' he said, 'out in Monkton, Ontario, some old dame read my hand. She was a palmist or somethin'. She took one look an' she said: "You know what I can see in your hand?" I told her no – that's what I was payin' her for. She said: "You got women in your hand." '

He felt in his coat pocket; produced a packet of Lucky Strikes; extracted one; lit it. She threw him another look.

'And had you?' she said.

Nikolls went on: 'I don't like the sorta way you say that. Maybe you think I'm no Casanova, but believe me, baby, I've had my moments.'

'They must have been very nice for you,' she said.

'All right . . . all right . . . !' said Nikolls. 'I get it. You're sittin' there lookin' at the woods, restin' your chin on your hands an' thinkin' about the big boy upstairs. I know all about it. Just because he kissed you outside the buttery last night you're gettin' ideas, hey? Look, if that guy had a dollar for every woman he'd necked he could buy up Rockefeller about forty times over and not even notice the difference in his pass-book.'

Suzanne said: 'You're quite wrong, Mr Nikolls.' Her expression was demure. 'I was merely thinking that Mr Callaghan has rather a way with him. In spite of oneself one is attracted. He has definitely a technique.'

'Yeah,' said Nikolls. 'So you've discovered that too.'

She asked: 'Could I have one of your cigarettes?'

Nikolls produced the packet; gave her a cigarette; lit it. He sat down on the step beside her.

She said: 'You know the telephone's been ringing the whole evening, don't you? It stopped just before dinner; then it started again.'

Nikolls said: 'Well, why don't somebody answer it?'

She said: 'We've only two maids. One of them is off duty; the other one's in the village seeing her Ma who's ill. There are no guests here except Mr Callaghan and yourself at the moment, and anyhow you know *who* is ringing. I answered the phone three times this afternoon. It's Miss Thompson from Mr Callaghan's office. She says she wants him urgently and she's *very* annoyed.'

Nikolls grinned. 'I bet she is,' he said. 'I can just see her. I've got a picture of that baby.'

She drew on her cigarette. She said: 'I take it that Miss Thompson is Mr Callaghan's confidential secretary?'

Nikolls said: 'You take it right. You hit it right on the nose first time, Gorgeous.'

She said diffidently: 'I suppose she's one of the very efficient, prim, bespectacled type?'

Nikolls said: 'Come again, Suzanne. She ain't. I could write an ode to that baby. She's got one of them figures – you know, the sort of thing you think about for no reason at all. She's very easy on the eyes. She's got a graceful walk an' a nice voice. She's got red hair an' green eyes an' a whole lot of intelligence.'

Suzanne Melander sighed. There was a touch of annoyance in the sigh. She said:

'Quite a paragon. We girls in the country trying to run inns miss a lot of fun, I should think.'

Nikolls grinned. 'You ought to be confidential secretaries to private detectives like Slim.'

She said: 'It might have its points.'

Nikolls said: 'I'd like it. Maybe it'd be good if there was a little bit of competition in the office.'

She said: 'I see. It's like that! Is Miss Thompson an admirer of Mr Callaghan's – I mean outside the normal admiration which a secretary sometimes has for her employer?'

Nikolls said: 'If you mean is Effie struck on him, the answer is yes. She's nuts about that mug. That's what burns me up.'

She asked coolly: 'Why?'

Nikolls said: 'Look, I'm a big kind-hearted guy and I got brains. I'm one of those clever sorta detectives, see? I reason things out. I could tell you stories about that guy that'd make your hair curl.'

She said: 'I bet!'

She stubbed out her cigarette on the top step; threw it into a nearby rhododendron bush.

Nikolls said: 'What's on your mind, Gorgeous?'

She said: 'Nothing . . . much! I was wondering. I was wondering when Mr Callaghan is going to decide to stay sober for a little while.'

Nikolls said: 'Don't you worry about that. He gets that way. We just finished a big case, see? We pulled it off. We won one of the biggest cheques we've ever made in this business.'

She said: 'Of course he's *very* clever, isn't he?'

'Yeah,' said Nikolls. 'He's clever enough an' he's got me behind him.'

She said: 'Yes, I'd forgotten that.'

'Well, he's sorta lettin' down his hair,' said Nikolls. 'He's relaxin'. I don't mind tellin' you this was a helluva case. Anyway we cracked it. So he thinks it's indicated that we come down here, stick around and do a little drinkin'. He'll get tired of it in a minute.'

Somewhere in the house the telephone bell began to jangle. It went on and on.

Nikolls said: 'Don't that mug at the local exchange ever get tired of ringin' that telephone bell?'

She said: 'No, they just keep on. Sometimes we're on the other side of the house. They do it out of kindness.'

Nikolls said: 'Look, baby, somebody ought to answer that telephone, and it's a helluva long way away. Who's it goin' to be – me or you?'

She said: 'It's not going to be me. I'm off duty. It's going to be you.'

Nikolls sighed. He said: 'I'm sorry for that, and not for the reason you're thinkin' of either. I'll go take that call with pleasure, but I'm disappointed. I wanted you to go.'

She asked: 'Why?'

Nikolls said: 'Because I like to see you walk. You got something. You don't walk – you sorta float along, with that little graceful sway – you know what I mean – that some dames would give a million pounds for. I could just sit around all day an' watch you walkin' about. I like the way you put your feet on the ground. You wear nice shoes an' you got pretty ankles. Maybe I didn't tell you, but I go for ankles in a very, very big way. They're a sorta hobby of mine. I reckon when you walk you look like some sort of goddess. I think you're terrific.'

She sighed. She said: 'Oh, well, now I suppose I'll *have* to answer the telephone!'

Nikolls grinned. He lit another cigarette.

She got up; walked slowly along the balcony; turned the corner. She was a slim, graceful thing. The telephone bell stopped. She came back; sat down again. She said:

'It would seem that Miss Thompson's hung up. Or else the exchange have got tired of keeping the plug in.'

Nikolls said: 'What does it matter? There's a fate that looks after these things. Maybe if you'd answered that telephone call, all sorts of things woulda happened. But you didn't get there in time so we stay here and look at the rain.' He sighed heavily. 'It reminds me of a Russian Countess I used to know.'

She pretended to yawn. She asked: 'Was she beautiful?'

'Was she beautiful!' said Nikolls. 'That woman was indescribable.'

She said: 'She was mad about you, wasn't she?'

'How did you know?' said Nikolls.

She said: 'During the last four days I've heard that story about the Russian Countess at least six times, and you've told me that one about the strawberry blonde from Oklahoma eleven times. I'm beginning to feel quite familiar with your conquests, Mr Nikolls.'

He said: 'Look, why don't you call me Windy?'

She looked at him along her eyes. She said: 'That is a most sensible request. I will. The name suits you, Windy, dear.'

Nikolls scratched his head. He said nothing.

Effie Thompson opened the door of her sitting-room in Knightsbridge; slammed it behind her; threw her handbag into one corner, her hat on the table. She was white with rage. She stood in the centre of the floor, her hands were clasped behind her back.

She said: 'Damn . . . damn . . . damn . . . !'

She walked to the mantelpiece; took a cigarette out of a box, lit it petulantly; went to the kitchen; put the kettle on. She came back to the sitting-room.

She was of middle height – attractive figure. Her clothes hung on her in the way they should. She wore a neat black coat and skirt, a cream silk shirt. Her red hair was a superb foil for her milk-white complexion.

The telephone rang. She looked at it for a moment angrily. Then she walked across the room and jerked off the receiver. It was Wilkie, the night porter at the Berkeley Square block where Callaghan's offices and flat were housed.

He said: 'Sorry to bother you, Miss Thompson, but the phone's been going like blazes. It's your main line that you put through to my office before you left.'

She said: 'I see, Wilkie. It is still Mrs Denys?'

'Yes,' said Wilkie, 'it's still her. She's pretty worried about something too. She seems to want Mr Callaghan pretty badly.'

Effie said: 'I'll try to get him again from here in a few minutes. When she comes through next time tell her I'm trying to reach him from my flat. If I do I'll call her back.'

Wilkie said: 'All right, Miss Thompson. I'll tell her. Oh, there's another thing – a messenger came round from the bank just after you left. He ought to have been round earlier but something hung him up. He's got a note marked "Urgent." '

'I see,' she said. 'Look, Wilkie, would you mind - tearing the note open and reading it over to me?'

He said: 'Righto, Miss Thompson, hang on.' She heard the sound of the envelope being torn. He came on again. He said: 'The note says this: "The Manager presents his compliments to Mr Callaghan, and regrets to inform him that the cheque for four thousand pounds paid into the account two days ago has been returned marked 'R.D.' Cheque enclosed." '

Effie said: 'I see.' She began to smile. It was a wicked little smile. She said: 'Well, perhaps I'll get an answer now. Good night, Wilkie.' She hung up.

She stood looking at the instrument for a moment; then she said: 'I *ought* to try to ring again but I'm not going to. I'm going to have two cups of tea, two cigarettes and a warm bath. And then perhaps one of you will be sober enough to answer that telephone.'

She flounced out of the room.

The rain had stopped. From behind a rift in the clouds over the hills the sun came through.

Nikolls said: 'Say, look at that rainbow. Now, that's what I call a beauty. You know, Suzanne, I got a developed sense of beauty.'

She said: 'What does that mean?'

He said: 'Well, it means when I see that rainbow I think of you.'

She said: 'Now, I'll tell one.' The telephone began to ring again. She said: 'Somebody ought to answer that telephone and somebody ought to do it quickly, so I'd better go. That'll give you another treat, won't it?'

Nikolls said: 'Go on, honey. The exercise will do you good.'

She got up; tripped quickly along the verandah round into the house. She went through the French windows into the dining-room, across it into the hallway; into the office on the other side of the hallway. She picked up the telephone. The girl at the exchange said:

'You've been a long time, haven't you, Miss Melander?'

'Yes, we've been busy.'

'Hold on,' said the exchange. 'London wants you.'

Effie Thompson's voice – prim and demure – came through. 'Is that The Crescent & Star? Is it possible now to speak to Mr Callaghan or Mr Nikolls? Or are they still indisposed?'

Suzanne said: 'This is Miss Melander, the proprietor's daughter. Would that be Miss Thompson?'

Effie said: 'Yes, it would.'

Suzanne said: 'I've been hearing so much about you, and you have such a delightful voice, I can almost visualize you.'

Effie said: 'That must be very nice for you. Should I be very curious if I asked why you're so interested? I suppose Mr Nikolls has been talking to you?'

Suzanne said: 'Yes, he's an interesting man, isn't he?'

'Very interesting. Of course you're not at all interested in Mr Callaghan are you? That wouldn't be the reason for your curiosity?'

Suzanne said: 'Well, Miss Thompson, I hope I haven't said anything to annoy you. We all think Mr Callaghan is most charming.'

Effie said: 'Well, it seems that you know. Do you think you can get either Mr Callaghan or Mr Nikolls to come to the telephone?'

Suzanne said: 'I think it might almost be impossible. They're having a holiday. They don't seem very keen on answering telephones, especially Mr Callaghan. Mr Callaghan is indisposed.'

Effie said: 'You mean Mr Callaghan is drunk?'

Suzanne said diffidently: 'Well, I think he *is* a trifle high.'

Effie said: 'How is Mr Nikolls?'

'Mr Nikolls is *very* well,' said Suzanne. 'We've been sitting on the back porch talking about the weather and Mr Callaghan.'

Effie said: 'All right. That must have been very delightful for you. In the meantime I've been ringing The Crescent & Star from the office and my home since five o'clock this afternoon; and nobody has taken the slightest notice. So would you please go and tell Mr Nikolls to tell Mr Callaghan, no matter what state he may be in, that the cheque for four thousand pounds that went into the bank two days ago has been returned marked "R.D." '

Suzanne said: 'Oh dear! I'll tell Mr Nikolls at once. That's terrible, isn't it?'

Effie said: 'I'll hold on. And it isn't *so* terrible, Miss Melander. You needn't worry about your bill anyway. In any event I expect Mr Callaghan would find *some* means of paying it.' Her voice was caustic.

Suzanne gurgled happily. She said: 'What a *charming* idea, Miss Thompson. I'm so sorry if you feel neglected. Will you hold on?'

Nikolls was at the bottom of the verandah steps throwing stones at a large frog in the lily pond. He said to her as she came down the steps:

'You know that frog is sorta like me – nothin' disturbs the fat slob. I got him a direct hit right on the snitch a minute ago, but he just sorta grinned at me.'

She said: 'That's Miss Thompson of your office on the telephone. She sounds awfully terse. I think she's annoyed about something. She asked me to tell you that the cheque for four thousand pounds which was paid into the bank two days ago has been returned marked "R.D." '

Nikolls threw his cigarette end into the water. He said: 'Jeez! Can you beat that one? Stick around, Suzanne, an' consider the weather till I get back. This is gonna be good.'

He went up the steps to the house.

Suzanne sat down on the bottom step and began to throw little stones at the frog. He had an odd lugubrious expression, she thought – not unlike Nikolls.

She began to think about Nikolls . . . and Callaghan. She thought they were fun. Especially Mr Callaghan. She liked Mr Callaghan, she thought Mr Callaghan had something. When he kissed you he did it in a remote and impersonal sort of manner – almost as if he were thinking of something else at the time. Perhaps he was! She felt mildly shocked. She made a mental note to ask him about this.

But it was fun having them at The Crescent & Star. It made the place feel sort of adventurous . . . and rather mysterious. Mr Nikolls . . . Windy . . . told the most impossible stories about his amazing adventures. And Mr Callaghan said very little. But a lot went on in his head. Definitely a great deal. Suzanne sighed a little. She wished that she were Miss Thompson and worked for Callaghan Investigations. She thought life might be amusing. She sighed a little more.

Inside the house Nikolls walked slowly to the deserted hotel office. He picked up the telephone.

He said: 'Hello, Delightful. What's cookin' around there?'

Effie Thompson said: 'Mr Nikolls? Thank you for coming to the telephone *so* quickly. It was kind of you.' Her voice was like ice.

Nikolls said, with a grin: 'I'd do anything for you, babe. It's just too bad about that cheque, hey?'

'Have you told Mr Callaghan?' she asked.

'Nope,' said Nikolls. 'The boy's what they call unapproachable right now. He's just comin' outa one of the finest hangovers on record. I reckon that when I tell him about that cheque bouncin' he's gonna blow up.'

She said: 'You might tell Mr Callaghan that I'm supposed to finish at six o'clock at the office. When you went away you were supposed to be back in four days. That was three weeks ago. Most evenings I've left at about nine . . .'

Nikolls said: 'Babe, you're wonderful. It's marvellous what a dame will do when she's struck on her boss, ain't it? I knew a sugar once in Arkansas –'

'I don't want to hear about her,' said Effie, 'I'm not stuck on my boss – as you call it. And I wish you wouldn't call me "babe". I don't like it.'

Nikolls sighed. He said: 'O.K. . . . babe.'

A strangled note came over the line. Nikolls grinned happily. She said:

'When Mr Callaghan is sufficiently sober to listen, you might tell him that a Mrs Denys has been trying to get him all the afternoon and evening. She wants to consult him. She says it's terribly important.'

'Yeah?' said Nikolls. He considered for a moment. 'Maybe we're gonna need some business after that rubber cheque.' he said. 'D'you know anything about this Denys baby?'

'I know nothing except that she wants to see Mr Callaghan and that she says money is no object. She says she's prepared to make *any* appointment to suit his convenience. I think she's a little scared about something.'

'You don't say,' said Nikolls. 'What does she sound like?'

'If you're talking about her voice, I would say it was a cultured voice. If her looks are as good as her voice even Mr Callaghan might be interested . . .'

Nikolls came to a conclusion. He said: 'Look, Effie, Slim's gonna be goddam difficult. He's in one of them moods, see? He's been tearin' this place open . . . kissin' all the daughters, an' generally makin' a lot of nonsense . . . you know . . .'

She said: 'I know . . .'

Nikolls went on: 'I got an idea. When this Denys dame comes through again you tell her to go around to the office. Go back there an' see her. Sorta size her up, see? If she looks O.K. send her down here. If she ain't got a car, ring Hyde an' tell him to drive her down . . .'

'She has a car,' said Effie. 'She said so.'

'O.K.,' said Nikolls. 'Well, you see her an' get the strength. See? If she looks O.K. you tell her to come down here, an' give me a tinkle when she's gonna make this dump.'

She said: 'Very well . . . but I think you've got a nerve.'

Nikolls said: 'Do your stuff, honey. Tell me somethin'. What're you wearin', Effie?'

She said: 'I'm wearing a black coat and skirt and a cream silk shirt if you *must* know. Why?'

Nikolls said in a dreamy voice: 'I was just tryin' to visualize you, Effie. You're my dream girl an' you got the finest hip-line an' ankles I ever met up with. Now I know just how you look I can sleep easy . . .'

She said: 'One of these fine days I'm going to throw something at you. Incidentally, my hip-line is none of your business . . .'

'You're tellin' me,' said Nikolls. 'Your hip-line is *nobody's* business. Listen, Effie . . . I remember some dame in San Louis Potosi . . .'

He heard her replace the receiver.

Nikolls hung up. He stood, for a moment, looking at the inanimate telephone; then, with a grin, he walked out of the office, across the oak-panelled hallway, and up the old-fashioned, curving staircase.

Callaghan was lying on the bed, his arms outstretched. He was wearing the legs of a pair of pale grey crepe-de-chine pyjamas, patterned with black *fleur-de-lys*. His head was turned sideways on the pillow. His breathing was almost stertorous.

His face was long, surmounted by an unruly mass of wavy black hair. The line from the ear to the apex of the jawbone would have inspired a portrait painter. The nostrils were sensitive. His shoulders were broad and tapered to a narrow hipline.

Nikolls stood by the side of the bed looking down at him; then he went to the window and drew the heavy velvet curtains. The evening sunlight came into the room. Callaghan stirred a little; muttered something under his breath. Nikolls went into the bathroom. He came back with a glass of seltzer water in one hand, an empty tooth glass in the other. He went to the dressing-table, on which stood a bottle of whisky; poured four fingers into the tooth glass. He went back to the bed. Placing one of the glasses on the flat top of the bottom bed-post, he pushed one of Callaghan's legs on to the floor. He picked up the glass.

He said: 'Hey, Slim! That Swayle cheque's bounced. What d'you know about that?'

Callaghan opened a baleful eye. He yawned. He opened the other eye and regarded Nikolls vindictively. Nikolls held out the two glasses.

'Which is it goin' to be?' he said. 'Seltzer or the hair of the dog?'

Callaghan took the whisky. He swallowed it; grimaced. He put his hands behind his head and lay looking at the ceiling with eyes that still blinked at the unaccustomed daylight.

He said: 'What did you say?'

Nikolls said: 'Effie's been tryin' to get one of us most of the afternoon. She's pretty steamed up – that one. Nobody took any notice of her.'

Callaghan said: 'Why not? What were *you* doing?'

Nikolls said: 'Oh, I was discussin' things generally with Suzanne around the back.'

Callaghan said: 'I see. So the Swayle cheque's come back.' He raised his head from the pillow; swung his other foot to the floor; sat on the edge of the bed running his fingers through his hair.

Nikolls grinned. He said: 'I thought maybe that'd please you.'

Callaghan muttered: 'I'm going to do something to Swayle for this.'

'Yeah,' said Nikolls. 'It's not so good. An' after what we did for him. Are you gonna do anything about it?'

Callaghan regarded him malevolently. He said: 'Do I look as if I'm going to do anything about it?' He rubbed his eyes with his knuckles. 'Turn on a bath,' he said, 'and give me a little more whisky. And you might tell one of those Melander girls to bring some coffee up. After that get through to Grayson. Tell him to get in touch with Effie and get that stumer cheque from her and issue a writ against Swayle.'

'O.K.,' said Nikolls. He went into the bathroom.

Callaghan got up. He walked across the bedroom and stood looking out of the window towards the woods at the back of the house. After a moment he went to the dressing-table; picked up a cigarette, lit it, grimaced, threw it in the fireplace. He got the tooth glass; drank another three fingers of whisky. He began to feel a little better.

He put on a dressing-gown that matched the pyjamas and began to walk up and down the bedroom. He walked with the controlled anger of a caged tiger.

Nikolls came out of the bathroom. He said: 'I put a coupla pounds of soda in your bath. They tell me it's a very good thing.'

Callaghan asked: 'For what?'

'For whisky,' said Nikolls. 'I thought maybe you'd want to do a little thinkin'.'

Callaghan said: 'What do I want to think about?'

Nikolls said: 'I wouldn't know.' He went out of the room.

Callaghan was still walking up and down when Suzanne Melander knocked on the door. She came in with the coffee.

She said: 'Good evening, Mr Callaghan. I hope I find you well.'

Callaghan took the coffee. He said: 'I'm very well, thank you, Suzanne.'

She said: 'Please tell me something. Do you ever kiss anybody and while you're kissing them you find yourself thinking of something else?'

Callaghan sat on the bed and sipped coffee. He looked at her darkly. He said: 'When I'm kissing who?'

Suzanne pleated her skirt with two fingers. She said demurely: 'Well. . . *me*, for instance.'

Callaghan sipped some more coffee. He said: 'I wouldn't know. Did I ever kiss you at any time?' He smiled at her.

Suzanne swore mildly under her breath. She thought Well, my girl, you asked for it and you got it.

Callaghan looked at her sideways. He smiled pleasantly. He said: 'Suzanne, would you do something for me?'

She said: 'Of course, Mr Callaghan.'

Callaghan said: 'Just close the door very quietly . . . from the outside . . . there's a good girl . . .'

Suzanne gasped a little. She went away. Outside, in the corridor, she said one or two very trenchant things about Mr Callaghan. Then she went downstairs.

As she reached the bottom of the staircase, the telephone bell began to ring. She started to walk towards the office. Nikolls came from the dining-room; got there first. He said as he passed her in the hallway:

'It's all right, honey. This is for me.'

It was Effie Thompson. She said: 'Mr Nikolls, I'm speaking from the office. Mrs Denys has just gone. She seems an extremely responsible person. I should say she has money. She's prepared to pay Mr Callaghan a retainer of a thousand pounds if he'll look after the business she wants him to.'

'Nice work, Effie,' said Nikolls. 'What did you tell her?'

She said: 'I told her what you said. She's on her way down now. She ought to be with you in about an hour.'

Nikolls said: 'That ought to be fun. O.K., Effie.'

She asked: 'How did Mr Callaghan like hearing about the Swayle cheque?'

Nikolls said: 'It did the trick. He's up. He's taking an interest in life. First thing in the morning ring through to Grayson; send him that cheque round and tell him to issue a writ against Swayle. You got that?'

She said: 'Yes, I've got that.' She paused; then: 'By the way, does Mr Callaghan know Mrs Denys is coming down?'

Nikolls grinned. He said: 'No, I didn't tell him. I thought he might like a pleasant little surprise.'

She said: 'I hope you're right. Anyhow, as far as looks are concerned his surprise at seeing Mrs Denys should be pleasant enough.'

'You don't say!' said Nikolls. 'So it's like that! She's a looker, hey?'

'Yes, Mr Nikolls,' said Effie. 'She's what you'd call a looker. Well, is that all?'

Nikolls said: 'Yeah, I think you've done a swell job.'

She said: 'I'm glad you like it.' She hung up.

Nikolls went out into the hallway. Suzanne Melander said:

'Mr Nikolls, Mr Callaghan is going to have supper in an hour. What do you think he'd like to eat?'

'I wouldn't know,' said Nikolls. 'If he eats at all I'll be surprised. But I'm glad you mentioned it. We'll have that nice table by the French windows, and you'd better lay it for three. We got company.'

He began to walk up the stairs towards Callaghan's room.

CHAPTER TWO
LA BELLE DAME

IT WAS eleven-thirty. Callaghan stood before the fireplace in the small office parlour. He was wearing a blue pinhead suit, a light blue silk shirt and collar, navy blue tie. He had a glass of brandy in one hand; a cigarette hung from the corner of his mouth. He was not so tired as bad-tempered.

Nikolls, stretched in one of the big leather armchairs that flanked the fireplace, blew a ruminative smoke ring.

He said: 'She oughta be here by now – that dame. If she left at ten o'clock she oughta been here just after eleven. Maybe she didn't like it because the roads are wet. Maybe she's a bad driver. Maybe she's just indifferent.'

Callaghan said: 'Perhaps she put the car in a ditch. I don't think I'd mind a bit.'

'Yeah?' said Nikolls. 'That's the way you're feelin'. You'll be all right in the morning. Me – I been thinkin' about your stomach. I been talkin' about it with Mrs Melander. She reckons she only knew one guy who drank more than you do. She's got an idea that you got yourself so goddam pickled inside that you're practically waterproof. You musta drunk two bottles of whisky this afternoon besides the Bacardi you had this mornin'. You must be built like a battleship.'

Callaghan said: 'Maybe, but that doesn't help. How do I know I want to see this Mrs Denys? This is supposed to be a holiday.'

'I know,' said Nikolls, 'but I reckon it's been goin' on too long – this holiday. I reckon if something don't get you back to work you'll turn into a rustic with hay in your hair. Besides, Effie thinks this Denys dame is a proposition.'

Suzannne Melander came in. She carried a coffee service on a silver tray in her hands. She put it down on the table near Callaghan. She said:

'Believe it or not, Mr Callaghan, but a most beautiful person has just arrived in a *very* large car. A unique creature. She wants to see you.'

Nikolls sighed. 'The customer's arrived,' he said. 'Say, Suzanne, what does she look like?'

She said: 'Too amazing for words. She's a brunette with the most marvellous skin and a very attractive nose. I liked the shape of her face and she has a delightful mouth – also a charmingly mischievous look in her eyes.'

Callaghan yawned. He said: 'Wonderful! I can hardly wait.'

Nikolls said: 'Sounds sorta interestin'. What was she wearin'? Did her clothes look good?'

Suzanne sighed. 'They looked very good to me. I'm burning with envy. Would you like an exact description, Mr Nikolls? Well . . . she's wearing a very well-cut grey flannel coat and skirt and a pale grey organdie blouse with red pin-spots. A grey felt pull-on hat with silk corded ribbon in red and grey, very attractive court shoes and brown pigskin driving gauntlets. Definitely a sight for tired eyes.'

Callaghan asked: 'Where is this wondrous being?'

Suzanne said: 'She's powdering her nose. She should be here in a minute. She stopped for supper on the way.'

Nikolls heaved himself out of the chair. He followed Suzanne Melander out of the room. He stood in the hallway looking down the passage; then he turned quickly and came back into the room. He said:

'Boy, is she wonderful! Now I've seen everything.'

The woman came out of the shadows of the hallway across the threshold. She looked from Nikolls to Callaghan with a smile – an attractive friendly smile. She was entirely poised, absolutely at ease. She said:

'I'm Paula Denys. I expect you're Mr Callaghan.'

Callaghan said: 'Correct. At your service, I hope.'

She said: 'I hope so too.'

Nikolls pushed up one of the big armchairs. He said: 'I reckon you're tired. Take your weight off your feet, Mrs Denys. Relax. You're with friends.'

She smiled at him. 'I'm glad of that,' she said. 'I've an idea I'm going to need them.' She looked at Callaghan. She said demurely: 'Are you going to help me, Mr Callaghan?'

Callaghan said: 'I'm not sure. I came down here for a holiday, but it seems that the holiday's been getting the better of me.'

'Too bad,' she said. 'Too much rain?'

Nikolls said: 'No – too much whisky. For the last three or four days this place has been like Chicago under prohibition.'

'Dear . . . dear . . .' said Mrs Denys. 'It seems as if I've come at the right time.'

Callaghan said: 'I wonder. Would you like to pour out the coffee?'

She said: 'I'd love to. And I see there's a cup for me.'

'You bet,' said Nikolls. 'Callaghan Investigations thinks of everything. We *give* our clients coffee –'

'And what do they give you?' she asked.

Nikolls sighed. 'Practically everything they've got,' he said. 'We're an expensive firm.'

Callaghan said: 'Mrs Denys, this is Windemere Nikolls, my assistant. He's a Canadian. His bark is very much worse than his bite.'

Nikolls said: 'Don't you take any notice of him, lady. I never bite the customers.'

She said: 'You know I think I'm going to like you both very much. I've only been here a few seconds and I feel I'm with friends.'

She poured out the coffee. Most of the time her eyes were on Callaghan. Without making any pretence, she took in every detail of his face and clothes. She gave the impression of submitting him to the closest scrutiny.

Callaghan yawned again. He lit a fresh cigarette and stood looking straight in front of him. He said:

'All this is very nice, but I think my secretary may have been a little premature in sending you down here, Mrs Denys. I think I ought to tell you that I haven't made up my mind as to whether I'll handle your business.'

She said: 'Mr Callaghan, I hope you will. And just to show that I mean business may I produce to you one excellent reason for your handling it?'

Callaghan said: 'I'd like to hear it.'

She said: 'It would be much better for you to see it.' She opened her handbag; brought out a wad of banknotes. She handed them to Callaghan. 'There is a thousand pounds there, Mr Callaghan,' she said. 'That is your retainer if you consent to help me. Naturally, I expect you to put a further bill in if the matter is completed successfully. You'll find that I seldom argue about money.'

Callaghan put the banknotes behind him on the mantelpiece. He said: 'What exactly is the trouble, Mrs Denys?'

She sighed. 'It's rather stupid, I'm afraid,' she said.

She handed Nikolls his coffee, brought a cup to Callaghan. She went back to the chair, sat down, crossed her legs and leaned back. Callaghan realized that when Suzanne Melander had said that Mrs Denys had a superb figure, she was not exaggerating. He drank some coffee.

'Most of the cases we get are rather stupid, Mrs Denys,' he said. 'Somebody starts off by being stupid and somebody else gets tough. Most cases are like that. Who was stupid in this one – you?'

She nodded prettily. 'Yes, I was,' she said. 'Just how stupid, only I know. Briefly, the facts are these: I've been married for three years. I didn't want to get married in the first place. I've never even liked my husband. When we were married I was foolish – I had no marriage settlement and our finances were very soon mixed up.' She smiled wryly. 'I mean *my* money got mixed up with *his*,' she said. 'My husband was a man who was rich, of good family, wildly extravagant and a drunkard. In point of fact,' she went on, 'our marriage was merely a marriage in name, although we lived in the same house.'

Callaghan nodded. He said: 'This isn't a divorce case, is it? I don't like divorce cases.'

She said: 'I know, Mr Callaghan. Your Miss Thompson told me that. No, this isn't a divorce case. I told you it was stupid. In a minute you'll realize what a terribly stupid case it is,' she went on. 'Some months ago I decided to leave my husband. I asked him if he would allow me to divorce him. He refused. Not only did he refuse, but in order to prevent my leaving him he stopped my allowance. That made me rather angry.'

Callaghan nodded. 'I can understand that,' he said. 'Would you like a cigarette, Mrs Denys?'

She said: 'Yes please.'

Callaghan gave her a cigarette; stood over her, lighting it. A breath of the attractive perfume she was wearing came to his nostrils. He went back to the fireplace.

She continued: 'I decided to leave him, but I made up my mind that I was going to get some money *somehow*. Then I had an idea. We were living in a house called Mayfield Place, near Chessingford in Buckinghamshire. My husband had a collection there of valuable antique jewellery, amongst which was a box. Possibly you've heard of it. It's called the Denys Coronet, and it's been in his family I believe for several hundred years. The box is in the shape of a coronet and is richly encrusted with jewels; the lid raises on a hinge that is worked by a secret spring. It is supposed to be very precious. It's valued at seventy thousand pounds.'

Callaghan nodded. 'So you made up your mind that when you went you'd take the Denys Coronet with you?'

'Yes and no,' she said. 'I wanted the Coronet. I thought I was entitled to it. I should tell you that my husband had had very much more than seventy thousand pounds of *my* money. But I did not propose to take it with me. I thought that would be too obvious.'

Callaghan said: 'I see. So what did you do?'

She said: 'I arranged to have the Coronet stolen. I arranged this with a man I'd met casually at a club where I used to dance – a man named De Sirac. He was hard up and when I talked to him about it he said that he'd do it – for a consideration.'

'Nice work,' said Nikolls. 'Did it come off?'

She nodded. 'Oh yes, Mr Nikolls. It came off. It was very simple. You see the jewellery was kept in a wall safe in the library, but I knew the combination. My husband rarely went to the safe. In point of fact it is seldom opened except once or twice a year when the jewellery is taken out for cleaning. So I thought it might easily be some time before the robbery was discovered.'

Callaghan said; 'So you gave the combination to De Sirac. And I suppose somebody let him into the house?'

'No,' she said, 'there was no need. I'd supplied him with a key. He opened the safe and removed the Coronet.'

Callaghan asked: 'Has the theft been discovered yet?'

'Not yet, Mr Callaghan,' she replied. 'As I told you, the Coronet is only taken out of the safe once or twice a year for cleaning, and as it had been cleaned a few weeks before De Sirac took it, some time may elapse before my husband discovers the theft.'

Callaghan nodded. 'And when he does discover it?' he queried. 'Do you think he'll suspect you?'

She shook her head. 'Why should he?' she asked. 'He doesn't even know that I knew the safe combination.'

Callaghan asked: 'Mrs Denys, what sort of a man is your husband? You say he didn't like the idea of divorce. Did he think you'd return to him? Is he very much in love with you?'

She said: 'I don't know. He's a strange possessive sort of man, but I've told you that we never really lived together as husband and wife. I think the idea of losing his wife didn't appeal to him very much. His pride was hurt, but that was probably all.'

Callaghan said: 'I see. And now what is it you want me to do, Mrs Denys?'

She said: 'Mr Callaghan, I want you to get the Denys Coronet for me.'

Callaghan raised his eyebrows. 'You haven't got it?' he queried.

She shook her head. 'I've never had it,' she said. 'That's the trouble. I told you this was rather a stupid case.'

Callaghan grinned. 'I take it that the enterprising De Sirac refuses to part with it,' he said. 'In other words, he's got you where he wants you, Mrs Denys. He's doing a little blackmail on the side.'

She said: 'That's right, Mr Callaghan.' She smiled. 'Life can be so disappointing, can't it? Or possibly my trust in human nature is too great.' She sighed again. 'Of course I was stupid,' she went on, 'I ought to have known better than to trust a person like De Sirac. But then I'm afraid I'm rather a trusting sort of individual.' She looked from Callaghan to Nikolls with a delightful smile. 'You realize how I'm trusting you,' she said demurely.

'That's right,' said Nikolls. 'Only *we* haven't got the Coronet, lady, have we?'

'I wish you had, Mr Nikolls,' she said.

Callaghan lit a fresh cigarette. 'Tell me what happened,' he asked. 'Did you expect De Sirac to bring you the Coronet?'

She said: 'The arrangement was that he should bring me the Coronet at a hotel in London four weeks after I had left Mayfield Place. When he didn't do so I became a little worried. I knew his address. I got in touch with him. First of all I tried ringing on the telephone, but no one ever replied. Then I wrote him a note. Two days after the note was despatched, he rang me up. He said that he had the Coronet, but that he didn't intend to hand it over until I had paid him some more money. He wanted ten thousand pounds.'

Nikolls whistled through his teeth. 'A nice guy,' he said, 'this De Sirac. A crooked basket that one. The boy sorta knows his way about. It looks to me as if he's sittin' on top of the heap right now.'

She nodded sadly.

Callaghan asked: 'How much did you pay De Sirac originally to do the job, Mrs Denys?'

'Two hundred and fifty pounds,' she said, 'and there was to be another two hundred and fifty when he handed the Coronet over.'

'And he wants ten thousand?' said Callaghan. He stubbed out his cigarette end in the ashtray on the mantelpiece behind him. He said: 'I still don't know what it is you want me to do.'

She smiled at him. Her smile was very slow, very sweet. He noticed the beauty of her mouth and teeth.

She said: 'I want you to get that Coronet back, Mr Callaghan. You see, I know where Mr De Sirac is living and I think you might possibly persuade him that it would be to his advantage to hand it over to you.'

Nikolls said: 'Yeah, I know – a little strong-arm stuff. I think it would be good for this guy, an' he couldn't very well squeal about it.'

Callaghan said: 'No, he couldn't do that. But if he talked he could make things very tough for you, Mrs Denys.'

She said: 'Yes, I suppose he could.'

Callaghan said: 'Tell me where did this thousand pounds come from?' He indicated the packet of banknotes on the mantelpiece behind him.

She said: 'I had a little money when I left my husband.'

Callaghan grinned. He said: 'You're certainly taking a chance on us, aren't you – parting with this thousand and hoping we'll get you the Coronet? By the way, what would you do with it if you got it? You couldn't sell a thing like that in the open market, you know.'

She said: 'I know that, Mr Callaghan, but the precious stones in the Coronet are very rare. I thought I might prise a few out at a time and sell them.'

Callaghan said: 'It's an idea.' He half turned; picked up the packet of banknotes. He counted them over.

She said: 'So you're going to help me, Mr Callaghan?' She smiled at him.

Callaghan said: 'I don't know, Mrs Denys. I've got to think about it. Probably you'll be staying here the night. It's very dark and the roads are bad. I expect you'll go back to town tomorrow. I'll think this over. I'll let you know in the morning. In the meantime you'd better have these banknotes back.'

She got up. She said: 'Oh no, Mr Callaghan. They're quite safe with you. If you decide in the morning that you're not going to do this job for me, then you can give them to me back.'

Callaghan said: 'Very well.' He put the notes in his pocket. 'Where is De Sirac living at the moment?' he asked. 'Is he in London?'

She nodded. 'He has a flat,' she said, 'on the third floor – 267a Long Acre.'

'And what sort of man is he?' asked Callaghan.

'Not very nice,' she said. 'In fact not at all nice, and I should say very tough – quite a proposition.'

Callaghan said: 'I'll think about it, Mrs Denys. I'll let you know in the morning.' He picked up the glass of brandy; finished it.

She said: 'Now I think I'll go to bed. I'm rather tired. I wonder where that charming girl is – the one who met me when I arrived.'

Nikolls said: 'You mean Suzanne. A nice kid, that, hey?'

He went out into the hallway and bellowed. After a minute she appeared.

Nikolls said: 'Hey, Suzanne, Mrs Denys wants to be shown her room. You've got another guest. See she gets an egg for breakfast – maybe two.'

Suzanne said: 'Of course. Will you come this way, please?'

She went away. Mrs Denys, with one final smile at Callaghan, followed her.

It was midnight. The rain had ceased and the moon came out from behind the clouds. Callaghan, an unlit cigarette between his lips, walked up and down the gravel path that bisected the lawn at the back of the house.

He was thinking about Mrs Denys, her husband and the man De Sirac. He concluded that De Sirac must have a good nerve; yet taking the line he had, he had not been taking *too* many chances. What manner of man was De Sirac? And why should he allow himself to commit burglary for two hundred and fifty pounds down and a like sum when the business was completed? Unless, of course, De Sirac had made up his mind, from the start, that he would not part with the Coronet until he was paid a much larger sum of money.

In which case he would be a fairly tough proposition. And he was in a strong position. A position in which he could still – if he wanted to – drive a hard bargain.

Callaghan lit his cigarette and pondered on this point. Then he began to walk towards the garage.

Arrived there, he opened the door with a key he took from his pocket and went in. His own car was obstructed from view by the very smart Daimler which had brought Mrs Denys to the inn. Callaghan, carefully closing the garage door, switched on the light and examined it. A fine car, he thought. He opened the door of the driving seat and glanced at the petrol indicator. The tank was nearly full. He inhaled a mouthful of tobacco smoke and wondered where Mrs Denys got her petrol from.

Callaghan sat down on the running board of the car and considered life generally. It was a bad business about that Swayle cheque and, although the loss of four thousand pounds did not mean the world to Callaghan Investigations, yet it was a rather nasty blow. Of course they *might* get the money. Callaghan thought it seemed indicated that he earned Mrs Denys' thousand pounds.

He began to think about Mrs Denys and women in general. Women were funny things. They did things which were incongruous if not directly contradictory. He wondered why in the first place it had been necessary for her to marry Denys whom she did not like; but having married him, and continued to dislike him, he wondered why it was that she should consider that he would be prepared to accept that situation permanently.

Callaghan thought it was odd. He came out of the garage; walked back across the lawn. He threw his cigarette stub into the lily pond and walked up the verandah stairway, through the dining-room into the hall. He went into the office. Suzanne Melander was sitting at the desk, busy with accounts.

Callaghan said: 'It's a nice night, Suzanne.'

She said: 'Is it?'

'Would you like to tell me something?' he asked.

She said: 'I'd like to tell you anything I can. I thought perhaps you were going to ask me to go for a walk.'

Callaghan said: 'That's a good idea, but maybe I'm going to be busy.'

She said: 'Yes? Doing what? And what was it you wanted me to tell you?'

Callaghan asked: 'What's the number of Mrs Denys' room?'

She said: 'She's in number eleven on the first floor. Of course I'd be awfully curious if I asked why you wanted to know.'

Callaghan said over his shoulder: 'The reason's obvious, isn't it?'

He crossed the hall; went up the stairway. On the first floor he stopped at No. 11 and rapped with his knuckles.

Mrs Denys said: 'Yes, who is that?'

Callaghan said: 'This is Callaghan. I had an idea to go for a little drive, but I can't get at my car because you've parked yours between it and the garage doors. I wondered if you'd let me have your key.'

She said: 'But of course. Just a moment.'

Callaghan leaned against the wall. He lit a cigarette. He began to blow smoke rings. After a minute the door opened. She came out. Over cyclamen silk pyjamas she was wearing a cyclamen dressing-gown, with white silk facings. Her hair was tied back with a black watered silk ribbon. Her face expressed a mild concern.

She said: 'I'm sorry about my car, Mr Callaghan.' She held out the key towards him.

Callaghan said: 'Think nothing of it.'

She said: 'Tell me something, Mr Callaghan. Do you often go driving about the countryside at dead of night?'

He said: 'Sometimes it's a good time to think.'

She asked: 'And you have lots of important things to think about?'

He said: 'Well, at the moment I have one very important thing – Mrs Denys!'

She put her hands behind her head. She smiled. Callaghan thought she looked very attractive.

She said: 'And may one ask what Mr Callaghan is thinking about Mrs Denys?'

Callaghan dropped the key into the side pocket of his coat. He said: 'I think Mrs Denys is a very delightful and very charming woman. A very beautiful woman too. I've been trying to pick holes in that story of hers.'

She said: 'I see.' She was still smiling. 'And have you succeeded, Mr Callaghan?'

He said: 'I'm not quite sure. Maybe you've told me the truth, the whole truth and nothing but the truth. Maybe you haven't.'

She said: 'So you're going to reason it out. You're going to go for a little drive and work it all out, and tomorrow morning you'll tell me *all* about it. If I haven't told the exact truth Mr Callaghan will unerringly place a finger on the weak point in my story. Is that it?'

Callaghan said: 'Who knows? Good night to you, Mrs Denys.' He grinned amiably at her.

'And good night to you, Mr Callaghan,' she said. She went back into her room.

He went down the hall stairs. At the bottom, Suzanne Melander was locking the office door. She said:

'Did you have a pleasant conversation?'

'Not too bad,' said Callaghan. 'Suzanne, what do you think of Mrs Denys?'

She considered for a moment. She said: 'She's charming. She has style. She dresses well. I like her – I *think*. And what does Mr Callaghan think?'

Callaghan said: 'I'm rather inclined to agree with you – I *think*. So long, Suzanne.'

'Good night, Mr Callaghan,' she said. 'Pleasant dreams.'

Callaghan walked across the hallway towards the dining-room.

She said: 'Are you going out?'

He nodded.

'Well, what about your hat?' she asked. 'Have you forgotten it?'

Callaghan came back. He said: 'I'm always forgetting something, aren't I?' He took her chin in his right hand, tilted it up, kissed her.

She said: 'Damn!'

Callaghan said: 'Why?'

She said: 'Oh, I don't know. But I'm perfectly certain you were thinking about something else.'

He grinned at her. He said: 'You'd be surprised, Suzanne.'

He picked up his hat from the stand in the hallway, disappeared into the darkness of the dining-room.

Suzanne stood looking after him. She thought: You're a strange and rather attractive man, Mr Callaghan. You'd be a terrible man to live with. One would never know where one was with you. But you'd never be boring . . . I wonder . . .

After a moment she gave up wondering. She said: 'Oh hell . . . !' – locked up the office and went to bed.

Outside the night breeze had freshened. Callaghan unlocked the garage doors; swung them open. He got into Mrs Denys' Daimler, switched on the engine, backed the car out of the garage. He got out of the car, closed the garage doors, locked them; then he got back into the Daimler, drove slowly along the drive, into the lane. Ten minutes later he was on the main road. He turned the head of the car towards London.

It was half-past one when Callaghan parked the car in a deserted turning off Endell Street; began to walk towards Long Acre. It was spitting with rain and the moon had disappeared. Five minutes afterwards he found himself outside 267a Long Acre. It was an old-fashioned apartment block.

Callaghan pushed open the folding doors and went inside. The single blued-out light burning in the hallway showed him that the glass-fronted porter's desk was empty. Down the corridor by the side of the lift he saw an address indicator. He walked quietly towards it, his hands in his coat pockets. It showed that Mr De Sirac lived on the third floor.

He walked on past the lift; began to ascend the stairs. He was thinking about De Sirac; wondered to what social category this young man about town, who was amiably prepared to lend himself to semi-professional jewel burglary, belonged.

He reached the third floor. Through the transom over the door of the flat a light showed. Callaghan rang the bell. Nothing happened. He waited a few minutes; then rapped sharply on the door with his knuckles. A minute afterwards the door opened.

Standing in the hallway was a tall, well-built man. He regarded Callaghan with an almost benevolent smile that showed his gleaming white teeth. His hair was black, of the patent leather type; his face round and amiably intelligent. Underneath the spotted foulard dressing-gown Callaghan could see that he had good well-set shoulders.

He said: 'Would you be De Sirac?'

The man nodded. His smile broadened a little.

He said: 'Yes. What can I do for you?'

Callaghan said: 'I want to talk to you. My name's Callaghan. I'm a private detective.'

De Sirac said softly: 'Yes? I wonder what you would want to talk to me about at this time in the morning, Mr Callaghan. It's not a conventional hour for calling, is it?'

Callaghan said: 'I haven't come to talk about conventional business.'

De Sirac said: 'I might not *want* to talk, Mr Callaghan.'

Callaghan said: 'Probably not, but you will – one way or another.' He concluded that he did not like Mr De Sirac. He went on : 'Supposing we don't waste time. I think I can make things fairly tough for you. On the other hand, If you're sensible –'

De Sirac said: 'I see. That sounds rather like the opening of a blackmail scene on the films, doesn't it?'

Callaghan said: 'You ought to know.'

De Sirac laughed softly. He said: 'Mr Callaghan, I find you quite amusing. Come in.' He held open the door.

Callaghan went into the hallway of the flat. It was well-furnished and there was an odd smell of perfume about the place. There was a lack of air too, which displeased Callaghan. He hung his black felt hat on the hallstand. De Sirac closed the front door, crossed the hall, opened another door. He said: 'Come in, Mr Callaghan.'

Callaghan went into the large well-furnished sitting-room. De Sirac closed the door softly behind him. He said:

'How about a little drink?'

Callaghan said: 'Thank you. I'd like some whisky if you've got some.'

De Sirac said: 'I've got whisky.' He went to a sideboard; produced a bottle of whisky, a syphon, two glasses. He mixed the drinks. He came to Callaghan, who was standing in front of the fireplace, a glass in each hand. He handed Callaghan a glass.

De Sirac said: 'Here's to our talk, Mr Callaghan. I hope it'll be successful from both points of view.'

Callaghan drank the whisky. He put the glass on the mantelpiece behind him. He said:

'I don't think it's going to be, De Sirac. This isn't the sort of talk that's going to be agreeable to both of us.'

De Sirac nodded. He brought out a gold and platinum striped cigarette case; offered it to Callaghan. Callaghan shook his head.

'I smoke Virginian cigarettes,' he said. 'I'll smoke my own if you don't mind.'

De Sirac lit a cigarette; put the case back in his hip pocket. The smell of the Turkish cigarette was strong and perfumed. Callaghan thought it matched the atmosphere of the flat.

De Sirac said: 'Well, Mr Callaghan, let's get on with this talk which is going to be disagreeable to one of us. I wonder which one that's going to be.'

Callaghan said: 'I'll tell you. It's going to be disagreeable to you. So I won't waste any words. A client of mine – Mrs Denys – tells me you've got a Coronet belonging to her – a rather valuable piece. I want it.'

De Sirac said: 'Just like that!' He was still smiling.

Callaghan said: 'Just like that.'

De Sirac said: 'Do you think it's going to be quite as easy as that?'

Callaghan grinned. He said: 'Why not? Mrs Denys made a little plot with you. She arranged for you to get into Mayfield Place. She gave you the combination of her husband's safe. The arrangement was that you should remove the Coronet and hand it over to her. You removed it but you haven't handed it over to her. I suppose the idea is that you blackmail her for what you can get, after which you'll leave her on the end of a string for as long as you want to keep her there. Right?'

De Sirac said: 'Yes, that's fairly correct. And I don't see that you can do anything about it. Perhaps you'd allow me to ask you a question or two. May I ask how long you've known Mrs Denys?'

Callaghan said: 'I don't see that helps. How long I've known Mrs Denys doesn't matter a damn. The only thing that concerns me is whether you're going to hand over that Coronet or not.'

De Sirac said: 'That's straight enough. That's a nice direct question.' He smiled again. 'The answer is I'm *not*. And I don't know exactly what you're going to do about it!'

Callaghan said: 'How's that for a start?' He hit De Sirac in the mouth. The sound of his fist against the other's teeth made a peculiar wooden noise. De Sirac fell flat on his back, his head against the side of an ottoman. A thin stream of blood began to trickle down his chin. But he was still smiling; his eyes, fixed on Callaghan's face, were malevolent.

Callaghan took a step forward. He reached out his left hand; put it into the top of De Sirac's shirt collar. He lifted his head and shoulders two or three feet; hit him again in the face. This time De Sirac's head hit the floor with a thud.

Callaghan said: 'It's going to be very much easier if you listen to reason.'

De Sirac slowly got to his feet. He said in his peculiar soft voice: 'I think that's where you're mistaken. I'd like to point this out to you. I believe –'

His right foot suddenly shot forward and upwards. Callaghan, who was waiting for it, side-stepped quickly, moved in, and before De Sirac could recover his balance hit him across the point of the jaw with his elbow. De Sirac fell sideways. His head struck a small ornamental table with a crash. The table ricochetted across the room, smashed against the wall.

De Sirac lay quite still in the middle of the floor. Callaghan looked at him for a moment. Then he lit a cigarette; began to walk round the flat.

It was a large well-furnished flat and if the *decor* was inclined to be on the theatrical side that, Callaghan concluded, was only to be expected of Mr De Sirac.

He looked casually into one or two drawers; opened a cupboard here and there. He saw nothing that looked remotely like the Denys Coronet. But then he hardly expected to.

He went back to the sitting-room. De Sirac was at the sideboard, pouring himself a whisky and soda. He looked at Callaghan over his shoulder. He said:

'Well, did you find it, Mr Bloody Clever Dick?'

Callaghan said: 'No, I didn't expect to.'

De Sirac said: 'It looks rather as if your journey's been wasted, doesn't it?'

Callaghan grinned. 'I wouldn't say that,' he said. 'It's been nice meeting you. We've had a lot of fun.'

De Sirac drank the whisky in one gulp. He put the glass down on the sideboard. He turned; stood leaning against the sideboard looking at Callaghan. He said:

'You're pretty tough aren't you, Mr Callaghan? Well, so am I. And you don't frighten me one little bit. So you might as well get something into your head here and now. I'm not parting with the Denys Coronet until I get what I want for it. And that isn't necessarily money. Do you understand that?'

Callaghan said: 'I hear what you say. You're a bluffer, De Sirac. You've got no possible right to that Coronet.'

De Sirac said: 'Has your client?'

Callaghan said: 'That isn't the point. Two wrongs don't make a right. If my client likes to do something that's odd and funny, that's her business.'

De Sirac said: 'Well . . . what can you do about it?' he was almost nonchalant.

Callaghan said: 'What can I do about it? Quite a lot. First of all you can't sell that Coronet, and even you haven't got the nerve to prise out the stones and sell them individually. You can take it from me I'm going to have it one way or another.'

He grinned at De Sirac. 'After all,' he said, 'there's a war on, you know. You can't get out of this country. You'll find it very difficult even to leave London, and from tomorrow morning I shall have somebody keeping an eye on this flat. Wherever you go, De Sirac, I'll have somebody on your tail. In fact,' said Callaghan, 'do you know what I think?'

De Sirac said: 'What do you think, Mr Callaghan?'

Callaghan said airily: 'I think you'll be very glad to hand me that Coronet in a couple of weeks' time.'

De Sirac said: 'We'll see.'

Callaghan lit a cigarette. He said: 'Well, I'll probably be seeing you sometime. Good night.'

He walked out of the sitting-room; took his hat from the hall-stand; opened the front door of the flat; closed it softly behind him. He walked slowly up and down the passage. The place was quite quiet. There was no one about.

Callaghan stubbed out his cigarette into a sand bucket and walked back past the lift and the stairs beside it. A few yards down the passage there was a short corridor leading to a flat. Callaghan turned the corner and stood with his back to the wall, his hands in his pockets. He was thinking about Mrs Denys.

He was wondering how a woman of her attraction, of her breeding and charm, could become associated with a man like De Sirac. He shrugged his shoulders. You never knew with women.

Twenty minutes went by. Callaghan heard a sound from the stairway; put his head round the corner. De Sirac emerged from the stairs into the main passage. He was carrying a suitcase. He began to walk towards the entrance. Callaghan, moving noiselessly, came up behind him.

He said softly: 'De Sirac . . .'

De Sirac spun round. As he did so, Callaghan raised his right arm and, using the fist and forearm as a sledge hammer, hit the other on the jaw. He caught him as he fell; propped him up against the side of the passage.

The suitcase was locked, but the key was on a ring in De Sirac's pocket. Callaghan opened the suitcase. At the bottom, under some silk shirts, was a square wooden box. Callaghan opened it. Inside the box was the Denys Coronet. Callaghan put the box on the floor; closed the suitcase. He arranged the suitcase artistically under De Sirac's head in the manner of a pillow; then, picking up the box, he went out.

Five minutes later he was on his way back to The Crescent & Star.

It was half-past three. Callaghan parked the car in the garage at The Crescent & Star, locked the garage doors and went into the inn through the side window. He walked quietly up the stairs to the first floor. He stood at the top of the stairs looking down the corridor. From under the door of Mrs Denys' room came a gleam of light. Callaghan walked along the corridor; tapped on the door.

She said: 'Who is that?'

Callaghan said: 'This is Callaghan. I've got something for you.'

She said: 'Would you like to come in?'

Callaghan opened the door; went into the bedroom. She was sitting up in bed, propped up with pillows, reading. She was wearing a lacy bedjacket and the light from the rose-coloured shaded lamp on the bed-table at her side helped an attractive picture. She closed her book with a snap.

'So you've got something for me, Mr Callaghan?'

Callaghan nodded. He put the box on the foot of the bed.

He said: 'There's your Coronet. Are you surprised?'

She smiled. She said: 'Candidly, no. Do you know, I had an idea when you came to me for the car key that you *might* be considering going to see Mr De Sirac. Apparently you found him at home?'

Callaghan said: 'Yes, I found him at home all right. He's inclined to be tough.'

She raised her eyebrows. 'Even so,' she said, 'you seem to be all in one piece, Mr Callaghan.'

He grinned. He said: 'Possibly I'm a little tougher. Anyway, you've got your Coronet.'

She said: 'Have you seen it?'

He nodded. 'A very nice piece of work,' he said. 'It must be worth a great deal of money.'

'It *is* worth a great deal of money,' she said. 'Does that mean that you're not satisfied with your fee?'

He said: 'Oh no, it doesn't mean that. I'm quite happy.'

She said: 'So am I. I have the Coronet. You have a thousand pounds. I think that's a very nice friendly deal, don't you?'

Callaghan said: 'Yes, I do.' He went on: 'You're an odd sort of person, aren't you?'

'Why do you say that?' she asked.

Callaghan said: 'I should never have thought that a woman like you would even have known a person like De Sirac. He's pretty bad medicine, you know.'

She nodded. 'So I've gathered,' she said. 'But when one's in a bad spot, Mr Callaghan, one chooses the lesser of two evils. De Sirac is, as you say, not very nice, but then neither is my husband.'

Callaghan said: 'Well, you ought to know. Good night, Mrs Denys.'

She smiled whimsically. She said in a humorously formal voice: '*Must* you go?'

Callaghan said: 'I think so. Mrs Melander might wonder what's going on at her inn.'

She said: 'That would worry you an awful lot, wouldn't it, Mr Callaghan?'

Callaghan said: 'Like hell! Good night.'

He went out.

The grandfather clock in the hallway struck four as he got into bed. He lay for a minute, his hands clasped behind his head, looking at the ceiling. He was thinking that Callaghan Investigations had made up a thousand of the Swayle cheque anyhow.

He switched off the light.

At ten o'clock Suzanne Melander came in with Callaghan's morning tea. She drew the curtains. The sunshine flooded into the bedroom.

Callaghan sat up and rubbed his eyes.

She said: 'Here's your tea, Mr Callaghan. And I ought to tell you that Miss Thompson wants to speak to you. She's on the phone.'

Callaghan said: 'Where's Nikolls?'

Suzanne said: 'I don't know. He's out somewhere. Don't you want to speak to Miss Thompson?'

Callaghan said: 'Is it important?'

'I don't know,' said Suzanne. 'Miss Thompson seemed to think so.'

Callaghan said: 'I'll come down. Tell her to hold on.'

He got up, put on a dressing-gown and slippers, went down to the office. He took the telephone from Suzanne Melander.

He said: 'Hello, Effie. What's the trouble?'

Effie Thompson's voice was cool. She said: 'There isn't any trouble, Mr Callaghan, but something has occurred to me which I think you ought to know. After I saw Mrs Denys yesterday evening I thought I ought to make a few enquiries about her just in case you decided to do anything about her business.'

Callaghan grinned. 'I think the enquiries were a little bit late,' he said. 'Mrs Denys' business is finished. We've handled that case.'

'Oh, have you?' said Effie. 'I think that's rather a pity.'

Callaghan said: 'What are you getting at, Effie?'

She said: 'Only this, Mr Callaghan. I've found out one or two things about Mrs Denys. She's a very responsible and charming person. I hear she's a brunette – a real brunette.'

Callaghan said: 'So what!'

Effie said: 'I think you ought to know that the Mrs Denys I saw yesterday evening – the one I sent to see you – wasn't a *real* brunette.'

Callaghan said: 'No?' His eyebrows were raised. 'What was she?' he asked.

'I don't know what she was,' said Effie. 'But I thought I'd better ring you and tell you that her hair was dyed.'

Callaghan said: 'I see.' He hung up; went into the hall. Suzanne Melander was ascending the stairs. He said:

'Suzanne, where's Mrs Denys?'

'Didn't you know?' she said. 'She left early this morning. She said she had an urgent appointment. Shall you miss her?'

Callaghan grinned. He said: 'Like hell!'

CHAPTER THREE
THE CUSTOMER IS ALWAYS RIGHT

CALLAGHAN pressed the bell-push at 17 Palmeira Court and waited. Somewhere in the neighbourhood a clock struck eight. He removed the cigarette from his mouth as the door opened. A neat maid looked at him enquiringly.

Callaghan said: 'Mrs Denys?'

The maid said: 'I don't know if she's in. And what name shall I say?'

Callaghan said: 'I don't suppose my name will mean anything to Mrs Denys, but it's Callaghan. *I* think my business is important.'

The maid said: 'Will you wait?'

She went away.

Callaghan threw his cigarette into the ashtray in the corner of the corridor. By the time he got back to the door, the maid had returned.

She said: 'Will you come in, sir?'

Callaghan went into the hallway of the flat, which was large, attractively furnished. He gave his hat to the maid and followed her through the open doorway on the other side.

The girl said: 'Mr Callaghan,' and went away.

The woman who was sitting at the writing desk on the far side of the room got up. She came towards Callaghan. She was tall, very graceful, quite beautiful. She wore a black dinner frock and a single rope of pearls. Her attitude was one of polite interest.

She said in a very soft voice: 'Yes, Mr Callaghan? Would you like to sit down?'

Callaghan said: 'Thank you.'

He waited for her to sit down in the large tapestry-covered armchair that stood by the fireplace; then he said:

'Mrs Denys, a rather odd thing's happened. I felt I ought to see you about it because it concerns you.'

She raised her eyebrows. 'Really, Mr Callaghan,' she said. 'How interesting.' She smiled politely.

Callaghan said: 'I'm a private detective. I've been on holiday. Yesterday, in the evening, my secretary rang me from London, and told me that a Mrs Paula Denys wanted to see me urgently. Usually we like to know something about a client before we do any business, but as this seemed to be rather an important case, and for one or two other reasons which don't matter (Callaghan thought of Swayle's cheque), I asked my secretary to form her own opinion of the lady. She seemed satisfied. She was quite satisfied that Mrs Denys was a responsible person.'

She said: 'You're talking about Mrs Paula Denys. This isn't supposed to be *me* by any chance, is it?'

Callaghan smiled. He said: 'That's the whole point. It *is* supposed to be you.'

She said: 'Please go on, Mr Callaghan.'

Callaghan continued: 'This lady arrived at the inn where I was staying in the country late last night. She told me a very interesting story. She said that she was Mrs Paula Denys and that she had been married to a gentleman whom she didn't like very much. She told me that some six months ago she decided to leave Denys; that she had a showdown with him; that she discovered that he'd spent most of her money.'

Callaghan stopped talking. 'Do you mind if I smoke?' he asked.

'Please do, Mr Callaghan,' she said. 'Let me give you a cigarette.'

She brought a silver box of cigarettes to him. Callaghan took one; lit it. He was watching her. If she had been surprised by the story she did not show it. At the same time he sensed a certain watchfulness, an interest that she was endeavouring to conceal under an obvious attitude of nonchalance.

She said coolly: 'I'm beginning to be quite intrigued.'

'You're going to be more intrigued before 'I'm through,' said Callaghan. 'The lady went on,' he continued, 'to inform me that her husband was the owner of a very valuable piece of antique jewellery called the Denys Coronet – a piece that was worth something like seventy thousand pounds. This Coronet was kept in a safe at Mayfield Place where they lived, and was examined only once every six months for cleaning – sometimes not even then.

'The lady, finding that her husband was not particularly sympathetic about her leaving him, and also that she had very little money, decided that when she went the Coronet should go with her.' He smiled at her. 'Are you still interested, Mrs Denys?'

She smiled. She said: 'This is *most* extraordinary. I'm most curious to hear the rest of it.'

He went on: 'Mrs Denys then arranged with a gentleman by the name of De Sirac, whom she knew and who apparently was not very particular what he did, that he should remove the Coronet. She gave him the combination of the safe and a key to get into the house.'

'How enthralling,' she said. 'And did this Mr De Sirac remove the Coronet?'

Callaghan nodded. 'He removed the Coronet all right,' he said. 'Then apparently the trouble started.'

She said: 'I see. And what was the trouble, Mr Callaghan?'

He said: 'De Sirac, having got the Coronet, refused to hand it over to Mrs Denys, or –' said Callaghan, 'the lady who we *thought* was Mrs Denys. Apparently she tried for some time to get him to see reason, but he wasn't playing.'

She nodded. 'So she came to you?' she said.

'That's right,' said Callaghan. 'She came to me, and she told me the story. She gave me a thousand pounds as a retainer. I told her I wanted to think the matter over; that I'd let her know my decision next day. So she stayed the night at the inn.'

'I see,' she said. 'And then what happened?'

Callaghan said: 'I thought it might be rather amusing to come up to town immediately and see if I could interview Mr De Sirac.'

'And did you?' she asked.

Callaghan nodded. 'I went up soon after Mrs Denys had gone to bed,' said Callaghan, 'and I was lucky. I found Mr De Sirac. We discussed the matter and he decided to hand over the Coronet.'

She said: 'As easily as *that*?'

Callaghan grinned. 'Well,' he said, 'perhaps not quite as easily as that. Anyway, I got the Coronet.'

'And then?' she queried.

'I went back to the country,' said Callaghan, 'and I handed over the Coronet to Mrs Denys. She left in her car early this morning.'

She said: 'I see. And what was the next act in this rather amusing comedy – or drama, Mr Callaghan?'

Callaghan said: 'The next sequence was when my secretary rang me up with a piece of very interesting information. It seems that when she saw Mrs Denys she noticed that this lady's hair had been recently dyed. She did not think anything of it at the time, but this morning she remembered having seen a notice in the papers some months ago of a petition for divorce issued by a Mrs Denys who was supposed to be a very beautiful woman, and she looked up the cuttings. She found that Mrs Denys was a real brunette; that her hair was not dyed. So she rang me up on the telephone.'

He blew a smoke ring, watched it sail across the room. 'So I thought I'd better come and see you about it, Mrs Denys,' he continued.

She got up. She went to the silver box on the table; took a cigarette; lit it with a lighter that stood beside the box.

She said: 'Exactly what am I supposed to do or say, Mr Callaghan?'

Callaghan smiled at her. He said: 'Having regard to the fact that *you* are Mrs Denys; having regard to the fact that this woman – whoever she may be – was impersonating you, I should have thought that you might have managed to work up a little more interest.'

She said: 'But why should I, Mr Callaghan?'

Callaghan got up. He walked over to the fireplace; stood leaning against it, looking at her. The cigarette was hanging out of the left-hand corner of his mouth. He said:

'Mrs Denys, I want to know if the story this woman told me is true as it applied to you. Don't you realize –'

She said coolly: 'Mr Callaghan, I don't realize anything at all. Candidly, I don't see why I should even be interested.'

Callaghan said: 'Well, I'll be damned! I take it that you're the Mrs Paula Denys who lived at Mayfield Place – who was married to Denys; who left him some months ago and who issued a divorce petition against him?'

She said: 'That is absolutely correct. And having established that fact, what am I supposed to say or do?'

Callaghan said: 'Mrs Denys, somewhere in England is a rather good-looking woman casually walking about with the Denys Coronet under her arm. Apparently that Coronet has been successfully stolen by herself and De Sirac. The fact that I have had something to do with it – except that I was quite innocent, of course – almost makes me an accessory to the business. But that isn't the interesting part. The interesting part is how did this lady know all this? You see she was able to tell me this story which seems to be entirely correct. How was she able to get the combination of the safe and give it to De Sirac? How was she able to get the key with which he let himself into the house?'

She said airily: 'Mr Callaghan, it would be very interesting to answer all those questions, wouldn't it? Do you think that I shall supply the answers?'

Callaghan said: 'I think you might try.'

She said: 'Do you really? So you think I might try. Perhaps you'll give me a reason for my even *wanting* to try, Mr Callaghan.'

Callaghan said: 'I could think of half a dozen, but just at the moment I think this one is enough. This woman, who was pretending to be you, was in a position in which she could know things which would normally only be known to you. Through her and her know-ledge, De Sirac was enabled to get that Coronet. Don't you realize, Mrs Denys, that even if we manage to catch up with that woman, she is going to have a very good story?'

'Really!' said Mrs Denys. 'And what do you think her story is going to be, Mr Callaghan?'

Callaghan said: 'I think her story is going to concern you. I think her story's going to be that when you found your husband had spent most of your money, Mrs Denys, when you left him, you arranged to steal that Coronet; *that you arranged it with her;* that in fact De Sirac stole it for you; that in point of fact the job was done *for* you. Unfortunately,' said Callaghan, 'De Sirac refused to hand over that Coronet. He thought he'd do better if he tried a little blackmailing. Probably he was afraid of trying to sell the Coronet on the open market, and he knew if he broke it down and sold the stones singly the value would have materially decreased.'

She said: 'I see.' Her voice was like ice. 'So I arranged this, Mr Callaghan! And I couldn't get the Coronet from De Sirac. So I arranged this other little plot?'

Callaghan said: 'Why not? Anyway, I'm entitled to think that, aren't I – if I want to think it? Don't you see that if I'd been prepared simply to take the thousand pounds, get the Coronet back and hand it over; if I'd been content to leave the job there, I should have thought it was you, wouldn't I? I shouldn't have known that the other lady *wasn't* you.'

She said nothing. Callaghan went on:

'Anyway, you're in quite a good position, Mrs Denys, if you were behind this, because unless the other lady gives you away nobody's going to know that, are they? That seems to be the only danger, doesn't it?'

She got up. She said: 'Really, Mr Callaghan, you are a most extra-ordinary person. I don't like you at all.'

She rang the bell. The neat maid appeared. Mrs Denys said:

'Lucille, will you show this gentleman out?'

Callaghan got up. He was smiling. He said: 'Mrs Denys, I'd like to say just one thing before I go.'

She nodded to the girl, who left the room.

She said: 'Say on, Mr Callaghan. You've said so much you couldn't make matters any worse even if *you* tried.'

Callaghan said: 'Either you knew that scheme about the Coronet, and it was your idea, or you didn't. If you knew it; if you were responsible for it, I can understand your attitude at the moment; but, if you didn't know anything about it . . .' He shrugged his shoulders.

She said: 'Mr Callaghan, will you tell me why I should be at all interested?'

Callaghan looked at her. She was smiling. She was entirely poised; seemingly quite happy. Obviously, she did not give a damn for Mr Callaghan.

He thought: She's stalling for time. For some reason she *can't* talk about it. She's much more interested than she cares to show.

He said: 'I can give you three or four reasons. But I'm not going to bother. Sooner or later I think you'll get in touch with me.'

She laughed. She said: 'But what makes you think I shall do that?'

Callaghan said: 'You'll have to.' He walked to the door.

She said: 'So I shall have to come to you, Mr Callaghan. I can conceive nothing more annoying than having to come to you about anything.'

Callaghan smiled at her almost happily. He said:

'Don't worry, Mrs Denys. You'll be quite safe with us when you do come. With us the customer is always right!'

The Chinese Dragon was just another of those places. This carefree habitat of vice was a 'club,' situated in a basement not a hundred miles from Piccadilly Circus. The walls, the ceilings and the furniture were intended to be Chinese, but the proprietor, whose artistic sense was not adequately developed, had rather mixed his periods, and the red, yellow and blue dragons which decorated the walls in profusion resembled the sort of things that one expected to crawl out from under a stick on the lawn.

Of the habituees of The Chinese Dragon, the less said the better. They were ladies and gentlemen who toiled not but spun plenty, and even if the webs they wove were sometimes inconvenient for the victims who found their way into them, still their argument would have been that people must live.

To those bright citizens who wonder why such a place as The Chinese Dragon is allowed to exist by the extremely efficient Metropolitan police force, I can say that those gentlemen in blue are not half so stupid as some of our less informed fiction writers try to make out, and it is a habit of theirs on occasion to allow sprats to exist in order that mackerel may eventually be caught. Hence The Chinese Dragon.

This resort of peace and happiness was owned by an individual known to his more intimate companions as Konky The Red – a title acquired from a proclivity towards nose bleeding in moments of anger. He was a fat, olive-skinned gentleman, with a nose of gigantic dimensions set in a face which was invariably smiling. Whatever wars and alarms took place outside The Chinese Dragon little perturbed its proprietor who, when not engaged in serving behind the bar, occupied himself upstairs in the bathroom in the creation of fresh supplies of liquor.

By this it must not be taken for granted that he supplied only hooch made on the premises. There were two sorts of liquor and two sorts of clients; proper branded spirits secured in that mysterious manner which leaves the Excise and Revenue officials dumbfounded in these days; and the second sort – the result of an apprenticeship served in Chicago during the years of Prohibition – which was manufactured in the bath upstairs, and the flavour of which was undoubtedly enriched by slight touches of rust which emanated from the adjacent geyser.

In another room were young ladies of much charm and undoubted ability, who also contributed in devious ways to the proprietor's income, and if the knowledge that such a place as The Chinese Dragon can exist in the heart of a great city like London is inclined to perturb the more serious-minded citizen, I can only point out that, as the sailor said, 'worse things happen at sea.'

Callaghan and Nikolls were seated at a small table in the corner of the bar. They were drinking large whiskies.

Nikolls said gloomily: 'I wonder if I got a liver. Every time I look at that dragon on the wall opposite it looks as if it's got a squint. I'm worried. I don't know whether it's the dragon or me that's squintin'.' He sighed. 'You know, Slim,' he said, 'I reckon we was wrong to come away from The Crescent & Star. We shoulda stayed there. That place has atmosphere.'

Callaghan asked: 'Are you sure he comes here?'

Nikolls said: 'Yeah – as sure as I can be. Three or four of the people who live around that apartment block of his said he used to drop in here every evening. The hall-porter – where there was a hall-porter – used to phone him here with messages sometimes. But maybe he's not gonna come here any more.'

'Why not?' asked Callaghan.

Nikolls sighed. 'Maybe he reckons you're gonna be on his tail,' he said.

Callaghan said: 'Why should I be? His attitude is going to be that once I have the Coronet I'm through with him. He won't expect to see me again.'

Nikolls said: 'I wonder *who* that dame was. Anyhow, whoever she was, she's got something. I reckon that baby's got a nerve bustin' in on our holiday, pretendin' to be Mrs Denys, sellin' you that fake story about the Coronet, an' gettin' away with it too.'

Callaghan said: 'Maybe she hasn't got away with it.'

Nikolls sighed again. 'I don't know why you're interestin' yourself in this thing. What have you got to worry about? You've got the thousand, haven't you?'

Callaghan said: 'Yes.' He lit a cigarette.

Nikolls said: 'But you feel sorta burned up. I know. You feel you've been taken for a ride – sorta gets you, don't it? I wonder who she was,' he continued.

Callaghan said: 'She was somebody who was pretty close to Mrs Denys – somebody who knew her very well – possibly a cousin or something like that.'

Nikolls said: 'How come?'

Callaghan said: 'When I went into her bedroom she was wearing pyjamas with the initials P.D. on the pocket. Those are Mrs Denys' initials – Paula Denys.'

Nikolls said: 'You mean she didn't have those pyjamas made especially for you to see those initials? She was in a position where she could borrow some of Paula Denys' pyjamas?'

'That's right,' said Callaghan. 'Obviously, she's a woman who takes trouble. She knew she had her own initials on her own pyjamas and she wasn't taking a chance.'

Nikolls said: 'A wise dame, this unknown *femme*, thinkin' of a thing like that. Anyway, how did she know you were goin' into her bedroom?'

Callaghan said moodily: 'She didn't.'

Nikolls said: 'No, maybe not.' He grinned. 'This baby's one of them frails who get ready for anything – or maybe she's heard of Callaghan Investigations,' he said.

Callaghan said: 'I didn't know that we usually did our business in bedrooms.'

'No!' said Nikolls. He lit a cigarette. The expression on his face might have been described as whimsical.

There was a long silence. Nikolls took the glasses to the bar; ordered fresh drinks; brought them back. He sat down.

He said: 'So your idea is that Mrs Denys knew something about this?'

Callaghan said: 'I haven't got any ideas.'

Nikolls said: 'Well, if she hadn't known something about this she'd have been surprised, wouldn't she? She wouldn't have been so sorta cool about it.'

'No,' said Callaghan, 'not unless she thought she knew who might have done such a thing.'

Nikolls said: 'I get it. You mean that she might have an idea that this dame who was close enough to her to have a pair of her pyjamas might be going to pull something like that. I get it.'

Callaghan looked at his watch. It was nine o'clock.

He said: 'When you've finished that drink, go back to the office. Get Haden and Gilmour working on the Denys family background. I want to know all about Mrs Paula Denys and all about her husband. And I want to know particularly what relatives she's got – whether she's got any cousins or sisters, or anybody who checks up with the description of that woman who came down to The Crescent & Star.'

Nikolls finished his drink in one gulp. He said: 'When d'you want that by?'

Callaghan said: 'By tomorrow midday. You'll have to get busy.'

Nikolls said: 'You're tellin' me.' He went out.

When he arrived at the office in Berkeley Square, Effie Thompson was tidying her desk. She looked at Nikolls as he passed through her office on his way to Callaghan's room.

Nikolls planted himself in Callaghan's big leather armchair. He reached down, opened the bottom drawer, took out a half bottle of Canadian rye. He put the neck of the bottle in his mouth and took a long pull.

He was replacing the bottle when the door opened. Effie Thompson stood in the doorway. She had put on her hat and was ready to leave.

She said: 'What's he going to do?'

Nikolls yawned. 'What do you think, Luscious?' he said. 'He's steamed up, see? That dame you sent down to The Crescent & Star has taken him for a ride an' he don't like it. It's given him a pain. You know what he's like.'

She said: 'So he's going to start something?'

Nikolls grinned at her. 'There're all the symptoms he's going to start plenty. He's hangin' around waitin' to pick up that De Sirac guy.'

She asked: 'What then?'

Nikolls said: 'Search me. If I know anything about it, he's going to play it straight off the cuff. I reckon he's in the frame of mind when he's not going to sleep till he's evened things up with that baby.' He stretched. He went on: 'What he wants to do it for beats me. Even if Swayle did take him for that four thousand, he's still got the thousand off the phoney dame.'

Effie said: 'Swayle didn't take him for the four thousand. Swayle's lawyer has been through to say that they're taking up the dishonoured cheque tomorrow. They're paying cash.'

Nikolls said: 'That won't make any difference. You know him when he gets started. He's sort of interested in this set-up, see?'

Effie said slowly: 'I see.'

Nikolls asked: 'Meanin' what?'

She said: 'He didn't feel so badly about it until he'd been to see the real Mrs Denys. Perhaps *she* started something. Is she very beautiful?'

'I wouldn't know,' said Nikolls. 'But I've got an idea that she gave him the air. He didn't like that.'

She said: 'So he's going to make trouble? One of these days he'll make a great deal of trouble for himself.'

Nikolls said: 'I think you're right, Gorgeous.'

He looked at her happily.

He said: 'Gee, Effie, you're lookin' swell tonight. That's a very nice line in coat and skirts you're wearin' – sorta makes your figure look very good.'

She said: 'Mr Nikolls, I'm going home now. I shall be here at nine-thirty in the morning. I've told you before that my figure's my own business.'

Nikolls said: 'I know, that's the trouble.' He sighed. 'I wish it was mine,' he said.

She turned away. As she went into the outer office she said over her shoulder: 'Don't you ever think about anything except women's figures?'

Nikolls considered deeply for a moment; then he said: 'I reckon I don't – much. But then I'm sorta artistic, see? Sorta poetic. It's the artist in me. Yeah . . . that's it.'

She said: 'If you're artistic, why don't you go to some of the art galleries?'

Nikolls looked at her in astonishment. 'For what?' he said: 'Be your age, Effie . . . whoever heard of tryin' to neck a picture!'

He grinned as the door slammed behind her.

It was midnight. The Chinese Dragon began to fill up. Callaghan was still sitting in the corner, his chair tilted back against the wall, his eyes fixed moodily on the dragon on the wall opposite. He had drunk a considerable quantity of whisky. He was unhappy. He flicked his cigarette end expertly into the bran-filled bowl set against the wall opposite; lit a fresh one.

De Sirac came in. He pushed aside the curtain that guarded the doorway; stood in the entrance looking into the bar. He saw Callaghan. He smiled; then he went to the bar.

Callaghan watched him out of the corner of his eye. After a moment he said: 'De Sirac!'

De Sirac looked over his shoulder. He picked up his glass. He walked over to where Callaghan was sitting. He stood on the other side of the table looking down at Callaghan. De Sirac was beautifully dressed. Even if the shoulders of his cleverly cut coat were a little too padded, the waist a little too slim, still the effect was quite good if you like that sort of thing.

He said: 'Well, Mr Callaghan?'

Callaghan said: 'Sit down, De Sirac.'

De Sirac sat down. He put his glass on the table and looked at it. He said:

'You're not trying to tell me you've got some *more* business you want to discuss with me?'

Callaghan said: 'I don't know very much about you and what I do know isn't good. All right. Well, from your point of view somebody's taken you for a ride over this Coronet business. Right?'

De Sirac picked up his glass. He regarded the amber fluid in it. He said: 'Who are you working for now, Callaghan?'

'I'm not working for anybody,' said Callaghan. 'I'm just being curious.'

De Sirac said: 'That being so, what you said about me was more or less right. I've been a mug.'

Callaghan said: 'You mean you were a mug to go to all that trouble of getting the Coronet and then have it taken off you by me. What did you get out of that job?'

De Sirac said: 'Don't you know? I got two hundred and fifty before I did it. That's all. And it doesn't look as if I'm going to get very much more, does it?' His smile widened. 'I wonder what *you're* unhappy about,' he said.

Callaghan's eyes wandered over the grotesque figure of the dragon. He was wondering what line would be best suited for the purpose he had in mind; what story De Sirac would swallow most easily.

He said: 'I don't like women to make a fool of me. I'm not used to it.'

De Sirac said: 'So she took you too?'

Callaghan nodded. 'That's right. She took me too. A clever woman. I suppose *you* wouldn't know that she wasn't even Mrs Denys. She was somebody else.'

De Sirac raised his eyebrows. 'Imagine that!' he said. He smiled at Callaghan sideways. 'It just shows you how careful you've got to be with women, doesn't it?'

Callaghan said nothing.

De Sirac asked: 'And you're going to do something about it? You could make things pretty warm for her, couldn't you?'

Callaghan said: 'I'm going to.'

De Sirac grinned. 'So you're coming round to my way of thinking?'

'Maybe,' said Callaghan.

The other considered for a moment. He said: 'What exactly do you propose to do?'

Callaghan said: 'I don't know. Maybe you can get an idea.'

De Sirac said: 'Why not?' He got up. 'Look, give me till tomorrow. Perhaps you could drop in at my flat and see me. That'd be better than me coming to your office.'

Callaghan said: 'All right. I'll be there at eight o'clock.'

'Right,' said De Sirac. He smiled pleasantly at Callaghan. 'Till then . . . *au revoir*.' He wandered away.

Callaghan drank another whisky and soda. He lit a cigarette, smoked it, nodded to the girl behind the bar, left The Chinese Dragon. He walked slowly in the direction of Haymarket, his hands in his pockets.

He was thinking about Paula Denys. There was something unique about her, something remote, that you couldn't quite put your finger on, but that was definitely very attractive.

He switched his mind over to the woman who had come down to The Crescent & Star; had pretended to be Mrs Denys. He began to smile to himself. She had something. Very definitely she had something. She knew what she wanted and having made up her mind she went out to get it.

Callaghan stopped suddenly in the darkness. He fumbled in his pocket for his cigarette case. An idea had occurred to him – a very odd idea – a hell of an idea.

He lit the cigarette. He was grinning. Life could be funny; or could it?

He was almost happy!

CHAPTER FOUR
SOME MORE BELLE DAME

CALLAGHAN lay back in his office chair. His feet were on the desk. He blew smoke rings; watched them sail across the office.

There was a knock on the door. Callaghan said: 'Come in!' without moving. Effie Thompson came into the office. She looked faintly amused.

She said: 'Mr Callaghan, the lady with the dyed hair whom I sent down to see you at The Crescent & Star is here again, only this time she doesn't say she is Mrs Denys. *Now* she says she is Miss Irana Faveley.'

Callaghan said: 'Just fancy that.' He inhaled cigarette smoke. 'How does she look, Effie?' he asked. 'Does she look pleased with herself?'

Effie Thompson shrugged her shoulders delicately. She said: 'I'm afraid that I don't make a point of noticing *everything* about our lady clients, Mr Callaghan. She seems to look quite normal to me. She's very well-dressed. Her coat and skirt came from a first-class tailor. I should say that her hat cost not a penny less than five or six guineas; her shoes are by Raoul, and the perfume she is wearing – *Vie D'Amour* – costs something like ten guineas for the tiniest flask. She doesn't seem horribly ashamed or miserable or anything like that. Should she?'

Callaghan said: 'How should I know? And as for your not noticing *everything* – well, you don't seem to have done so badly. The only thing you missed is the shade of the lady's *lingerie* . . .'

She said: 'I don't consider *that* concerns *me*, Mr Callaghan . . .'

Callaghan grinned. He said: 'You're quite right, Effie. Ask her to come in.'

Irana Faveley came into the office. Callaghan looked at her appreciatively. She was entirely self-possessed, smiling.

He got up. He said: 'Good morning, Miss Faveley. I think you look very nice.'

She said: 'That's very kind of you, Mr Callaghan. I think one ought to look nice, don't you?'

He said: 'Why not? Besides, it must be useful for you.'

She raised her eyebrows. 'Really!' she said. 'What exactly do you mean?'

Callaghan said: 'If you're going about the country saying you're somebody you're *not*, it's much better to be thoroughly attractive, don't you think?'

She made a little moue. Callaghan pushed forward a chair for her; went back to his seat behind the desk.

She said: 'Mr Callaghan, I wonder what you think of me.'

Callaghan grinned at her. He said: 'You didn't come here to ask me that, did you?'

She said: 'No, I came here to apologize – I hope prettily – and to say I'm sorry.' She smiled at him.

Callaghan said: 'That's very nice of you. Your apology is accepted. But I want to know *why* you're sorry.'

She made a little gesture with her hands. She said: 'Don't be unkind to me, Mr Callaghan. I'm not half as bad as I seem. I've come here to tell you the truth.'

Callaghan said: 'That would be a nice change. I'd be interested to hear it.'

She said: 'I had a good motive for what I did.'

Callaghan said: 'The road to hell is paved with good intentions. Tell me about the motive.'

She said: 'Well, the story I told you down in the country – some of it at least – was true. But I'd better explain why I pretended to be my sister Paula. You see, she did conceive that idea of taking the Coronet with her when she left Arthur Denys. Well, she didn't do it, and I didn't know *why* she didn't do it. I thought she *should* have done it, so I made up my mind I'd do it for her. When I make up my mind to do something,' she went on demurely, 'I do it.'

'So it seems,' said Callaghan. 'So you went to De Sirac, gave him the key of the house and the safe combination, so that your sister could have the Coronet?'

'That's quite right,' she said.

Callaghan said: 'After which De Sirac, having got the Coronet, refused to give it to you, and you had to find some way of getting possession of it.'

'You're perfectly right, Mr Callaghan,' she said. 'I was in a jam and had to get out of it. I reasoned that if I came to you and told you the truth, you'd probably refuse to have anything to do with me. So I conceived the idea of coming to you and telling you that *I* was Paula Denys.' She smiled at him suddenly. 'I thought you couldn't refuse your help to a wife who was being given a very bad deal by her husband.'

Callaghan shrugged his shoulders. He said: 'You know I've been to see your sister?'

She nodded. 'Paula's furious with me. At least she's pretending to be furious.'

Callaghan said: 'Well, she seemed to take the news coolly enough – almost as if she expected it.' He smiled at her. 'I don't think she likes me an awful lot,' he said.

She said: 'Well, perhaps she doesn't like private detectives. But then she only knows one side of you, Mr Callaghan, doesn't she? She doesn't know you as well as I do.'

Callaghan said: 'No, maybe she doesn't. Perhaps that's a pleasure she's got to come.'

She looked seriously at him. She asked: 'Are you going to see her again?'

Callaghan said: 'That depends on the next move in the game.'

She settled herself back in her chair. She said: 'That's really what I've come to see you about. I'm going to do the right thing and I want you to help me.'

He grinned amiably. He said: 'I thought there'd be a catch in it somewhere. And what am I to do this time?'

She said: 'Mr Callaghan, please believe me when I say that I don't want you to do anything. It's what you're *not* to do that matters to me.'

Callaghan said: 'That would be a nice change. Well, what am I not to do, Miss Faveley?'

She said: 'I wish you wouldn't call me that. It sounds so formal. My name's Irana.'

Callaghan said: 'A delightful name too. It's nice of you to let me call you by your first name, but I'm much more intrigued to know what I'm *not* to do.'

She said: 'I'm going to ask you not to say anything to anybody about this, Mr Callaghan. Just to forget it. I think you'll do that for me.'

Callaghan said: 'Why?'

She said: 'I'll tell you. I'm going to return the Coronet. Quite obviously, no one's discovered that it's gone. Well, I have a key to the house. I know the combination of the safe. I'm going down there tonight and I'm going to put it back.'

Callaghan said: 'You've got a good nerve, haven't you? So you're not going to ask Mr De Sirac to do it for you this time?'

She looked at him demurely. She said: 'No, I'm not. Once bitten twice shy! All that remains for me to do is to go and put the Coronet back, after which I can sleep easily – at least I can if you promise that you're going to forget about this. Please say you will.'

Callaghan said: 'Why not? If you intend to put the Coronet back, I don't see why I should say anything about it. Besides, who should I talk to about it? So far as I'm concerned the business is finished. There's only one thing . . .'

'And what is that?' she asked.

Callaghan said: 'That thousand pounds. I think I earned that a little too easily. I think I'm going to give it back to you.'

He opened a drawer, took out the packet of banknotes. He walked over to her; threw them into her lap. He said:

'For once Callaghan Investigations has really done something for nothing.'

She said: 'Really, you're the most delightful man, Mr Callaghan. I don't know how to thank you.'

Callaghan said: 'You don't have to. There's just one other point interests me and that is this: Aren't you scared of De Sirac?'

She hesitated for a moment; then she said: 'That's something I hadn't thought of.'

Callaghan said: 'I should think it would be worth while thinking about. He's not going to be very pleased with you, is he? And you've got to realize that at the moment he thinks you have the Coronet. He doesn't know that you're going to return it to its rightful owner.'

She said: 'No. I think he ought to know about that. I wonder . . .'

Callaghan looked at her sideways. He said: 'And what do you wonder?'

'I wonder if you'd do one more little thing for me,' she said, 'and tell him. Naturally, I don't want to have anything more to do with him. How could I? I never want to see him again. But if you were to tell him, Mr Callaghan – if you were to tell him that the Coronet had been returned – it would sort of tie the ends up, wouldn't it? It would close the De Sirac episode.'

Callaghan said: 'Yes, I suppose it would. All right, I'll tell him.'

She said: 'And I shall be able to sleep in peace. Mr Callaghan, do you know what I think you are?'

He smiled at her. He said: 'No, I don't. Lots of people have thought I was all sorts of things.'

She said: 'I think you're a darling. You've been awfully good to me. I'm going to take this money back again because, candidly, I need it. I think you've been very *very* generous.'

She got up; came towards Callaghan, who was standing in front of the fireplace. She stood quite close to him. He caught a suggestion of her perfume. Then, quite suddenly, she put her arms round his neck; kissed him full on the mouth; turned and walked out of the office. Callaghan heard the outside office door shut behind her.

After a minute he called to Effie Thompson. When she came in, he said: 'Aren't there some letters to be dictated?'

She looked at him. Then she said: 'Yes, Mr Callaghan, there are. And would you like to wipe your mouth? I don't think the shade of lipstick that Miss Faveley wears suits you an awful lot.'

Callaghan was drinking tea when Nikolls came in. He looked up enquiringly.

Nikolls said: 'Well, it's pretty easy. That dame was the sister.'

Callaghan said: 'Yes, go on.'

'There is a pair of 'em,' said Nikolls. 'They usta be called the lovely Miss Faveleys. One of 'em – Paula – married this Denys guy. I think she was sorta pushed into it by her people. They're dead now. The other one is Irana. A pair of classy babies by what I can hear of them – expensive educations an' everything that opens an' shuts, you know – all the right social sorta backgrounds. A swell pair of beautiful brunettes.'

Callaghan asked: 'Why didn't Irana get married?'

'I wouldn't know,' said Nikolls. 'She just didn't, that's all. But she gets around plenty. She's travelled a lot. I reckon she's a bit more frisky than her sister.'

Callaghan said: 'So it seems. Anything else?'

'Nothin' much,' said Nikolls. 'Paula was fairly well off when she married Denys and he had some money too. But Denys is a sorta playboy. He spends a lot an' drinks a lot. Beyond that he seems a popular sorta guy.'

Callaghan asked: 'What about Irana's finances?'

'She oughta be fairly well off. She was left some dough by her folks,' said Nikolls, 'but I'd say she was a pretty good spender. She likes clothes.'

He lit a cigarette. 'I wonder what she did this for. I wonder what the big idea was.'

Callaghan said: 'I know. She's been in today.'

Nikolls said: 'For cryin' out loud! She's got her nerve all right, that one.'

Callaghan said: 'She did it for her sister.'

Nikolls said: 'Ain't she a pip?'

Callaghan went on: 'The idea was that it was Paula's scheme originally to take the Coronet when she left Denys, but she got scared of it so she didn't do it. Irana thought she ought to take the law into her own hands and do it herself. She got De Sirac to do the job and he turned sour on her.'

Nikolls said: 'Well, that's logical. He had her where he wanted her. She didn't leave the Coronet with you by any chance?' He flopped into a leather armchair.

Callaghan said: 'No. She's going to return it.'

Nikolls grinned. 'You don't say!' he said. 'Well, maybe she's right.'

Callaghan said: 'Maybe she is. Anyway, that's what she is going to do.'

Nikolls said: 'She certainly is a pip – that one. What about that lug De Sirac?'

Callaghan said: 'I'm going to tell him all about it. I'm seeing him tonight.'

Nikolls said: 'He won't be pleased. It looks as if he's had the thin end of the stick on this job. I'm sorta sorry for that guy. Anyhow, you got a thousand, so it looks like the end of the story.'

Callaghan said: 'No, I didn't. I've given her the thousand back.'

Nikolls' eyes widened. He said: 'For cryin' out loud! What's the idea?'

Callaghan said: 'Well, the Swayle money is paid, and I didn't think we'd done enough work for a thousand on this job.' He smiled. 'Besides,' he said, 'I rather like Irana.'

Nikolls said: 'I see. That's an expensive sort of like, hey? I wonder if we'll ever see that honeypot again.'

Callaghan said: 'I wonder.'

At eight o'clock precisely Callaghan stood in the passage at the doorway of De Sirac's flat and pressed the bell. Almost immediately the door opened. De Sirac stood smiling in the hallway. He said:

'I think I like this visit rather more than I did your last one.'

Callaghan followed De Sirac into the sitting-room. He put his hat on a chair. He said:

'Mrs Denys' sister – Irana Faveley – came to see me this afternoon. Apparently it was her sister Paula Denys' idea in the first place to take the Coronet, and then Irana thought she ought to go on with the scheme. She realizes now she's made a mistake. She's going to do her best to put it right.'

De Sirac went to the sideboard; mixed himself a whisky and soda. He said:

'How's she going to do that?'

Callaghan said: 'That's relatively simple. She's going to put the Coronet back in the safe at Mayfield Place.'

De Sirac laughed.

Callaghan said: 'What have you got to laugh about?'

De Sirac said: 'Nothing. I'm the fall guy, aren't I, Callaghan – the sucker? That Irana has certainly got something, hasn't she? She pulls me in to do this thing, and heaven knows it's not in my line. Any risk and trouble I've taken have been for nothing.' He shrugged his shoulders. 'I wonder she didn't ask me to put it back for her,' he said.

Callaghan said: 'Well, I should think she'd hardly do that.'

De Sirac grinned. 'She'd be right there,' he said. 'I wonder if she proposes to pay me the other two hundred and fifty pounds.'

Callaghan said: 'No, she won't do that. Why should she? You've got two hundred and fifty out of this and the thing's finished. I think everybody ought to be very happy.'

De Sirac said: 'Including me.' He finished his whisky and soda. 'I suppose this story of Irana's is true?'

Callaghan said: 'Meaning what?'

De Sirac said: 'When I saw you yesterday you rather suggested that Mrs Denys might have been behind this. That might still be true, mightn't it?'

Callaghan said: 'How should I know? And what do I care?'

De Sirac said: 'Your attitude seems to have changed since yesterday. I had an idea that you had something in your mind – something in which we might co-operate.'

Callaghan said: 'I had a lot of things in my mind yesterday, but yesterday isn't today. Besides, Miss Faveley's attitude about returning the Coronet rather puts an end to things, doesn't it?'

De Sirac said: 'I suppose it does.' He shrugged his shoulders. 'Well, that's that!'

Callaghan picked up his hat. 'You're perfectly right,' he said. 'That's that! It looks as if there aren't going to be any more pickings in this for you or anybody else.'

He stopped at the door; looked over his shoulder and smiled. He said: 'It looks as if you haven't even got anything to blackmail Miss Faveley about now, have you?'

De Sirac was at the sideboard pouring another drink. He returned Callaghan's smile over his shoulder. He said:

'No, I haven't. That's a pity, isn't it?'

Callaghan said: 'I don't suppose it'll worry you a lot.'

De Sirac said: 'Why should it? Good night, Mr Callaghan.'

Callaghan said good night.

It was half-past ten. Callaghan and Nikolls sat on high stools against the bar at The Triton Club in Albemarle Street. They were drinking double Bacardis. Nikolls put his glass down on the bar. He signalled to the henna-haired young woman behind it to refill the glasses.

He said: 'I feel sorta depressed about the Denys business. It didn't do us any good. It didn't do this De Sirac guy any good –'

Callaghan said: 'De Sirac got two hundred and fifty pounds.'

Nikolls shrugged his shoulders. 'What's that?' he said. 'Just chicken feed to a guy like that. Funny that boyo sorta bein' contented with the situation, hey?'

Callaghan said: 'What else can he do?'

Nikolls said: 'That's true enough. I suppose he thinks if he tried to make any trouble he'd have you on his tail.' A thought struck him. 'But why should you be worryin'?' he said. 'You're not workin' for anybody in this case now. It's finished.'

Callaghan said: 'Yes, that's right. It's all over.' He went on: 'What do you propose to do now?'

Nikolls said: 'I don't propose to do anything. I thought I'd have two or three more Bacardis an' go home. I need sleep.'

Callaghan said: 'That's an idea. I think you need sleep too. I'll see you in the office tomorrow morning at ten-thirty. Good night, Windy.'

He got off the high stool; went out of the bar.

He began to walk down Albemarle Street. He turned down Hay Hill. Half-way down he stopped; lit a cigarette. A taxi crawled along the kerb. Callaghan stopped it.

He told the driver to go to Palmeira Court.

Callaghan arrived at Palmeira Court at half-past eleven. The neat maid who opened the door looked a trifle surprised.

Callaghan said: 'It's very late, but it's necessary that I see Mrs Denys. Will you tell her?'

The maid asked him to come into the hallway and wait. She returned in a few minutes. She said:

'Will you come this way, sir?'

Callaghan followed her across the hallway; went into the drawing-room. Mrs Denys, in a black velvet house-coat, was writing letters at her desk.

She got up, came towards him. She was smiling. Callaghan thought: She's come to the conclusion that it would be better for us to be friends.

He said: 'I'm sorry to disturb you at such a late hour, Mrs Denys. I haven't very much of an excuse, except that I think you ought to know that the lady who called herself Mrs Paula Denys, and who is apparently your sister – Irana Faveley – came to see me this afternoon. She cleared up the situation. She told me she proposes to return the Coronet to Mayfield Place.'

'In that case,' said Mrs Denys, 'the matter can be considered at an end, don't you think?'

'It might be,' said Callaghan. 'But I'm curious, Mrs Denys.'

She asked: 'About what, Mr Callaghan?'

Callaghan said: 'I would like to know a little more about the story your sister Irana told me when she came down to see me in the country, when she was pretending to be you.'

She said: 'Exactly what did she tell you, Mr Callaghan?'

Callaghan said: 'It was something like this: She said that you and your husband had never lived together as husband and wife; that you weren't at all keen on him. She said that six months ago you decided to leave him; that you had a talk to him about his allowing you to divorce him, but he didn't like the idea. Is that right?'

She said: 'Yes, that is correct. But I don't see what this has to do with you, especially now.'

Callaghan said: 'What do you mean by "especially now"?'

She said: 'Mr Callaghan, my sister, pretending – for what she thought was a good motive – to be me, came to you and asked you to get the Coronet returned to her. You did it and I'm very grateful that you did. And you were paid a thousand pounds for doing it. Don't you think that that rather settles the matter? Do we have to go into anything else? Do we have to go into my private affairs?'

Callaghan said: 'Why not? First of all I'd like to tell you that I haven't been paid a thousand pounds for getting that Coronet back. I returned the money to your sister this afternoon.'

She looked at him in amazement.

Callaghan said amiably: 'That surprises you, doesn't it? The idea of a private detective returning a client's money?'

She said: 'I must say I never conceived the idea of your doing something for nothing.'

Callaghan grinned. He said: 'You're perfectly right, Mrs Denys. I seldom do.'

She asked: 'Then why did you give the thousand pounds back to my sister?'

Callaghan said: 'That ought to be obvious. I'm a private detective, and I don't like to fall foul of the police.'

She said: 'But, Mr Callaghan, I see no reason why you should.'

Callaghan said: 'You never know. After all your sister planned to steal the Coronet – that's an offence, you know – a criminal offence. And the fact that I got it away from De Sirac and handed it back to her, might, in some circumstances, make me an accessory. You see, I haven't any guarantee that the police would believe me if I told them that I *thought* that Irana was the real Mrs Denys. They might possibly think I ought to have taken a little more trouble in the first place to find out.'

She said: 'I wonder why you didn't do that, Mr Callaghan. It might have saved a lot of trouble.'

He said: 'Do you think so? The position would be rather worse, wouldn't it? If I'd found out that she *wasn't* Mrs Denys, I *might* have gone to the police.'

She said: 'You might have done that.'

Callaghan thought he detected a little insolence in her voice.

'You might have done that,' she repeated. 'Or you might have done something else.'

'Such as what?' Callaghan asked.

She said: 'You might have kept quiet about it – for a consideration.'

He smiled at her. He said: 'That puts me in rather the same class as Mr De Sirac, doesn't it? Well, I don't mind that, Mrs Denys, but in point of fact I've been rather the guardian angel in this job, haven't I? That's why I think you ought to satisfy my curiosity.'

She said: 'Exactly what is it you want to know, Mr Callaghan?'

Callaghan said: 'I want to know this: Quite obviously, when you asked your husband if he'd allow you to divorce him, you hadn't any evidence against him. You couldn't have had, otherwise you wouldn't have had to ask him if he would agree to the divorce. Well, shortly after that you began divorce proceedings against him. So you *had* got some evidence?'

She said: 'Yes, I had.'

Callaghan asked: 'Where did you get it from, Mrs Denys?'

She said: 'If you must know, I received an anonymous letter. The letter said that my husband had been staying at an hotel in the country with a woman.'

Callaghan said: 'Anonymous letters are annoying things, aren't they? I suppose your lawyer has that letter, Mrs Denys?'

She said: 'As a matter of fact, he hasn't. It's been returned to me. I have it here with some papers.'

Callaghan said: 'Mrs Denys, should I be asking too much if I asked to see that letter?'

She said coldly: 'I really don't see why you should. I see no reason why I should continue to satisfy your curiosity.'

Callaghan said: 'I'm going to give you one. Mrs Denys, if you don't produce that letter, tomorrow morning I shall take a trip to Mayfield Place. I shall tell your husband the whole story. That's not going to be very convenient, is it?'

She said: 'Do you think he'll believe it? Irana has returned the Coronet by now. He'll never even know it's gone.'

Callaghan grinned again. He said: 'No? What about De Sirac?'

She said: 'What do you mean?'

Callaghan said: 'I'm not the only person who's annoyed, you know, Mrs Denys. De Sirac's not very happy either. He feels he's been done down. He describes himself as the sucker in this business. Well, he could corroborate my story, couldn't he?'

She said: 'That wouldn't be very easy for him, would it, Mr Callaghan? He'd be confessing to a crime.'

Callaghan shrugged his shoulders. 'If you like to put it that way,' he said, 'yes. But not such a terrible crime if he thought he was doing it for you. Do you see what I mean?'

She said: 'Yes, I see what you mean.' She considered for a moment. 'Do I understand that if I show you this letter you will not go to my husband.'

Callaghan nodded.

She asked: 'How do I know that I can believe you, Mr Callaghan?'

Callaghan said: 'You don't. That's one of the chances you have to take.'

She looked at him for a moment; then she turned; went to the writing desk. She unlocked a drawer, took out a folder, looked through it. She came back to him. She handed him the letter.

He took it. It was written on a half sheet of good notepaper. There was no address – merely the word '*London*' at the top. It said:

'*Dear Mrs Denys,*

For the last five or six days your husband Arthur Denys has been having a very good time at the Waterfall Hotel near Laleham. He's been staying there with a most delightful blonde. Personally I think she's ugly and I don't like his taste a bit. But I think you ought to know about it.

A Friend in Need'

Callaghan read the letter through twice. He handed it back to her. He said:

'Thank you very much, Mrs Denys. It only remains now for me to say good night. I expect you'll be glad to be rid of me.'

She said: 'I agree with you, Mr Callaghan. Unfortunately, I'm not quite certain that I shall be rid of you.'

Callaghan said: 'Meaning what?' He was smiling.

She said bitterly: 'You might want something else; mightn't you, Mr Callaghan?'

Callaghan said: 'You never know. Life is full of surprises. Good night, Mrs Denys.'

He went out.

Callaghan got out of the cab in Piccadilly. He began to walk down Piccadilly towards Berkeley Square. He was thinking. He was thinking that women were strange things. They did the weirdest things at the oddest moments. They said anything that suited them. Callaghan thought they never realized the efficacy of truth.

He began to think of The Crescent & Star. He felt annoyed with Irana Faveley for interrupting his holiday. After a moment he crossed over to the call box on the corner of Hay Hill. Inside he lit a cigarette, dialled a number. He waited patiently. After a few moments Effie Thompson's voice answered. Callaghan said: 'Effie, I'm awfully sorry to disturb you. Were you asleep?'

She said: 'Yes, Mr Callaghan. But does a little thing like that matter?' Her voice was acid.

Callaghan said: 'Thank you for reassuring me on that point, Effie.'

She said: 'Mr Callaghan, is this a social conversation, or did you want to tell me something?'

Callaghan said: 'Effie, I wanted to tell you something. I'm walking over to the flat now to pack a bag. You might get through to Nikolls and tell him to bring the car round. He'd better bring a suitcase with him.'

Effie said: 'Are you going away, Mr Callaghan?'

He said: 'Yes, I'm going back to The Crescent & Star. I'm going to finish my holiday. Let me know if anything happens, will you, Effie?'

She said: 'Mr Callaghan, you know there've been two enquiries today. A gentleman who owns a brick firm has been missing his bricks. They have been disappearing in large quantities.'

Callaghan said: 'Tell him I haven't got 'em. Why should I trouble about his bricks?'

She said: 'Very well, Mr Callaghan. The other enquiry was from a lady. She's worried about her husband.'

Callaghan said: 'That's not unique, Effie. Most women are worried about their husbands.' He continued: 'Sleep well, Effie. If anything really important turns up you know where to get me.'

She said: 'If it does turn up I hope I shall be *able* to get you, Mr Callaghan. I wasn't very successful before.'

Callaghan grinned into the transmitter. He said: 'I know, Effie. But from now on everything's going to be *so* different!'

As he hung up he heard her say: 'Like hell it is!'

CHAPTER FIVE
THEY SELDOM SAY NO

THE afternoon sun tinted the rhododendron bushes on the lawn of The Crescent & Star. Long shadows stretched over the hot over-grown paths. In the corner of the verandah Nikolls lay extended at full length. By his side were two bottles of lager beer and a glass. He was reading a detective story.

Mrs Melander came on to the verandah. She looked at Nikolls. She thought to herself that he looked like nothing so much as an overgrown seal. She said: 'It's strange to see you reading a detective story, Mr Nikolls.'

Nikolls looked up. He said: 'Yeah! But I'm a guy who is always out to learn. Now this feller in this story – he's like me. He's a detective who relies on instinct. I gotta helluva instinct.'

Mrs Melander said politely: 'I'm sure of that, Mr Nikolls.'

Nikolls looked at her. He said: 'Now I can look at you and I can tell you plenty about what you been doin' today. Just by instinct . . .'

Nikolls looked at her mysteriously. His eyes wandered over Mrs Melander's trim figure. He said eventually:

'Look . . . you gotta fish scale stickin' to the sleeve of your right arm, hey? Well . . . that tells me a lot. It tells me that that second maid of yours has been duckin' again; that you had to go down to the village to get the fish. O.K. Well, there's a salvage drive on, so the fishmonger hadn't any wrappin' paper. So you had to bring the fish out without any paper. You carried it under your arm.'

Mrs Melander looked surprised. She said: 'Really, Mr Nikolls, you're quite wonderful . . .' She went into the house through the French windows. Just inside she met Suzanne Melander with a bundle of newspapers under her arm. She said to her mother:

'You just don't know how marvellous he is!'

Mrs Melander said: 'Well, my dear, what he said was perfectly true.'

Suzanne nodded. 'Quite,' she said. 'When I went down to the village for the newspapers I saw him standing in a doorway opposite the fishmongers. He saw you come out!'

She walked round the verandah towards the back of the house. At the bottom of the lawn where it joined with the thick undergrowth, Callaghan lay in a hammock swung between two trees. On a table by the side of the hammock was a bottle of brandy, a syphon and a glass. Callaghan lay relaxed in the hammock, looking up towards the sky, his arms hanging down over the sides.

Suzanne put the newspapers on his chest. She said: 'Here are your papers, sire!'

Callaghan said: 'Thanks.'

She stood looking at him, her hands clasped behind her back, primly. She asked: 'Aren't you going to kiss me?'

Callaghan said: 'Why not?'

Suzanne approached the hammock; leaned over him. He kissed her.

She said: 'You're the laziest person, aren't you. I don't even know why I want to be kissed by you. I suppose it's because you don't give a damn whether you kiss me or not.'

Callaghan yawned. He said nothing at all.

Suzanne sighed heavily. She said pleasantly: 'Damn you, Mr Callaghan.' She went back into the house.

Callaghan began to look through the papers. On the front page of *The Times*, under the 'Legal Notices' column, his eye stopped at an advertisement. He read:

Messrs Dyatt, Wilmot & Hayle, Assessors, give notice that the sum of £1000 will be paid to any person giving information which will lead to the recovery of a piece of antique jewellery known as the Denys Coronet, consisting of a gold box shaped as a Coronet, studded with diamonds, rubies and pearls, lately stolen from Mayfield Place, near Chessingford, Bucks. Information received will be treated in the fullest confidence.

Callaghan dropped the paper on to the ground. He reached for the brandy bottle, poured four fingers, splashed in some soda, drank it. He put the glass back on the table, folded his hands on his chest. He lay gazing at the sky drowsily.

Nikolls, carrying a bottle of lager beer and a glass, came across the lawn. He said to Callaghan:

'You know, I've been thinkin' about this guy De Sirac. A funny guy that, hey?'

Callaghan said: 'Most people are funny.'

Nikolls said: 'Yeah, but this guy is so funny that it creaks out loud.'

Callaghan folded his hands behind his head. He asked why. Nikolls poured out a glass of lager beer. He drank it off at one gulp. He said:

'Look, I reckon this Irana baby has gotta know this De Sirac bozo pretty well, ain't she – in the first place I mean.'

'Exactly what do you mean by in the first place?' asked Callaghan.

Nikolls said: 'Well, you don't go to a guy and ask him to pinch a Coronet outa somebody's safe; you don't give him the key of the house and the safe combination, unless you know the palooka pretty well, do you?'

Callaghan stretched. He said: 'You never know with women.'

Nikolls said: 'Maybe not. But I still think I'm right.'

Callaghan said: 'I think you're right too, Windy.' He felt in the inside pocket of his coat for his cigarette case; produced it, lit a cigarette. He lay back exhaling a thin stream of tobacco smoke.

Nikolls poured another glass of beer.

Callaghan said: 'Windy, pack your bag and get the next train back to town. Get a line on De Sirac. I want his background and anything else you can get. And find out what you can about Denys. That ought to be fairly easy. Mayfield Place is near Chessingford – a small place – and there's always talk in a village. Have you got that?'

Nikolls put down the glass. 'Yeah . . . I got it,' he said. His tone was dolorous. 'Say, is this journey really necessary?' he went on. 'We ain't workin' for anybody on this case!'

'No?' said Callaghan. He looked at his wrist-watch. 'You'd better get going,' he said. 'Don't waste any time.'

'O.K . . . O.K . . .' said Nikolls. He began to walk towards the house.

Callaghan lay back in the hammock relaxed. Above his head the foliage of the trees met in an archway. Through the leaves he could see the blue and white summer sky above him. He lay there content-edly for five minutes; then he got out of the hammock; went across the lawn up the back verandah steps into the house. He walked through it into the front office. He sat down by the telephone; dialled his office number.

Effie Thompson answered.

Callaghan said: 'Effie, go out and get a copy of today's *Times*. There's an Insurance Assessors' notice on the front page under the Legal Notices heading. Ring through to Mrs Paul Denys at Palmeira Court. Read it out to her.'

She said: 'Very good, Mr Callaghan. Anything else?'

'Yes,' said Callaghan, 'when you've done that you can tell her I shall be very glad to see her if she likes to come down some time this evening to The Crescent & Star.'

She said: 'I understand, Mr Callaghan. Supposing she doesn't want to come.'

Callaghan grinned. 'She'll come,' he said.

He hung up.

Dusk was falling. The evening shadows made grotesque patterns on the floor of the small parlour off the hallway. Callaghan, seated in the big leather armchair before the fireplace, his feet on the mantelpiece, smoked placidly. On the floor by his side was the bottle of brandy, now three-quarters empty, a syphon and a glass.

Suzanne Melander came in. She said: 'Mr Callaghan, a lady wants to see you – she says she's Mrs Paula Denys, but she's not the one who came before.'

Callaghan said: 'No, she wouldn't be.'

Suzanne said archly: 'She's very beautiful, Mr Callaghan.'

Callaghan said: 'I know.'

She asked: 'Are all your clients as beautiful? It must be very interesting being a private detective.'

Callaghan said: 'It is sometimes. We haven't had an ugly client for years. Plain women seldom get into trouble. Maybe you can work that one out for yourself?'

She said: 'Yes, I think I can. Shall I tell her to come in?'

Callaghan nodded.

He took his feet off the mantelpiece; got up. He was standing in front of the fireplace when Mrs Denys came in.

She stopped just inside the room. Callaghan, looking at her carefully, thought she *was* very beautiful. She wore a coat and skirt of small navy and white check, a navy blue shirt blouse, blue glacé kid court shoes. The small blue turban accentuated the colour of her eyes.

Callaghan said pleasantly: 'You look very beautiful. It's nice seeing you.'

She said: 'It's very kind of you to say that, Mr Callaghan, but I don't know that I'm awfully interested in your opinion.'

Callaghan grinned amiably. He said: 'No, you wouldn't be, would you?' He looked at the newspaper under her arm. He said: 'I see you got a copy of *The Times*.'

'Yes, it's terrible, isn't it? I wonder what it means.'

Callaghan said: 'Sit down, Mrs Denys. I think you and I ought to have a little heart-to-heart talk, don't you?'

She said coldly: 'I suppose we *should* talk, Mr Callaghan, although I don't know exactly what we're going to talk about.'

Callaghan lit a cigarette. 'But you've some sort of idea, haven't you? Otherwise you wouldn't have come here. I don't suppose it was particularly pleasant for you to have to make the journey.'

She said: 'No. But I regarded it as a necessity.'

She sat down in a high-backed chair by the table. She folded her gloved hands in her lap. She sat there quite still, looking at Callaghan. There was a long silence.

Eventually he said: 'You're intrigued as to what that Insurance Assessors' notice in *The Times* means?'

She shrugged her shoulders. 'It means only one thing, Mr Callaghan, doesn't it? It means that the Denys Coronet is not at Mayfield Place.'

Callaghan inhaled tobacco smoke. He nodded. 'That's perfectly right, and that in turn can mean a lot of things, can't it?'

She raised her eyebrows: 'A lot, Mr Callaghan?'

He said: 'Well, two or three. It could mean in the first place that Irana didn't return the Coronet. It could mean that Denys discovered the loss of it before she had time to put it back. And of course there's the third thing.'

She asked: 'What would that be, Mr Callaghan?' She was looking at him intently. Her eyes never left his face.

Callaghan said: 'The third solution is that De Sirac might have stolen the Coronet for the second time.'

She looked at him in astonishment. 'Would he dare?' she asked.

Callaghan said: 'Why not? He had the key of the house, so conveniently supplied by your sister. He knew the combination of the safe, which he also got from her. He knew that she was going to replace that Coronet. He knew she wouldn't waste any time about it. He knew she'd do it the same night.'

She said: 'Mr Callaghan, do you really believe that that is what has happened? Do you really believe that De Sirac has the Coronet?'

Callaghan said: 'How should I know?'

'Then what do you think has happened?' she asked.

Callaghan shrugged his shoulders. He said: 'You know as much about this business as I do.'

She said softly: 'I wonder. Tell me something, were you expecting that Insurance Assessor's notice to appear in *The Times*? Were you surprised when you saw it?'

'I always read the legal notices on the front page of *The Times*,' Callaghan replied. 'It's a habit of mine. I can't say I was awfully surprised.'

She said: 'I suppose it hasn't struck you, Mr Callaghan, that there might be another solution to my husband having discovered that the Coronet was missing?'

Callaghan raised his eyebrows. He said: 'Really! That's interesting.'

She said coolly: '*You* could have told him, couldn't you?'

Callaghan grinned. He said: 'You're perfectly right. I could.'

She went on: 'You could have let him know that the Coronet was missing before Irana had a chance to return it.'

Callaghan said: 'Quite. But why should I do that?'

She considered for a moment; then she said: 'I don't know. I don't profess to understand you very well, Mr Callaghan. You might have all sorts of unknown reasons. You might have seen a way to make some money out of it.'

Callaghan said: 'That isn't logical, is it, Mrs Denys? You forget that I had a chance to make a thousand out of your sister.'

She said: 'I realize that. But I think you considered there was some danger in taking that money.'

Callaghan said: 'So you thought I might get something from Denys for telling him that the Coronet wasn't there.' He smiled at her. 'You're guessing wildly, Mrs Denys. If I wanted to make anything out of this business I could do it very much more easily.'

She said: 'Yes, I suppose you could, Mr Callaghan.'

There was a pause; then Callaghan asked: 'Do you know where your sister Irana is at the moment?'

She shook her head. 'No, I don't. That's rather bothering me.'

Callaghan asked: 'Is that what you came to see me about?'

She said: 'Yes, I suppose it is. I remember you told me once before that eventually I should have to come to you. It seems that you're right, doesn't it?' She smiled at him – a small sarcastic smile.

Callaghan said casually: 'We always do our best for our clients.'

'That remains to be see, doesn't it?' she said. She opened her blue leather handbag; took out an envelope. 'Inside this envelope are two hundred and fifty pounds. Perhaps you'll accept that as a retainer.' She held out the envelope towards him. Callaghan walked over, took it from her. He put it in the side pocket of his jacket. He said:

'That's fine. Now, Mrs Denys, exactly what is the two hundred and fifty pounds for? Are we to do something or are we *not* to do something?'

She said: 'That's rather cryptic, isn't it, Mr Callaghan?'

Callaghan said: 'Let me put it a little more plainly. Do I take it that you're paying me this two hundred and fifty pounds to keep quiet about the fact that your sister Irana was originally responsible for the stealing of the Denys Coronet – whatever may or may not have happened to it afterwards?'

She said: 'I see no reason to believe that my sister Irana is a liar. I'm perfectly certain that she returned that Coronet.'

Callaghan shrugged his shoulders. He said: 'She telephoned you and told you she had. Isn't that right?'

She nodded. 'Yes, she did.'

Callaghan said: 'And you believed her?'

She said: 'I believed her.'

'All right,' said Callaghan, 'If you believed her, and if it's true, then somebody else re-stole the Coronet after she'd put it back. Well, it's not very difficult to guess who that would be. That would *have* to be De Sirac.' He grinned at her. 'Or would you *like* people to think it was De Sirac?'

She said: 'It *must* have been De Sirac'

Callaghan smiled at her. He said: 'All right. That's how it is!'

She got up. She said: 'Mr Callaghan, I don't like your attitude very much. I never have liked it, but I suppose I'm not in a position to complain. You're suggesting that by some means or other you can hang this thing on to De Sirac, believing that my sister Irana never returned the Coronet. I don't think I like that.'

Callaghan said: 'What you like or what you don't like has very little to do with it. I'm concerned with facts. I don't suppose your husband likes you very much. I don't suppose he likes your sister Irana. I'm perfectly certain that if he knew Mr De Sirac he wouldn't like him either. He has reason for dislike too, hasn't he? You are at the present moment in the process of divorcing him. Your sister plotted to have the Denys Coronet – his most valuable piece of property – stolen, and De Sirac carried out that theft. The very fact that that Assessor's notice has appeared in *The Times*, Mrs Denys, is an indication that the disappearance of the Coronet has been established and that your husband has put a claim in on the Insurance Society.'

Callaghan took out his cigarette case, selected and lit a cigarette. He was maddeningly slow about the process. When the cigarette was lit he inhaled deeply, blew smoke rings into the air. He went on:

'The Assessors are carrying out the usual custom of trying to get some information as to where the missing piece of jewellery might be. The next thing that happens is that the police will be brought into this. They must be. The Insurance Company are going to insist on that. Very well, there are several people who know quite a lot about the Denys Coronet. Who are these people? They are you, your sister Irana, myself and De Sirac. Of those four people only one is likely to do sufficient talking to upset the applecart, that is Mr De Sirac. You have suggested that I have talked, but I assure you I haven't.'

She interrupted. She said: 'I didn't suggest anything of the sort. I suggested that you *could* have done so.'

Callaghan went on: 'All right. I *could* have done so. But, believe it or not, I didn't.' He smiled at her. 'Do you know why? Because I made up my mind, Mrs Denys, that eventually you were going to be a client of Callaghan Investigations – and Callaghan Investigations never lets its clients down.' His tone was sarcastic. 'Well, not often. In any event, you have made it worth my while by paying me a retainer to treat anything that I may have discovered in this business as a matter of confidence. So it looks as if there's only one thing to be done.'

She said nothing. She stood looking at Callaghan. Then she said: 'There are moments when I think I have *never* disliked anyone so much as I do you.'

Callaghan smiled at her. He said evenly: 'We don't make any extra charge for that, Mrs Denys. And in any event somebody has got to shut De Sirac's mouth, haven't they? And the person best suited to do that is me. Isn't that what you wanted, Mrs Denys? Isn't that what you came down here for?'

She said: 'Candidly, Mr Callaghan, I was afraid that this man De Sirac might talk; that he might possibly do my sister some harm.'

Callaghan cocked one eyebrow. 'And not only your sister,' he said. 'What about you? Remember, won't you, that the *original* idea of stealing the Denys Coronet was yours.'

She said: 'Mr Callaghan, I don't think we need discuss that. Whatever ideas I may have had *I* was never responsible for their being carried out.'

'That's all right,' said Callaghan. 'I believe you, but I doubt if anyone else would.'

She moved over to the table; stood looking out of the window. She said quietly: 'I don't think there's anything else for us to talk about, is there?'

Callaghan threw his cigarette stub into the grate behind him. He said: 'I don't think there is, Mrs Denys, except I suppose you'd like me to try and find out where Irana is, wouldn't you?'

She said: 'I've been hoping very much to hear from her.'

Callaghan said: 'Well, of course, you may hear from her, and then you may not. One would have thought that when she heard about the Coronet, she'd have called through to you by now.' He grinned. 'But then perhaps she doesn't read the newspapers.'

She turned round. She said: 'Mr Callaghan, I am worried about Irana, not because I believe that she's done anything deliberately wicked, but because I'm worried about her in connection with this man De Sirac. I'm frightened for her. I *would* like to know where she is.'

Callaghan said: 'That's all included in the two hundred and fifty pounds. We'll try to take care of everything.'

She said: 'Thank you very much.' She walked towards the door. On the threshold she stopped suddenly as if she'd thought of something; half turned; then she said:

'Good evening, Mr Callaghan.'

Callaghan said: 'Good evening.'

She closed the door quietly behind her. Callaghan stood in front of the fireplace looking straight in front of him. After a while he began to smile. Then he reached down for the brandy bottle. He poured out a very stiff shot. He held the amber-coloured liquid up to the light and looked at it.

He said: 'Well . . . well . . . well . . . !'

He drank the brandy.

Effie Thompson was about to put the cover on her typewriter when Nikolls came into the office. He crossed into Callaghan's room, sat down at the desk, opened the lower drawer, found the whisky bottle, took a long swig. He sighed heavily.

He called: 'Effie!'

She came into the doorway. She said: 'What is it, Mr Nikolls?'

Nikolls said: 'I suppose the boss is still down in the country. I'll have to make a night train. Me – I hate goddam trains. Everybody stands on your feet an' there's always some momma wants to tell you her life story.'

'You needn't worry,' she said. 'Mr Callaghan's back. He said if you came in before seven you could reach him at The Silver Grill in Dover Street.

Nikolls raised his eyebrows. He said: 'You don't say. So we're workin'? Who're we workin' for, Precious?'

Effie smiled. It was a cynical little smile. She said: 'We're working for Mrs Denys – the real one.'

Nikolls grinned. He said: 'Can you beat it! What happened?'

She shrugged her shoulders. 'What do you think happened? Mrs Denys decided to go down and see Mr Callaghan at The Crescent & Star. He knew she'd go there eventually. She *had* to.'

Nikolls said: 'How come?'

'He called through here, told me to ring her up and read the Assessors' notice in *The Times* – the notice that said the Coronet was stolen from Mayfield Place.'

Nikolls said: 'Well . . . I'll be sugared an' iced. So that's why he sent me up to get this dope. He musta been guessin'.'

'It was good guessing,' she said. 'But he knew that when she heard about that notice she'd have to go down and see him. I bet he loved that.' She sniffed audibly.

Nikolls said: 'He's a funny guy sometimes . . .'

'Not so funny as sadistic,' she said.

Nikolls said: 'Yeah . . . what's that?'

She shrugged her shoulders again. 'What does it matter?' she said. 'Let's skip it. If his clients like to be treated like that – if they *like* to stand for it – that's their affair.'

He grinned at her. '*You* wouldn't stand for it, would you, Effie?' he said.

She said: 'This conversation isn't really necessary, Mr Nikolls. I'm merely Mr Callaghan's secretary. Beyond that I'm not interested.'

'I know,' said Nikolls. 'If you was wrecked on a desert island with him you wouldn't even ask him to knock a coconut offa tree for you. You'd just sit around and play with the sharks.'

She said: '*Good* night, Mr Nikolls.'

'O.K . . . O.K . . .' said Nikolls. 'It looks to me as if I'm the only good-tempered guy around this dump. Talkin' to you reminds me of a dame that I once knew in Saskatchewan. Did I ever tell you about that baby?'

Effie said: 'That was the brunette with eight divorces, wasn't it?'

Nikolls said: 'Nope. This was a red-head. She was terrific. She woulda been all right if she'd kept her fingers crossed.'

Effie said: 'Well – why didn't she?'

Nikolls said:

'I wouldn't know. Maybe it was my fatal charm. I'll get around to tellin' you about her sometime. So long, sweetheart.'

Callaghan was sitting at the corner table in the almost deserted Silver Grill. He was eating chicken salad, drinking whisky. He was wearing a dark grey suit with a black and white foulard spotted tie. He was freshly shaved. Nikolls, crossing towards the table, thought he looked happy.

Nikolls sat down.

He said: 'Well . . . here I am.'

Callaghan indicated the bottle. 'Give yourself a drink,' he said.

'Thanks,' said Nikolls. 'I could use one.' He helped himself to a whisky and soda. He went on: 'Effie tells me we're workin' for Mrs Denys.'

Callaghan nodded.

Nikolls said: 'About this De Sirac guy: The guy's about thirty-seven. He's a quarter French. He's been hangin' around the West End for years – always well-dressed – always with some dough. Nobody seems to know where he got it from. Dames go for him in a big way. They like him. Don't ask me why because I don't know.'

Callaghan asked: 'Was there any connection between De Sirac and Irana Faveley that you could put your finger on?'

Nikolls said: 'They usta dance together but not a lot. It looked as if she was just one of the usual run of dames that usta get around with him.'

Callaghan asked: 'Why should De Sirac think that she had a lot of money? He must have known her fairly well. He must have had a reason for thinking she had money.'

Nikolls drank some whisky. 'Search me!' he said. 'Why does he have to think she has money?'

Callaghan said: 'He was holding her up for ten thousand over the Coronet, wasn't he? He must have thought she had that amount.'

'Yeah . . .' said Nikolls. 'I never thought of that one. De Sirac musta thought she had a lotta jack. Maybe he was just hopin'.'

Callaghan shook his head. 'People like De Sirac don't just hope,' he said. 'He must have had some idea that there was money to be had – somewhere.'

Nikolls nodded. 'Yeah,' he said. 'Ten thousand . . . that's a lot of loose change.' An idea came to him. 'Say, look,' he said, 'maybe De Sirac thought Irana could get the dough offa Paula. See? Maybe he thought that if Paula got to hear that he's holdin' Irana up for the Coronet . . . he reckons that Irana has gotta go an' tell Paula about it. He reckons that she's gonna tell Paula that she fixed this Coronet liftin' business for *her*, an' that Paula is gonna stump up so's to keep Irana outa trouble. How's that?'

Callaghan lit a cigarette. He said: 'That could be; but if De Sirac thought that, he was wrong. Irana didn't go to Mrs Denys, did she? She came to us.'

'Yeah . . .' said Nikolls. 'That's right. She came to us. An' *we* went to Mrs Denys, didn't we? An' *we* got the Coronet back offa De Sirac an' we slipped the thousand back to Irana. Maybe *we're* the mugs.'

Callaghan grinned. He said evenly: 'You mean *I'm* the mug?'

Nikolls said nothing.

Callaghan asked: 'Just what do you think?'

Nikolls shrugged his shoulders. He fished in his pocket for the cigarette pack. He said:

'Search me. I don't think anythin'. You know what you're doin'. But why you hadta hand that thousand back to Irana beats me. You coulda kept that. There wasn't any strings on that dough.' He grinned. 'It looks like you gone overboard for somebody. Maybe Mrs Denys has got something . . .'

Callaghan said: 'Did she know De Sirac?'

'Not as far as I can make out,' said Nikolls. 'I can't get much on her except this: She was sorta pushed into this marriage with Denys by her people. Denys wanted to marry her but she didn't wanta marry him. Irana was against it too. She didn't like Denys. She did everything she could to stop her sister marryin' him. I'm not surprised. The guy's usually high; an' he has a weakness for heavy blondes.'

Callaghan said: 'Lots of them, I suppose?'

Nikolls nodded. 'There was plenty,' he said. 'Denys is a guy who apparently believes that there is safety in numbers. He always has one totin' around.'

'Who's the woman that Denys is getting about with now? I suppose there is one,' said Callaghan.

'Yeah,' said Nikolls. 'The babe on the menu at the moment is some frail called Juliette de Longues. Semble, the guy on the door at the Relinqua Club, told me about her. She's some *bona roba* that one. She's so goddam full of allure that you gotta look at her with blinkers.'

'Is she really French?' Callaghan asked.

'I wouldn't know,' said Nikolls. 'Semble says she's got a line in French accents that would open a sardine can. This baby can work enough basic English with her eyes to ask for anything she wants without sayin' a word. Any time she gets stuck she says "But definitlee . . .", an' lets it go at that. I sorta like the sound of Juliette.'

Callaghan asked: 'Would Juliette be the blonde who stayed at the hotel with Denys – the woman who was cited in Mrs Denys' divorce petition?'

Nikolls shrugged. 'Maybe,' he said. 'It was some unknown dame. I went into that. I went down to the hotel. Some firm of private dicks came around an' hiked round a picture of Mrs Denys; they asked the waiters an' everybody if that was the baby who'd stayed with him. They all said no, it wasn't. But nobody ever showed 'em a picture of the frail who did.'

Callaghan said: 'No, I can understand that.'

Nikolls said: 'About this Coronet thing, it's valuable all right, but the value is mainly in the fact that it's an antique – a bit of old stuff – beautiful hand-work. Mark you, the jewels in it are worth plenty, but I don't reckon it would be a lotta use for anybody to melt down an' prise out the stones.'

Callaghan said: 'What's it insured for and who wrote the policy?'

Nikolls said: 'It's insured for seventy thousand with the Globe and Consolidated. The policy's eight years old and the premiums have always been paid. Everything's O.K. there. Denys has put a claim in.'

Callaghan nodded. He said: 'Is that the lot?'

Nikolls said: 'That's enough to be going on with, hey? Where do we go from here?'

Callaghan did not reply. He asked: 'Where's Denys at the moment?'

'He's up in town,' said Nikolls. 'He's a great guy for dance haunts an' gamblin' dives. He uses The Chemin de Luxe. You know, that swell dump off Mount Street. He's there practically every night.'

Callaghan finished his whisky. He asked: 'Who runs The Chemin de Luxe?'

'Carlazzi runs it – frontin' for that guy Vanza who usta have The Bright Spot. You remember The Bright Spot?' Nikolls grinned at Callaghan.

Callaghan nodded. 'I remember it,' he said. He went on: 'All right, Windy, just keep on digging. Get anything you can on the de Longues piece and anyone else you think matters.'

Nikolls poured the last of the whisky into his glass. He said: 'That's O.K., but it would be a helluva help to me to know just what we're tryin' to do with this case. I suppose you wouldn't have any sorta idea about that?'

Callaghan said: 'At the moment – no. Except that we're trying to find Irana.'

'Just fancy that,' said Nikolls. 'Well, I hope we find her. Say, listen . . . what's a sadist?'

Callaghan considered. He said eventually: 'A sadist is a person who gets a kick out of seeing other people hurt.'

'I got it,' said Nikolls – 'a clever guy. One of those guys that dames hate like hell but go for in a very big way just because they don't know why . . . hey?'

Callaghan shrugged his shoulders. 'That's near enough, I suppose,' he said.

Nikolls got up. 'I'm gonna start readin' up to be a sadist,' he said. 'I reckon I've tried everything else. Maybe I'll get some place that way. Well . . . I'll be on my way.'

'Just a minute,' said Callaghan. 'About De Sirac. You might take a look at that apartment block where he lives. It's a pretty deserted sort of place. If he's not around; if the coast's clear and you get the chance, get inside that flat of his and have a look round. You might find something.'

Nikolls raised his eyebrows. 'Yeah?' he said. 'What do I find? An' what am I gonna look for? Maybe I'm gonna find the Denys Coronet on the hall table.'

'I don't think so,' said Callaghan. 'But you might find something else – you might find Irana.'

Nikolls looked at him in amazement. He said: 'Jeez! I give up. This case is breakin' my heart. O.K. If I do find her, where are you gonna be?'

Callaghan said: 'I'll be at my apartment – I hope – about two or three o'clock. You can call me there if you want.'

'O.K.,' said Nikolls. 'But I think this is a helluva case. In a minute somebody's gonna tell me I'm Julius Caesar an' I'm gonna believe 'em . . .'

He went out.

Callaghan lit a cigarette. He signalled the waiter; ordered more whisky.

He wondered where he was going to find Irana.

CHAPTER SIX
NIGHT PIECE

THE Chinese clock on the mantelpiece struck midnight. Callaghan opened one eye, cast a baleful look at the clock, got off the bed, began to walk up and down the bedroom. He was wearing a grey silk dressing-gown, red bedroom slippers. He was trying to concentrate on unimportant points.

Unimportant points – those details which seemed, in the first place, of little consequence – were usually the things that mattered in the long run. If they did matter they were like the concealed banana skin clue in the detective story upon which the detective, the reader and, very often, the author, all slipped up. Callaghan remembered things, in other cases, which had seemed unimportant. . . .

He walked into the sitting-room, went to the sideboard, found a bottle of rum, poured out a slug, mixed it with some synthetic lemon juice, swallowed it. It tasted awful. He shuddered a little, lit a cigarette and resumed his pacing.

It was understandable that Denys should not have wanted his wife to have a divorce. If you have divorces you have settlements and understandings; the Court want to know about finances; there are such things as alimony *pendente lite*. If Denys had been making ducks and drakes with his wife's money – *if* he had been – then his point of view was obvious.

But an incongruity became apparent for, having informed his wife that he would not consent to a divorce, he had promptly gone off to a hotel with a blonde and someone had been in a position in which they could write an anonymous note to his wife and inform her of the fact. And it had been a not too good-looking blonde. The writer of the anonymous letter had said that; had intimated that she was ugly. . . . That fact was interesting . . .

It was of course possible that Denys had thought his trip to the country would be undiscovered by his wife. Even so, his attitude was incongruous.

Callaghan began to think about Irana Faveley. Here at least was a woman who was consistent – definitely beautiful and beautifully consistent. She had objected in the first place to the marriage between her sister and Denys; then she had thought that, having married Denys, having realized that it was a complete failure, Paula was justified in going off and taking the Coronet with her.

Irana – who was a woman of nerve – had been annoyed that Paula had funked her fence at the last moment and left the Coronet behind. She had completed the business herself. She had arranged for it to be stolen and if, for this or that reason, the process had not come off, that was not her fault.

A definitely consistent person.

And Paula? Paula, just as beautiful, was not quite so consistent. But now, at last, she was being forced to take a line. Because, or so she said, she was frightened for Irana.

Callaghan wondered just *how* frightened Paula Denys really was. . . .

Then there was De Sirac. De Sirac was interesting because he seemed clever and did things which were, apparently, stupid. He had consented, in the first place, to steal the Coronet and hand it over, for the sum of five hundred pounds. Having got the Coronet, he had started a little blackmail on the side for an extra ten thousand without even bothering to draw the two hundred and fifty pounds, which were still due to him, *first*.

It would seem that De Sirac could be stupid. Yet his background was one in which stupidity was so redundant that the word was almost unknown. Surely De Sirac was not as stupid as that . . . ?

Callaghan's mouth was dry. His tongue seemed to be composed of a particularly dark brown plush. He stubbed out the cigarette in an ash tray, went to the sideboard, looked at the bottle of rum, decided to drink whisky. He found a bottle, poured out half a tumblerful, added a little soda water, drank it. He considered for a moment, decided that he felt better.

The telephone bell rang – the extension from the offices below. Callaghan walked across the room, picked up the receiver. He said: 'This is Callaghan Investigations.'

Somebody said: 'Hello, Mr Callaghan . . .' The voice was very soft, quite delightful, and a trifle tremulous.

Callaghan began to grin.

She said: 'You know who I am – of course.'

'Of course,' said Callaghan. 'I'm glad to hear from you, Miss Faveley, because you've saved me a lot of trouble. I'm supposed to be looking for you. Aren't you lost or missing or something?'

She said: 'Well . . . not really.' Her voice became serious. 'I'm in a jam,' she went on. 'A bad one. I need your help very badly. I don't know *what* to do.'

Callaghan said: 'In those cases the best thing to do is just nothing at all. What's the matter?'

'I can't talk to you on the telephone,' she said. 'I ought to see you. Please don't think that I've been deliberately stupid or wicked in seeming to disappear. I felt I had to . . .'

'I know that feeling,' said Callaghan. 'It becomes more marked when there's a possibility of someone getting a little tough, doesn't it, Miss Faveley?'

She said: 'I do wish you'd call me Irana. I feel I've known you for such a long time; that we're really such good friends . . . aren't we? I wanted to know if I could telephone you some time tomorrow. So that I could make an appointment for us to meet. I must talk to you but I don't want to meet anyone I know. You understand?'

'Perfectly,' said Callaghan. 'I take it that you're worried about something. I think I know what it is.'

She said: 'Do you . . . ? You *are* clever. I felt that about you when I first saw you.'

Callaghan grinned into the receiver. He said: 'Me too. . . . But getting back to cases, I think you rather wish you hadn't been so keen on doing what your sister originally planned to do. You wish you'd left it alone?'

She said: 'Yes, I do. I wish I hadn't done it. I wish She hesitated; stopped speaking.

Callaghan said: 'Let me make a suggestion about what you wish most of all. You wish that I hadn't gone to see your sister after we got that idea that you weren't Mrs Denys. You wish I'd never got the idea that you weren't. It would be so easy if I had still thought it was her . . .'

She said: 'Ye-es . . . Of course I must sound a fearful little beast to say that. I adore Paula . . . I'd do anything for her.

'Love's a wonderful thing,' said Callaghan. 'But don't worry too much. Perhaps I ought to tell you that I'm acting for Mrs Denys now. She's our client. She asked us to find you. . . .'

She said: 'Oh . . . that makes it rather . . .' She stopped speaking.

'Oh no, it doesn't,' said Callaghan. 'After all, you were our first client. We met you originally. Even if . . .' Callaghan's voice dropped a tone – 'we decide to forget it.'

She said: 'I always knew you were a sweet. Very strong and tough and fascinating and a sweet.'

Callaghan sighed.

She said: 'Will you tell me where I can telephone you tomorrow? So that I can arrange to see you.'

Callaghan said: 'Call through here – to my apartment. I'm speaking to you now on the extension line from the office. My private number here is Mayfair 66556. Perhaps you could call through in the morning.'

She said: 'Yes . . . I'll do that. I'm so *terribly* grateful to you . . . Good night . . . and thank you so much.'

Callaghan said good night. He hung up. He went back to the sideboard.

The rum tasted a lot better.

Callaghan parked the car halfway down Mount Street, began to walk. He stopped in the shadow of a doorway to light a cigarette, looked at his wrist-watch in the flame of the lighter. It was half-past one.

He continued on his way. The street looked delightful. The moon had come out and the buildings threw grotesque shadows across the pavements. He thought life was rather like that – a kaleidoscope of light and shade, and you picked your way gingerly in between the shadows – if you were lucky. . . .

Callaghan was intrigued. The conversation which he had had with Irana had opened up an entirely new aspect of thought – a very interesting one. He shrugged his shoulders. When you didn't know what to do you played it off the cuff and watched what happened. Something had to happen. Providing it was tangible enough you could make use of it.

He turned into a side street, turned again to the left and stopped at the entrance to an apartment block. The outer door was open.

Callaghan went in, closing the door quietly behind him. He found himself in a large well-furnished hallway, the passage in front of him leading towards the back of the building.

He walked along the passage, passing two lifts *en route*. He stopped at the end of the corridor opposite what seemed to be a service lift. He pressed the bell and waited.

The lift came down. A man in a pale grey and green uniform emerged. he was a tall thin man. He said:

'Good evening, sir. Can I do something for you?'

Callaghan smiled amiably. He said: 'I'm not a member of The Chemin de Luxe Club, but I'd like to be. I think I could be.'

The man grinned a little insolently. He said: 'I wonder what makes you think that?'

Callaghan said: 'I know Mr Carlazzi. In any event, it's something I'd rather discuss with him.'

The man said: 'You might be a dick.'

Callaghan said: 'I might be. I'm not. I might be a plain clothes man, but I'm not. You know that. I expect you've seen 'em in your time. The point is I'm going upstairs.' Callaghan grinned. 'The last time I had a little trouble with a lift attendant,' he said, 'he spent about three months in hospital trying to get them to put his jaw back into its normal position.'

The man said: 'You wouldn't be tough, would you?'

Callaghan said: 'I might.'

The lift attendant considered for a moment; then he said: 'Well, if you know Mr Carlazzi, there's no harm in your seeing him.'

Callaghan said: 'I'm glad of that.' He got into the lift.

The Chemin de Luxe was almost like its name. It was superbly furnished. It had atmosphere. The men and women who used it were the sort of people you found in places like The Chemin de Luxe. They were well-dressed. They had money. The women, in spite of war-time restrictions, still managed to find exotic perfumes, and the men seemed little worried with the coupon problem.

When you went through the door, which looked like the normal entrance of a flat, you found yourself in a long narrow room, effectively lighted from concealed globes, tastefully decorated in grey and black, with here and there a touch of silver. Six or seven doors led out of the hallway, which was entirely deserted except for a cloak-room, attended by a young woman, on the right-hand side.

On the left of the hallway was a door. The lift attendant knocked on it; opened it. He said through the half open door: 'Somebody wants to see you, Mr Carlazzi. He says he know you.'

A deep voice said: 'Ask him to come in.'

The man held the door open. Callaghan went in. The door closed behind him.

Vincent Carlazzi was sitting behind an ornate mahogany and rosewood desk that stood diagonally across the opposite corner of the room. He was of middle height, broad-shouldered and dark. His swarthy skin proclaimed his Italian parentage. His clothes, his linen, his tie, and the dressing that kept the superfine sheen on his hair, were all quite superb. It has been said by those who should know that Carlazzi was a specialist in looking after the vices of other people. Whether he was or not, the smile that showed his white teeth was open, almost benevolent.

Callaghan said: 'Good evening.'

Carlazzi got up. He stood looking at Callaghan. He said: 'I expect my memory's very bad, but I don't remember you.'

Callaghan said: 'You're a liar. You used to own a club called The Bright Spot. We had a client – a Mrs Vazey – I think her front name was Evette – she got into a lot of trouble at your club. I got her out of it. The name's Callaghan.'

Callaghan grinned. He took his cigarette case out of his pocket, selected a cigarette. As he lit it, he looked at Carlazzi through the flame of his lighter.

'Maybe you remember me now?' he said.

Carlazzi shrugged his shoulders. 'Of course,' he said. 'You know . . .' He spread his hands – 'one meets so many people.'

He came round the desk, went to a carved wall cupboard, took out a bottle and two glasses. He said:

'Perhaps my memory isn't so bad. Perhaps I remember that Mr Callaghan's favourite drink was bourbon neat with a water chaser.'

He put the bottle and glasses on the desk; went back for a carafe of water – more glasses.

Callaghan said: 'I'm glad you've remembered.'

Carlazzi poured the drinks. He said: 'You're not going to start anything, are you? You're not going to suggest that we've done something to another of your clients?' He looked at Callaghan. He smiled charmingly.

Callaghan said: 'No.' He went on: 'It's very necessary that I talk to Mr Denys. I though he might be here. If he is here he's going to thank you for letting me get at him. I think he's going to need me.'

Carlazzi raised his eyebrows. He said: 'You don't say? Well, I would do anything for you. Have your drink, and excuse me.'

He went out of the room. Callaghan drank his bourbon; helped himself to another three fingers; drank that; then a little water.

Three minutes later, Carlazzi came back. He said: 'My friend, you're lucky. Mr Denys is here. He's playing roulette. There's just one little thing. He says he doesn't know you.'

Callaghan said: 'That's all right. He will.' He grinned. 'And you can take it from me he'll like it a lot. I suggest the easiest thing is for you to show him to me.'

Carlazzi spread his hands. He said: 'All I can do is to try to please everybody. Come with me, my forceful friend.'

Callaghan followed him out of the office across the hallway. They went into the room at the top of the hallway. It was surprisingly large, very crowded. At one end was a large alcove in which was an American bar. In the main room were four roulette tables. A pall of smoke hung in the upper air in spite of the fact that two electric fans were working in the corners.

Carlazzi said: 'There's Mr Denys. I wish you good luck, my friend.'

Callaghan said: 'I'm invariably lucky. *You* ought to know that.'

He walked slowly through the room, edging his way here and there, to the American bar. He got some whisky from the white-coated attendant. He went back into the main room; stood leaning against the wall watching the crowd.

He looked at Denys. Denys was well-built, florid of feature, smiling. He looked prosperous. As he leaned over the table to stake, Callaghan noticed that he moved easily, quickly.

Callaghan looked at the woman who was sitting beside Denys. She was a blonde, and even if she was not good-looking – in fact Callaghan thought she might be described as ugly – she possessed that peculiar quality that some women enjoy – an allure that is indescribable, quickly recognized – a thing of movement, grace and personality – the thing that enables a man to 'go overboard' for a woman who, whilst not rating the adjective beautiful, has enough of what it takes to make a lot of trouble.

She was dressed in black, and when she got up to lean over the table to put some plaques on a number, Callaghan saw that her figure was exquisite. This, he thought, would be Juliette.

He walked over to the table. The croupier said: '*Mesdames, messieurs, rien ne va plus . . .*' He spun the wheel. There was the usual silence until it stopped. Denys shrugged his shoulders; threw a quick look at the woman beside him; stepped back from the table.

Callaghan said: 'Excuse me . . .' He stood at an angle to Denys, smiling. Denys looked at him.

He said: 'I don't think I know you.' His voice was brusque and incisive, well-modulated, curt.

Callaghan said: 'You *don't* know me. My name's Callaghan. I'm a private detective. I think it might be to everybody's advantage if you and I had a little talk.'

Denys said: 'I wonder why.' His tone was mildly curious.

Callaghan said: 'I've gone to quite some inconvenience to come up here to find you. I was on holiday. I saw the assessor's notice in *The Times* about the Denys Coronet. I thought I might be able to help.'

Denys said: 'Excuse me for a moment.' He leaned over the table; staked. His movements were deliberate. He backed *manque, impaire*, and six numbers. Then he came back to Callaghan.

He said: 'If you're particularly interested in that notice – if you know something that you think the assessors ought to know – it might be a good thing if you went to see them. I don't expect you're in business for your health, Mr Callaghan, and I think a considerable reward was offered.'

Callaghan said: 'I know. But I haven't anything of particular interest to say to the assessors.' He grinned. 'I thought I ought to talk to you.'

Denys said: 'I don't want to seem rude, but I still don't see why.'

Callaghan said: 'I'll try and tell you. I have an idea that somebody intended to remove that Coronet. I've an idea they removed it; I've an idea it was put back again, or maybe not. In fact I've got all sorts of ideas. But I don't think it would be awfully wise or clever of me to discuss them with the assessors.'

Denys said: 'No? Why not?'

Callaghan smiled. He said: 'Believe it or not, Mr Denys, if I did, eventually, one way or another, you wouldn't like it.'

The croupier called the winning number and colour. Denys was on the number. He waited until the plaques had been pushed towards him, picked them up. He dropped them casually into the side pocket of his jacket. He said:

'Mr Callaghan, I'll try anything once. Let's go and have a drink.'

They went into the bar in the alcove. Denys ordered the drinks. He said to Callaghan:

'You like whisky, don't you? You drink a lot of it?'

Callaghan said: 'A fair amount.'

Denys said: 'It doesn't stop you thinking?'

Callaghan said: 'No, I've solved most of my cases with the aid of a little whisky.'

Denys smiled. He said: 'Well, you'd better have some more whisky.'

Callaghan thought it was not an unpleasant smile.

The bar-tender refilled the glasses.

'Well, say on, my friend,' said Denys. 'I think I ought to tell you that I don't like private detectives. You may be the exception that proves the rule, but I think they're a funny lot.'

Callaghan grinned. He said: 'You'd be surprised if you knew how funny this one was. But I can understand you not liking them.'

'What do you mean?' Denys asked.

Callaghan said: 'It must have been awfully annoying for you to have private detectives stooging around that hotel at Laleham.'

Denys said: 'So you know about that too? What is this – a spot of blackmail?'

Callaghan shrugged his shoulders. He said: 'I'm not interested in the Laleham proposition. I'm interested in the Denys Coronet. I can tell you something about it. When I've told you about it, if you still think I ought to go and see the assessors and take that thousand pounds reward, I'll do it.'

Denys said: 'That's fair enough.'

Callaghan said: 'I was having a holiday in the country when a lady got into touch with my office. She wanted to see me urgently.

My secretary sent her down. This lady told me that she'd conceived the idea of removing the Denys Coronet from Mayfield Place; that she'd given a key to the house and the safe combination to a man she knew. The idea was that he was actually to remove the Coronet and return it to her at some later time. Interesting, isn't it?'

Denys drank a little whisky. He said: 'Very. Tell me some more. Why did she have to come and see you about it?'

Callaghan went on: 'Well, you see, the position got a little tough. Her boy friend decided he'd stick to the Coronet. He refused to hand it over. He wanted some money – a lot of money.'

Denys said: 'Well . . . well . . . Did he get it?'

'No,' said Callaghan. 'I undertook to try and get back the Coronet for her. I was lucky. I had an interview with the boyo and he listened to reason. I got the Coronet. I gave it back to her. It *is* interesting, isn't it?'

Denys said: 'That depends.'

Callaghan nodded. He said: 'Quite. Quite obviously whether it's interesting or not depends on who the lady was.'

Denys smiled. He signalled to the bar-tender for more whisky. He said: 'That is the part that's intriguing me. That's what I'm waiting to hear.'

Callaghan said: 'That's all very well, but the point is the assessors are prepared to pay a thousand pounds for that information they're asking for. If I don't go to them I shan't get it.'

Denys said: 'You mean that's because you've been a good fellow and told me about it first. Are you suggesting that I might give you a thousand?'

Callaghan said: 'You might. It depends on who the lady was, doesn't it?'

Denys considered for a moment; then he said: 'I'll have to be the judge of that, won't I?'

Callaghan said: 'Yes, that's only fair.'

The man in the grey and green uniform came into the bar. He came up to Denys. He said: 'You're wanted on the telephone, Mr Denys.'

Denys said to Callaghan: 'Will you excuse me for a moment? I'll have to hold my curiosity in check till I've taken this call.' He went away.

Callaghan finished his drink. He stood leaning up against the bar smoking a cigarette, looking into the roulette room. He felt happy. He felt he was swimming in a sea of ink. Whichever way one looked one couldn't see anything. So the only thing to do was to go on swimming.

A few minutes went by. Denys came back. He said: 'I'm sorry, Callaghan, but I've got to go. Something's turned up that I must attend to.' He said to the bar-tender: 'Do you think you could get a car for the lady who's with me?'

The bar-tender said: 'There's no hope, sir. You'll never get a cab or a car, or anything else, in London at this time of night.'

Callaghan said: 'Can I help? My own car's round the corner. Perhaps I could give the lady a lift.'

Denys looked at him. His eyes were smiling. He said: 'That's very nice of you. I think you're a very amiable fellow, and I'd be most grateful if you'd drop Miss de Longues – the lady who was with me at the roulette table – at her flat.'

Callaghan said: 'I'll be delighted. I'll go over and introduce myself in a minute.'

Denys said: 'I think you and I ought to have a little talk. I think in any event there's something we can talk about. Incidentally, I'd like to know the name of the lady.' He smiled. 'Who was this mysterious woman who went to such trouble to remove the Coronet?'

Callaghan grinned pleasantly. He said: 'It was Mrs Denys.'

Denys raised his eyebrows. He said coolly: 'It just shows how careful one ought to be, doesn't it, Callaghan? Women do the most surprising things.' He shrugged his shoulders. 'Perhaps after all you'd better have a talk with me,' he said. 'Telephone me tomorrow, at the Savoy. We'll make an appointment.'

Callaghan said: 'I'll do that. I'll be seeing you.'

'Good night,' said Denys. He turned away. He said, over his shoulder: 'As a detective I don't think you're quite so bad . . . but I still don't see what your game is.'

'You will,' said Callaghan. 'And I hope you'll like it.'

Callaghan stood leaning up against the wall of the roulette room watching Miss Juliette de Longues, who was having a run of luck. There was something fascinating about Miss de Longues, Callaghan thought. In some odd way her attraction was enhanced by the fact that she was plain. But that was because everything else about her was as it should be.

He walked over; stood behind her watching her as she played. Callaghan was considering whether it might be worthwhile to play another guess. He leaned forward. He said:

'Miss de Longues, my name's Callaghan. Mr Denys asked me if I'd take you home when you were ready to go. He's been called away, and it's practically impossible to get a cab at this time of night.'

She looked over her shoulder at Callaghan. She gave him a long searching look that took in every detail – from his shoes to his hair. She said precisely, with a vague touch of French accent:

'That is very kind of you. I am very grateful. Would you like me to go now?'

Callaghan grinned. He said: 'You're having a run of luck, Miss de Longues. Perhaps you'd rather play it out.'

She shrugged her shoulders. She said: 'If I go on playing I shall lose it, so I think I will go home. Shall I meet you in the hall?'

Callaghan said: 'Yes.'

She collected her plaques; went away. Callaghan went back to the bar and drank another whisky and soda. When he went out into the hallway she was waiting there. She stood in the centre of the large hall, quite relaxed, smiling vaguely at nothing. Callaghan got his hat. He said:

'If you will come downstairs in about three minutes, I'll have the car there.'

She said: 'Thank you very much.'

Callaghan went down in the lift. He was assessing the chance of playing another bluff, pulling it off or making a mistake. He concluded that if he made a mistake it might not be so good.

He fetched the car, sat behind the wheel smoking. He concluded that maybe the bluff was too good to be missed.

She came out of the entrance. Callaghan opened the door and she slipped into the car beside him.

He said: 'I think this is one of those nights – fresh but not cold. Where would you like to be driven to?'

'Not very far away,' she said, '– Lowndes Square will be very convenient for me. And can you give me a cigarette?'

Callaghan produced his case. He lit the cigarette for her, started the car. He turned towards Piccadilly.

She asked: 'Isn't this rather a funny way to go to Lowndes Square?'

He looked at her sideways. He said: 'Perhaps it is, Miss de Longues. It might take a little longer, but then I wanted to talk to you.'

She said: 'Ah, so you wanted to talk, Mr Callaghan. That's very interesting.'

Callaghan felt she was smiling in the darkness. 'So you're not surprised?' he asked.

She said: 'Mr Callaghan, nothing ever surprises me. Now . . . you talk!'

Callaghan said: 'First of all I think you should know that I'm a private detective.'

She said: 'That must be an interesting profession.'

Callaghan said: 'It is and it isn't. It's a very tough profession though, Miss de Longues – sometimes.'

She said softly: 'Are you trying to tell me, Mr Callaghan, that you are going to be tough with me?'

Callaghan accelerated a little. He turned into the Buckingham Palace Road. He said: 'I'm trying hard not to be tough with anybody. You see, the position is this. I came along tonight to see Mr Denys about something that required discussion. Then I saw you. You interested me very much, Miss de Longues.'

She said: 'Mr Callaghan, I think you are a very charming man to be interested in me. But why?'

Callaghan went on: 'We don't handle any divorce business in my firm. We don't like it. But sometimes we have a case which impinges on a divorce action. We've got something like that now. I thought I could save you a lot of trouble, Miss de Longues.'

She said: 'Ah . . . So Mr Callaghan wishes to save me trouble. How does he do that?'

Callaghan said: 'I'll be quite frank. Apparently Mr Denys stayed at an hotel at Laleham just about the time that the Denys Coronet was stolen – you know about that, of course – he didn't stay there alone. He stayed there with a woman – a blonde.'

She said: 'How very interesting.'

Callaghan said: 'It might be. Now, it seems that Mrs Denys received some information about this fact. She took action. Apparently a divorce petition has been issued citing this unknown lady.'

Callaghan stopped talking. Driving with one hand he fished out his cigarette case and lighter.

She said: 'Won't you let me help you, Mr Callaghan?'

She took the cigarette case, opened it, put the cigarette in her mouth, lit it. She slipped the case and lighter back into his pocket. In some odd way she made the process intimate and charming.

She said: 'So a divorce petition has been issued and an unknown woman has been cited. Go on, Mr Callaghan. I suppose in a moment we shall come to the crux of this business?'

Callaghan said: 'We're almost there now. The point is, Miss de Longues, it might be nice for the blonde lady who stayed at Laleham with Mr Denys to remain an unknown party. She might prefer that.'

She said: 'Mr Callaghan, why should I be interested?'

Callaghan grinned. He said: 'Because you were the woman, Miss de Longues. You are the blonde lady who stayed at Laleham. Well, not many people know that.'

There was a long silence; then she said: 'Mr Callaghan, what am I supposed to say or do? Supposing you are right – supposing I was the mysterious woman who stayed at the hotel at Laleham – supposing I wish to remain unknown – what do I have to do?'

Callaghan said: 'Just at this minute I don't know. But I can tell you this much. There is somebody isn't awfully well disposed to you. There's somebody knew you were staying there – somebody who wrote an anonymous letter to Mrs Denys – not a very nice person,' said Callaghan, still grinning, ' – he described you as being ugly. I don't think you're a bit ugly.'

She said: 'Mr Callaghan, I'm sure that you are always very charming.'

Callaghan went on: 'It may be that during the next two or three days, when a certain amount of public attention must be directed to Mr Denys because of the fact that the Denys Coronet has been stolen, that the writer of that anonymous letter might feel that the time had come when he might make himself a little troublesome. He might want something.'

She said: 'Yes, he might. You mean he might want money?'

Callaghan said: 'I don't know. How should I know? But he might want something. He might be difficult. I thought that you might like a little assistance from Callaghan Investigations, Miss de Longues. I thought you might like to give me your telephone number and address. Perhaps we might talk again.'

She said softly, in the same unperturbed voice: 'Mr Callaghan, you mean if this writer of unsigned letters becomes troublesome, then I might appeal to the charming Mr Callaghan for assistance?'

Callaghan said: 'Roughly, that is the idea.'

She said: 'A most delightful idea. Now if you will turn your car towards Lowndes Square I will give you a cigarette, a drink, and my card.' She smiled suddenly. Callaghan saw the flash of her teeth. She went on: 'Then I think I will feel much safer and much happier.'

Callaghan turned the car into Victoria Street. He smiled to himself. It looked as if the guess had come off.

It was ten minutes to three when Callaghan drove the Jaguar into the garage at Berkeley Square. He walked up the ramp, through the side door into the apartment block. Wilkie, the night porter, was seated in his glass-fronted box, reading the *Evening News*.

Callaghan said: 'Good evening, Wilkie.'

Wilkie yawned. He said: 'There's not much evening about it, Mr Callaghan. It's ten to three. Mr Nikolls is upstairs. He's in the flat. He's been there since half-past one.'

Callaghan asked: 'Any calls on the office lines?'

Wilkie shook his head.

Callaghan went up to his apartment. Nikolls was sitting in the big leather armchair in front of the fire. His hands were folded placidly on his stomach. A cigarette was hanging from the corner of his mouth. An empty glass was on the floor by his side. He said:

'I'm glad you got back. I wondered how long I'd gotta stick around here.'

Callaghan said: 'Wilkie tells me you've been here since one-thirty. You've had a drink?'

'Yeah,' said Nikolls. 'I had two-three drinks. You look sorta pleased about something.'

Callaghan said: 'I am. I've been doing a little guessing tonight. It seems to have come off.'

'Yeah,' said Nikolls. 'You're a good guesser. Effie said that.'

'Very nice of her,' said Callaghan.

He lit a cigarette.

Nikolls said: 'Well, is that all you gotta say to me, because I got some news for you.'

Callaghan said: 'Good news, I hope.'

Nikolls said: 'I wouldn't know. It's about that De Sirac guy. I hung around there tonight. I thought I might get a chance of casin' the place, seein' if I could find anything – even that Irana baby. I thought if I waited long enough I'd see De Sirac come out. Those guys always come out at the time when everybody else is goin' to bed. He didn't, so I sorta took a chance on it. I went up an' rang the bell. Nothin' happened, so I opened the door with a spider an' went in. It wasn't so good.'

Callaghan asked: 'What happened?'

'Nothing happened,' said Nikolls. 'But somebody's croaked that guy. In the sittin' room. An' how do you like that one!'

CHAPTER SEVEN
THE CLOVEN HOOF

CALLAGHAN stood in the centre of the sitting-room, looking at what was left of Mr De Sirac who, no matter how amusing his life may have been, was infinitely more interesting in the manner of his death. At the moment he was sprawled over the writing desk in the corner of the room, his head lying grotesquely to one side. A little trickle of blood came from the upper ear; from the underneath one a yellow viscous fluid stained the blotter.

Callaghan looked at the clock on the mantelpiece. It was a quarter to four. He lit a cigarette; put on a pair of gloves. Then, carefully wiping the electric light switch and door handles with his handkerchief, began systematically to search the flat. The search was not successful. If De Sirac had papers or documents that mattered he kept them in some other place.

Callaghan came back to the desk. He stood looking down at the dead man, wondering exactly what had happened in the apartment that evening. Callaghan thought he could make three guesses; that one of them would be right. He took the cigarette out of his mouth; flipped the ash into his right-hand jacket pocket.

Somebody had been very tough with De Sirac. Callaghan looked round for a possible weapon. In the grate were two brass dogs. Callaghan picked them up in his gloved hands, held them under the light, examined them carefully. He grinned. They were *too* clean. They had both been recently polished. In a room where everything was dusty, their brightness was suspicious.

Callaghan put the dogs back in the grate. He stood in front of it smoking. Out of the corner of his eye, protruding from under the edge of the blotter nearest to him, he could see a tiny piece of paper. Callaghan moved over to the desk and, holding the blotter in position with one finger, gently drew out the sheet of notepaper. He stood reading it, wondering why someone had been careful to remove the first page of the letter.

' . . . *The idea of my having the Coronet is I think a good one. It would be a lesson for Arthur, and one that he richly deserves. I am going to think about this. I shall make up my mind – that is if it is not already made up – because I think that if I do this I may at least put myself in a better position to negotiate something that is fairly satisfactory.*

I look forward to seeing you again soon, my dear,

All my love,

Paula.'

Callaghan dropped a little more ash into his right-hand coat pocket. He thought that this was a very interesting note. He read it a second time, stood smiling at it. He looked almost reminiscent.

He thought that it was quite obvious that whoever had killed De Sirac had left the sheet of notepaper – a portion of a longer letter – to be found, unless . . .

Callaghan toyed with the idea that this theory was wrong; that the letter had been written by his client, Mrs Paula Denys, to De Sirac! That *might* be so, in which case the use of the word 'dear' would seem to indicate that Paula as well as Irana had been friendly with the dead man.

Callaghan folded the sheet of notepaper, put it into his pocket. On the other side of the room, fixed against the wall, was a small carved bookcase. Callaghan, thinking of half a dozen things, moved towards it, began vaguely to read the titles of the books. Most of them were books of a serious nature. He took one down, flipped it open. On the fly-leaf was written *'The property of Anthony De Sirac.'*

Callaghan squeezed out his cigarette stub with his gloved fingers, put it into his pocket. Now he was smiling again. De Sirac, he thought, was possibly not such a fool, or more of a fool, than one had imagined. He remembered the handwriting of the anonymous note which had informed Mrs Denys that her husband was staying at the hotel at Laleham with the ugly blonde woman. The handwriting was the same as that on the fly-leaf of the book which Callaghan held in his hand. So De Sirac had written that letter.

For some reason De Sirac had been the instrument which had enabled Mrs Paula Denys to begin the divorce proceedings against her husband. Callaghan shut the book, put it back in its place on the shelf.

He began to wander round the flat, going from room to room, his restless eyes taking in everything, looking for something, important or unimportant, which might indicate anything at all. He found nothing. Except that the place was dusty, uncared for, the bed unmade, the windows dingy. He went back to the sitting-room, stood in the doorway, leaning against the doorpost.

He took one more look at the recumbent figure at the desk; switched off the light, closed the door softly behind him. He stood in the dark deserted hallway of the flat, listening. There was no sound. Callaghan opened the front door, closed it very gently behind him, walked gingerly down the stairs. Just inside the entrance he looked up and down the street. There was no one about. He stepped out into the dark street, turned down a side turning, began to walk in the direction of Berkeley Square.

The September sunshine came through the curtains, illuminating the floor of Callaghan's bedroom. Callaghan, sitting up in bed, a tray of tea and toast perched precariously on his knees, thought about De Sirac. He wondered whether there was some woman who came to clean the flat, or if not, just how long the murder would be undiscovered. Callaghan was not quite certain at the moment whether he would like a time lapse or not.

The telephone by his bedside jangled. Effie Thompson's voice came through from the office below. She said:

'Mr Callaghan, a lady is on the line. She wants to speak to you personally. I don't know who it is, and she doesn't seem very keen on giving her name.'

Callaghan said: 'You wouldn't recognize the voice, I suppose?'

'I haven't thought about it,' she replied.

Callaghan said: 'You're a wise girl, Effie. Put her through.'

There was a pause. Someone said: 'Good morning, Mr Callaghan.'

Callaghan said: 'Good morning. That would be Irana, I think.'

She said: 'Yes, you're quite right as usual . . .' Her voice was cool, pleasant.

Callaghan said: 'You're not quite so worried as you were last night?'

She said: 'No, I'm not worried *now*, because I hope to talk to you some time today.'

Callaghan grinned. He said: 'And that makes you feel safer?'

She said: 'Yes, it does. I've been very unfair to you once or twice. I haven't been quite truthful . . .'

'You're telling me!' said Callaghan. 'So now you're going to be truthful?'

She said: 'Yes . . . please . . .'

Callaghan said: 'The truth, the whole truth and nothing but the truth! I think it's a good idea, don't you? What would you like to do?'

She said: 'Well, I'm very busy, and I don't think I want to be seen about London.'

Callaghan said: 'Why not? Are you afraid that your sister Paula might see you – or who else?'

She said: 'Please don't be unkind. Can't I talk to you tonight somewhere?'

Callaghan said: 'Why not? That's a good time. Would you like to come here this evening?'

She said: 'Yes, but not too early. Could I come at ten o'clock?'

'Certainly,' said Callaghan.

She said: 'Very well, I'll be there. Thank you very much.'

He heard the receiver click. He waited a moment; then he called down to his office. He said:

'Effie, is Nikolls there?'

'He's been here ten minutes, Mr Callaghan,' she said.

Callaghan said: 'Send him up. And I'd like some more tea – strong tea.'

'Very good,' she said.

Callaghan put the tray on the floor. He lay back, his hands clasped behind his head, looking at the ceiling. He thought that in any event, whether he was a good or a bad guesser, the Denys case must of necessity develop in the next twelve hours. He thought the development might be quite interesting.

Nikolls came in. He asked: 'Can I have a drink?'

Callaghan said: 'This morning drinking is going to be the death of you.'

Nikolls said: 'You oughta talk. I can remember the time when you usta drink *before* breakfast.'

He went out of the bedroom; returned with a bottle of whisky and two glasses. He poured out two shots; handed one to Callaghan. He said:

'I'm not a curious guy, but it looks like a good case, hey – this Denys case? It's funny how things start.'

Callaghan said: 'It's very much funnier how they end – sometimes.'

Nikolls said: 'Who slugged that guy? Me – I'm not sorry, but somebody did it, didn't they? It wouldn't be our client, would it?'

Callaghan said: 'Why not? There was a very nice piece of evidence there.'

Nikolls raised his eyebrows. He flopped into the armchair, produced his packet of Lucky Strikes.

He said: 'You don't say?'

Callaghan went on: 'At some time or other our client wrote a letter to somebody saying that it might be a good idea if she took the Denys Coronet, suggesting that if she had it she'd be in a very much better position to negotiate something or other. That letter was stuck under De Sirac's blotter.'

Nikolls said: 'What d'you know about that? Maybe somebody planted it there.'

Callaghan shrugged his shoulders. 'That's possible,' he said.

Nikolls said: 'You know, it looks to me like we don't really know who stole this Coronet. Ever since this job started we've been hearin'' about the people who wanted to steal it an' who did steal it. They stole it, they put it back, an' so it goes on! I think it stinks a bit.'

Callaghan said: 'Maybe.' He opened a cigarette box on the bedside table, took a cigarette, lit it. He said: 'Mrs Denys started a divorce action against her husband because she received an anonymous letter telling her that her husband had been staying at that hotel at Laleham with a blonde – an ugly woman.'

Nikolls said: 'The ugly dame being de Longues, hey?'

Callaghan said: 'Why not? But that's not the interesting thing. De Sirac wrote that note.'

Nikolls said: 'For cryin' out loud! What is this? What's goin' on around here?'

Callaghan said: 'I've seen the note. Last night I saw a specimen of De Sirac's handwriting on the fly-leaf of one of the books in his library. It was the same.'

Nikolls said: 'I give up. I don't even know a thing about this job.'

Callaghan said: 'Neither do I. But I'm going to.'

Nikolls drank some whisky. He said: 'Look, have you seen de Longues?'

Callaghan said: 'I saw her last night. She's one of those peculiarly fascinating women who are plain but have something. You know what I mean!'

Nikolls said: 'You're tellin' me. I can remember a homely baby some time in Oklahoma . . .'

Callaghan said: 'Maybe, but it doesn't help. So skip it.' He went on: 'I had a talk with her. She's quite charming, very intelligent. I suggested to her that as there may be a little publicity about the Denys Coronet, people might begin to be curious as to who the unknown woman was who stayed with Denys at the Laleham hotel. I suggested somebody might do some talking; that it might be a good thing if their mouth was shut.'

Nikolls said: 'I get it. That would be De Sirac. Look, why shouldn't this de Longues baby have croaked him? She might have.'

Callaghan said: 'I don't know. It all depends on how long De Sirac had been dead.' He grinned. 'Incidentally,' he said, 'it's going to be pretty difficult for anybody to say at what time he died now – that is unless they found him.'

Nikolls said: 'Yes, that's something. Say, I wonder if they've found this stiff yet.'

Callaghan said: 'No, I don't think they would have. De Sirac was the sort of man who'd stay in bed half the morning. You saw how dusty and untidy the flat was. It's difficult to get help these days. If anybody goes in there it'll be this afternoon – if then.'

Nikolls said: 'You might be right. It might be a long time before somebody even misses this guy.'

Callaghan said: 'It might easily be a long time. Maybe we'll do something about that.'

Nikolls said: 'Yeah. An' what do we do about it?'

Callaghan did not reply. He finished his whisky, lit a fresh cigarette, poured himself another shot. He began to feel as happy as he ever did. He asked:

'What else did you get on the de Longues?'

Nikolls said: 'Not much – only one thing. Maybe it's a big thing. The baby has dough. Real dough. Where she got it from I don't know, but she's got a lot. So she ain't gold diggin' Denys – or if she is she don't have to. Maybe she loves the guy. It could be. There'll always be miracles.'

Callaghan shrugged his shoulders. 'It wouldn't have to be a miracle,' he said. 'Denys is an attractive man. He's got something.'

'Do I still go on diggin'?' asked Nikolls. 'Or do I lay off? I'm sorta tired. I could do with a day off. There's some baby out near Dorking, an' . . .'

Callaghan said: 'She'll keep. You go on digging. We can't always rely on guessing.'

Nikolls got up. 'No?' he said. 'Well, we always sorta have an' usually it works. Well . . . I'm on my way.'

He went out of the flat.

Callaghan, having drunk his afternoon tea, relaxed in his chair, put his feet on the desk, blew smoke rings into the air. He was thinking that the odd thing about life is not that things are not what they seem, but that often they *are* what they seem. He pondered on this. He allowed his mind to wander round a mental picture gallery composed of Arthur Denys, his wife, Paula, her sister Irana, the girl friend Juliette de Longues, and, vaguely in the background, Anthony

De Sirac, who probably considered himself the most clever person in the gallery, but whose cleverness had done him little good.

There was a knock on the door. Effie Thompson came in.

She said: 'Mr Callaghan, Mrs Denys is here. She said that if you were engaged she would go away as she has no appointment with you.'

Callaghan took his feet off the desk. He said: 'Ask her to come in, Effie.'

He got up as Paula Denys came into the office. Callaghan, who had clothes sense, appreciated the quality and line of her black coat and skirt, the daintiness of the frilled blouse, the chic of the small tailored hat. Definitely, he thought, Mrs Denys was a woman to be reckoned with. . . .

He said almost casually: 'Good afternoon. Won't you sit down? What can I do for you?'

She sat down. She folded her gloved hands in her lap, looked at Callaghan silently for a moment. Her eyes, large and lustrous, rested on his face as if she were trying to fathom the working of his mind.

She said: 'I wondered if you'd done anything about Irana. I'm very worried about her.'

Callaghan said: 'You know, it isn't very easy for a private detective to find missing people. The police have a much better organization. You didn't consider going to them about it?'

She said: 'No. There are reasons why that might not have been politic. I think you know what they are. Besides, I'd hoped you would have been able to do something. You said you would. Perhaps you only *said* that. Perhaps you didn't mean it.'

He grinned at her amiably. He said: 'So you've come to the conclusion that I'm a person who says things that he doesn't mean. You've found *that* out already?'

She nodded slowly. 'I think you're quite unscrupulous,' she said. 'Unscrupulous in your own peculiar way, I mean. I don't think I've ever met anyone quite like you. One doesn't quite know why one trusts you at all.'

Callaghan's grin became broader – almost insolent. 'I can tell you why,' he said. 'You haven't much choice, have you? If you don't trust me – whether I'm unscrupulous or not – what can you do?'

She nodded again. 'I understand that,' she said. 'So you only *said* that about trying to find Irana – you didn't really mean it?'

Callaghan said: 'I meant it all right. I haven't done anything about Miss Faveley because, candidly, I've been a little busy, but I'll do something soon. In the meantime I don't think you ought to worry about her a great deal.'

She said: 'No? Why not?'

Callaghan said: 'Surely your sister is a woman who can look after herself. I imagine she's got into difficult situations before. I should also think that she'd got out of most of them. Irana's nobody's fool.'

She said: 'That point doesn't interest me. I'm very fond of Irana – too fond perhaps. I'm terribly worried about her. I don't like her disappearing at a time like this. There must be a reason. Perhaps it's not a very happy one.'

Callaghan shrugged his shoulders. He said: 'I can think of a reason why Miss Faveley might have wanted to disappear. It's quite on the cards that she saw the assessors' notice in *The Times*. Well, if she returned the Coronet it would be obvious to her that someone else had stolen it.'

She said: 'Why obvious?'

Callaghan said: 'Why not? We know that De Sirac had the key of the house and the combination of the safe. She would naturally think that he'd stolen it. She wouldn't like that. You see, De Sirac's attitude might easily be that the Coronet had never been returned. Possibly that would be his story, and he'd stick to it. He might still be able to do a little blackmail.'

She said: 'Would he? Does he think my sister has sufficient money to be adequately blackmailed?'

'I wouldn't know,' said Callaghan. 'I don't know how much money she's got. But she had enough money to give me a thousand pounds. You don't give away your last thousand, do you?'

She sighed. She said: 'Irana could do anything. So you think she's hiding somewhere because she's afraid of De Sirac?'

Callaghan said: 'I think it's possible. Another thing is she might possibly think that both you and I believe that she'd never returned the Coronet.' Callaghan grinned again. 'Perhaps she didn't,' he said.

'That isn't true,' she said indignantly. 'Irana isn't a liar. She intended to return that Coronet, and I know she did it.'

'All right,' said Callaghan. 'You know she did it! And she's disappeared and you're worried about her. I've got to try to find her. I'll get round to it quite soon.'

She said: 'Mr Callaghan, you're a strange person, aren't you? Do you take a delight in tormenting people? Do you *like* being rude? Does it make you feel powerful or something like that?'

Callaghan lit a cigarette. He said airily: 'Mrs Denys, I assure you I'm not an introspective person. I never consider those points. And people usually manage to do their own tormenting without much assistance from me.' He smiled at her. 'I must admit I occasionally allow myself the privilege of adding a little fuel to the fire. But about Irana, perhaps I haven't worried as much as I ought to about your sister because I've got an idea that she'll turn up like the proverbial bad penny.'

She said: 'I don't like the way you talk about my sister, Mr Callaghan.'

Callaghan said: 'All right. Well, what are you going to do about it?'

She got up. She said: 'I don't think I'm going to do any good by talking to you. I'd hoped you'd do something about Irana. I paid you a retainer to do something about her. You're taking advantage of a situation, aren't you – a situation in which you're in rather a favourable position?'

Callaghan lit a cigarette. He said: 'Am I? That's interesting. Why am I in a favourable position?'

She said: 'You know that I had a foolish idea about taking the Coronet away from Mayfield Place. I didn't do it, but you know I had the idea. You know that Irana did it. You know that she allowed herself to be assisted by this man De Sirac. You know that the Coronet's disappeared again. Well, it might be that you could make all of us appear in rather an odd light if you wanted to, if there were an investigation.'

Callaghan said: 'Don't you worry about that, Mrs Denys. There'll be an investigation. Surely you don't think an insurance company is going to pay over seventy thousand pounds without finding out something about it?' He smiled. 'If the Globe and Consolidated knew the facts about this Coronet, I wonder what they'd really think. I wonder what they'd *do*.'

She said calmly: 'No one could accuse you of trying to help, Mr Callaghan.'

Callaghan said: 'That's where you're wrong, Mrs Denys. Let me tell you something. I rather like you. I like the way you stand, the way you talk, the way you wear your clothes. I even like you when you get angry; but I'm still not going to allow my likes and dislikes to affect my mentality or the way I carry out my work. That's a thing I decide.'

She said: 'So it seems. May I take it that when you've done something about Irana, when you've tried to find out something, you'll let me know?'

Callaghan said: 'Yes, of course I shall.' He went on: 'Possibly I took my instructions from you a little too seriously. You paid me a retainer of two hundred and fifty pounds, but you didn't pay that money primarily because you wanted Irana found. You paid me that money because you hoped I'd find some way of protecting her reputation. You hoped I'd find some way of keeping her out of this mess – a mess which becomes a little more involved each day. You may not have said so, but that's what you meant, isn't it?'

She nodded miserably. She said: 'Yes, I suppose if I told the truth, that is what I meant.'

'All right,' said Callaghan. 'You go home and relax. Drink a cup of tea; go to the movies. I'll take care of things.'

She moved towards the door. She said: 'I wonder just how you'll take care of things. I wonder whether they'll be better or worse for your taking care of them.'

He grinned at her. He said: 'Mrs Denys, that's one of the chances you take when you come to an organization like Callaghan Investigations.'

She said: 'I wish I'd known that in the first place. I wouldn't have come.'

'Wouldn't you?' said Callaghan. 'You hadn't a hope. I told you you'd have to come – not because you wanted to but because it seemed to me as if your sister Irana created a situation in which you'd have to. Well, I don't think you're doing so badly.'

She said: 'I wonder if you want some more money. I wonder if the sum I gave you wasn't enough. Is that it?'

Callaghan said: 'It's enough for the moment. When I want some more I'll ask for it. I expect I shall want some more.'

She said: 'I expect you will.' Her voice was hard.

'Possibly,' said Callaghan. 'And if I do –' he smiled at her again – 'I shall probably get it.' His tone changed suddenly. It became hard – almost menacing. He said: 'I suppose, Mrs Denys, if you were asked to account for your movements last evening – or last night – you'd have no difficulty? You'd be able to say just where you were – what you were doing?'

She said: 'I don't understand you. In any event that has nothing to do with you.'

Callaghan shrugged his shoulders. 'You've answered my question,' he said. 'Good afternoon, Mrs Denys.'

He held the door open for her. She went out.

He went back to his desk. He sat down in the chair, swung it round, put his feet up on the mantelpiece. He lit another cigarette. Women, he thought, were extremely difficult propositions. When they were beautiful they were even more difficult. A natural process, he supposed.

He called: 'Effie!'

The door opened. Effie Thompson stood in the doorway. Callaghan did not look round. He asked casually:

'Effie, how good is your memory?'

She said: 'I think I've remembered most of the things you've wanted me to.'

Callaghan said: 'Yes. I wonder if it could be a not very good memory.'

She said: 'Why not? Do you want me to forget something?'

Callaghan asked: 'Could you?' He looked at her over his shoulder. He was smiling.

She said: 'I daresay.'

Callaghan said: 'I've got a dozen pairs of rather good silk stockings upstairs. I think you ought to have them, Effie. I hope they're the right size.'

She said: 'That's very good of you. But I can still forget anything you want me to without the silk stockings.'

Callaghan said evenly: 'I'm sure you could.'

She said a little acidly: 'I hope I'm not doing somebody else out of them, Mr Callaghan.'

Callaghan said seriously: 'At the moment – no.' He went on: 'You remember that odd thing you noticed about the lady you thought was Mrs Paula Denys – the thing you told me about – that her hair had been dyed; that she wasn't a real brunette?'

She said: 'Yes, I remember.'

'At the time,' said Callaghan, 'when she saw you and when you sent her to see me at The Crescent & Star, we both of us thought that she was Mrs Paula Denys, didn't we?'

She said: 'Yes.'

Callaghan said: 'It was only when you told me about the dyed hair that I took the trouble to find out that she wasn't.'

She nodded.

Callaghan went on: 'We're going to forget all that. After all, the lady who came to see us in the first place *told* us she was Mrs Denys. We believed her. We still believe that. We don't know anything about anybody else. Do you understand that, Effie?'

She said: 'Yes, I understand.' She went on: 'But don't you think that behaving like that might be a little inconvenient for somebody?'

Callaghan said: 'Inconvenient for whom?'

'For Mrs Denys,' said Effie. She stood, leaning her shoulder against the doorpost, looking straight at him.

Callaghan said: 'I think it's very good of you to worry so much about my clients. But it's not necessary.'

She said: 'Very well, Mr Callaghan. It's just as you say. The lady was Mrs Paula Denys. I've never thought she was anyone else.'

'Thanks a lot,' said Callaghan. 'That's all, Effie. And don't slam the door as you go out, because I know you want to.'

She was white with rage, but she closed the door very quietly behind her.

Callaghan threw the cigarette stub into the fireplace, put his hands behind his head, looked at the ceiling. He sat there for quite a while, his feet poised precariously on the mantlepiece, gazing upwards.

It was ten minutes afterwards that he went into the outer office. Effie Thompson was busy at her typewriter.

Callaghan said: 'Effie, do you remember six or seven months ago we ordered some rather special quarto typing paper?'

She nodded. 'I remember,' she said. 'A rather good paper with a very odd and attractive watermark. It was handmade, I think.'

Callaghan said: 'That's right. Have we got any?'

She said: 'I think so. There's a little anyway.'

Callaghan said: 'You might find me a couple of sheets.'

She got up, went to a store cupboard at the back of the office, came out after a minute or two. She handed two or three sheets of the notepaper to Callaghan.

She said: 'Do you want something typed?'

Callaghan smiled at her. He said: 'No thanks, Effie – nothing that I couldn't type myself.'

She said: 'Very well. There are some letters for the post. I'll take them.' She went out.

Callaghan sat down at the typewriter. He inserted the sheet of notepaper. He typed these words:

'Mr "X" presents his compliments to the General Manager of the Globe and Consolidated Insurance Company.

If the Company are foolish enough to pay the claim made on the loss of the Denys Coronet without due investigation, then the Company are greater fools than even Mr "X" believes.'

Callaghan addressed the envelope, folded the sheet of notepaper, put it inside, stamped it. He put the letter in his pocket. He went back to his own room, sat down at the desk, lit another cigarette, opened the bottom drawer, took out the bottle of bourbon. He put the neck of the bottle in his mouth and took a long swig. He felt a lot better.

It was seven o'clock when Callaghan closed the door of his apartment behind him, took the lift to the ground floor. As he passed the night porter's box he said:

'Wilkie, I may be a little late. I've switched one of the office lines through to here, and also the private line to my apartment. Take any messages, will you?'

'O.K., Mr Callaghan,' said Wilkie.

Callaghan went out. He walked across the square, up Hay Hill. He stopped at a pillar box to post the letter to the Globe and Consolidated Insurance Company. He was smiling a little as he put the envelope into the letter box. That, he thought, would start something. Callaghan considered that it was time that somebody started something in the Denys case. The affair was too nebulous. It was time that something emerged and if things did not emerge of themselves you gave them a little assistance. Then *something* happened, and that would be good for *somebody* – if only Callaghan.

He walked down into Piccadilly, waited on the pavement for a taxicab. When one came, he told the driver to take him to Long Acre. It was half-past seven when he entered the block in which De Sirac's apartment was situated. Callaghan went in. He waited for a little while in the hall; walked down the two passageways. He found nobody. He began to walk up the stairs.

Outside the entrance to De Sirac's flat he lit a cigarette, rang the bell. When there was no answer he tapped noisily on the door. He waited a little while; then descended to the floor beneath. He walked along until he found the entrance to a flat in which a light was burning.

Callaghan rang the bell. After a minute a maid opened the door.

He asked: 'Is there a manager or a hall-porter to this block?'

The girl said: 'Yes – No. 6 on the ground floor, sir. There's no hall porter, but the manager lives there.'

Callaghan said: 'Thank you.' He went down the stairs.

The door of No. 6 was opened by a middle-aged man.

Callaghan said: 'My name's Callaghan. Some time yesterday morning a Mr De Sirac, who lives here, telephoned me. He wanted to see me urgently. I arranged to see him this afternoon. I've just managed to get round here. I've rung the bell at his flat and banged on the door. There isn't any answer. I'm a little bit worried about him.'

The man said: 'Maybe he's asleep. He's usually in during the day. He's one of those people who go out late at night.' His tone was caustic.

Callaghan said: 'That's as may be. But I banged on the door loudly enough to wake anybody who was asleep. Would I be troubling you a lot if I asked you to open the flat so that we could see?'

The manager said: 'What's on your mind? Do you think he's committed suicide or something?'

Callaghan shrugged his shoulders. He said: 'I don't know, but I think it's possible.'

The man said: 'Very well. We'll go up and look.' His tone was resigned.

He went into the flat, returned a minute later with a bunch of keys. They went up the stairs. Outside De Sirac's flat the apartment manager rang the bell, tapped on the door. When there was no answer, he found the key, opened the door. They went in.

The place smelt musty. Callaghan thought that his guess that no one had been in since the night before was right. The manager switched on the light in the hallway, walked across to the sitting-room, opened the door. The blinds and blackout curtains were drawn. The room was very dark.

As he switched on the light, the man said: 'My God! It looks as if you're right.'

Callaghan, standing just behind him, could see De Sirac's body. He went over. He said:

'Not quite right. This fellow never committed suicide. He's been hit on the head with something. He's dead.'

The manager said: 'Murder, hey! That's going to do us a lot of good.'

Callaghan said: 'You'll get over it. People forget very quickly, you know, if that's any consolation to you.'

The other said: 'Well, what do we do?'

Callaghan said: 'You'd better leave it to me. There's one thing only to do, isn't there?'

He walked across to the telephone, picked up the receiver. He dialled Whitehall 1212. He said:

'Is that the Information Room? My name's Callaghan. I'd like to have a word with Detective-Inspector Gringall if he's in. It's rather important.'

He held on. A minute later Gringall's voice came on the telephone.

Callaghan said: 'Good evening, Gringall. It's quite nice to talk to you again.'

Gringall said: 'How are you, Slim? So you're still at large?'

Callaghan said: 'What do you mean – at large?'

Gringall said: 'One of these fine days somebody's going to catch up with you.' His tone was humorous. 'Well, what can I do for you? What's your trouble?'

Callaghan said: 'It's not my trouble. It's yours. I've been doing a little business with a fellow called De Sirac. He lives at 267a Long Acre – a flat on the third floor. I'm speaking from there now. I was supposed to see him this afternoon. It was something which he considered important, so I knew he'd be here. I couldn't get any reply so I got the apartment manager to open the door. He's dead. Somebody killed him.'

Gringall said: 'I see. You weren't expecting that he was going to be killed or anything like that, were you?'

Callaghan said: 'No. Why should I be? I know very little about him.'

Gringall said: 'Were you awfully surprised to find that you got no reply? Mightn't he have been out?'

Callaghan said: 'No. He wanted to see me particularly. He was in a jam. I was pretty certain that he would be waiting for me. That's why I was a little worried.'

Gringall said airily: 'So you're worried. That's a nice change, isn't it?'

Callaghan replied: 'Well, not exactly worried. Shall we say a little perturbed. After all, I don't *like* finding dead bodies, you know.'

Gringall said: 'I'm surprised to hear that anything concerns you. All right, I'll send a waggon round. Will you wait there?'

Callaghan said: 'I'd rather not if you don't mind. I've a very busy evening in front of me. Lots of important things to attend to. The apartment manager's here. He'll wait.'

Gringall said: 'All right. Oh, by the way, do you think you might look in some time tomorrow. I'd like to have a little talk with you about this De Sirac. You might be able to help us. You'd want to do that, wouldn't you?'

Callaghan said sarcastically: 'You know I've always been a great help to you, Gringall. I don't know what you'd have done without me.'

Gringall said: 'All right. Well, you be a little more help. You wouldn't forget to come in tomorrow, would you?'

'How could I?' said Callaghan. 'I'm looking forward to seeing you. I'll come in the afternoon. Perhaps you'll give me a cup of tea. Well, so long, Gringall.' He hung up.

The apartment manager was standing by the door. He looked unhappy. Callaghan said:

'The police are going to send a waggon round here. They'll look after everything. Don't touch anything. They wouldn't like that. And you won't go away till they come, will you? If you don't like it inside, I should wait out in the passageway.'

He took a last look at De Sirac, went out of the flat. Outside in Long Acre, he walked briskly in the direction of Piccadilly. He turned into Albemarle Street, went into The Silver Triton bar. He ordered a large whisky and soda. He drank it slowly.

Something had got to happen now.

Chapter Eight
Money from Home

It was eight o'clock when Callaghan was shown into Denys' sitting-room at The Savoy. He said:

'I'm sorry I couldn't telephone before. I've had rather a busy day.'

Denys said: 'That's all right. You're here – that's the great thing. Have a drink?'

Callaghan said: 'Thanks.'

Denys poured out two stiff whiskies and sodas. He brought one to Callaghan; offered him a silver cigarette box.

He said: 'You know, I've been thinking about you. I don't think you're a bad detective at all.'

Callaghan said: 'Having regard to the fact that you don't like private detectives, that's a compliment. But why don't you think I'm bad?'

Denys said: 'I've always regarded them as an unintelligent class.' He carried his own drink back to the fireplace; stood looking at Callaghan, smiling. 'But I don't think you're unintelligent.'

Callaghan drank a little whisky. He said: 'No? Why?'

Denys shrugged his shoulders. 'I think you did the right thing,' he said, 'to come to me and tell me that it was my wife who removed the Coronet from Mayfield Place. Of course you could have gone to the assessors and told *them*. That wouldn't have been very nice for *her*, would it?'

Callaghan said: 'Are you worrying about that? Do you mind whether it's nice or not for her? After all, she's in the process of divorcing you, isn't she? One imagines you haven't a great deal of time for each other . . . or have you?'

Denys shrugged his shoulders. 'I'm very fond of my wife,' he said. He looked at Callaghan. His glance was almost mischievous. 'You can imagine that,' he went on. 'But in any event, if what you say is true, she's put herself in a very odd position – the position of . . . well . . . almost a common thief. And that isn't very nice now – is it?'

'No,' said Callaghan. 'It isn't very nice. So that's what is worrying you?'

Denys drank some whisky. He said: 'Nothing's worrying me. I'm not the worrying type. Surely you've guessed that. Neither are you.'

Callaghan said: 'Quite – you just don't want a scandal?'

'Right,' said Denys. 'That's just it. I don't want a scandal.'

Callaghan nodded. 'I can understand that,' he said. 'But the situation is a little bit odd, isn't it?'

Denys lit a cigarette. He smoked silently for a moment; then he said:

'I don't think so. So far as I am concerned, the Coronet was stolen from Mayfield. It was insured, and the premiums have been paid for years. I've put a claim in on the insurance company. You come to me and tell me that it was stolen by my own wife, but I've only got your word for that, and you don't suggest I'm going to do anything about it, do you?'

Callaghan said: 'Yes, I do. There's one little thing that you ought to do about it.'

Denys smiled. He said: 'I think I know what's coming. Well, what's the little thing?'

Callaghan said: 'If I went to the assessors they'd certainly conclude that I was eligible for that reward of a thousand pounds. They offered that sum for information leading to the recovery of the Coronet.'

Denys walked across the room to a bureau. He opened a drawer. He came back with a packet of banknotes. He said: 'If you count those you'll find there are a thousand pounds there. I think that'll straighten things up pretty well between you and me.'

Callaghan said: 'More or less.' He put the notes in his pocket. He went on: 'I take it that I'm supposed to forget what has happened?'

Deny s said: 'I don't know what's happened so far as you're concerned. You haven't told me yet.' He smiled amicably at Callaghan.

'I told you most of the story at The Chemin de Luxe,' said Callaghan. 'But perhaps you weren't listening?'

'I was listening,' said Denys with a little smile, 'but I wasn't taking in all the implications. Candidly, I was a little preoccupied. I was concerned with one or two other little things. And, if you remember, I was interrupted. I had to take a telephone call. Perhaps you'd like to tell me the story again. Just so that you and I wouldn't make any mistakes about it at any future time.'

Callaghan grinned. He said: 'Well, briefly, the story is this. I was, as I told you, on holiday in the country. I was staying at a place called The Crescent & Star. Mrs Denys got in touch with my office. She wanted to see me urgently. I don't know where she got my name from, but she must have heard it somewhere. To cut a long story short, she came down the same evening. She told me what had happened.'

Denys said: 'Actually what did happen? This ought to be very interesting.'

Callaghan said: 'It seems that she asked you to let her have a divorce and you wouldn't agree. She didn't like that so she planned to leave and take the Coronet. For some reason or other the idea of actually stealing it herself didn't seem to please her so she employed a man whom she knew to steal it for her. She must have thought he was an awful fool. 'Naturally,' Callaghan went on, 'once he got it, he intended to hold her up on a little blackmail. So she was in a jam. That's why she came to me. You know the rest of the story. I got the Coronet back from De Sirac. I gave it to her, and that's that.'

Denys said: 'It seems to me that the situation is quite in order. She has the Coronet. She's either going to keep it and do nothing about it, or she's going to try to get rid of it. If she gets rid of it the police will soon find out about it.'

Callaghan asked: 'And what about the insurance company? Supposing they pay in the meantime. They've got to pay this claim, haven't they – sometime or other?'

Denys said: 'There's no reason why they shouldn't pay. So far as I'm concerned the Coronet's been stolen. I haven't got it. I'm entitled to the money. If they pay it I shall take it. Incidentally – that might not be a bad thing for you.'

Callaghan raised his eyebrows. 'No?' he queried. 'Why not?'

Denys said: 'There might be a little more money in it for you. That thousand' – he smiled suddenly – 'might be considered a payment on account. If the insurance company pay up – and they will pay up because they've got to – there'll be another thousand.'

Callaghan said: 'Aren't you trusting me rather a lot?'

Denys shrugged his shoulders. 'Am I?' he asked. 'I don't think so. Supposing you work out that angle for yourself.'

Callaghan rubbed his ear reflectively. He said: 'I see what you mean. In taking this thousand from you I am in fact making myself an accessory more or less to whatever has or has not happened.'

Denys grinned. He said: 'That's how it looks to me. Does that suit you?'

Callaghan said: 'Why not? A thousand's a thousand. I've got a bad memory. I don't know anything about the Coronet.'

Denys said: 'I thought you were intelligent. Shall we have another drink?'

Callaghan said: 'I think that would be a very good idea.'

Denys busied himself with the drinks. Callaghan lit a fresh cigarette. He said: 'I saw Miss de Longues home last night. She's a very charming person. I like her a lot.'

Denys handed Callaghan his glass. He said: 'I'm glad of that. She's amusing. I expect you found something to talk about.'

Callaghan said casually: 'Yes – we found something to talk about. We talked about the hotel at Laleham and the private detectives who went down there looking for evidence and one or two other things. . . .'

'I see,' said Denys. 'I suppose I'd be *very* curious if I asked what the "other things" were?'

'No,' said Callaghan, 'you wouldn't be. Anyhow, you're entitled to know.'

Denys smiled. He said: 'I think that's very nice of you.' His tone was slightly caustic.

Callaghan went on: 'We talked about an anonymous note that somebody sent to Mrs Denys. The note that told her you were staying at the hotel at Laleham with Miss de Longues. It seemed to me that if she wanted her name kept out of this business – now that there's likely to be a little publicity in connection with the disappearance of the Coronet – it might be a good thing if I looked after her interests. I rather think she agreed.'

Denys said: 'You're a most refreshing bastard, aren't you? Is there anything you'd stop at?'

Callaghan said: 'I wouldn't know. I've never come up against anything yet that I've wanted to stop at.'

'So I imagine,' said Denys. 'So I take it that you think that the writer of the anonymous note is going to get busy with Miss de Longues – you think he might see some pickings there?'

'Not now,' said Callaghan. 'I said I was looking after him. I told her that. When I take care of something I'm fearfully conscientious.' He grinned at Denys.

Denys said: 'I feel that Miss de Longues is safe in your hands.'

'You'd be surprised,' said Callaghan. He handed his glass to Denys. 'I think one for the road,' he said. 'To seal the bargain – don't you?'

Denys filled the glasses.

They had one for the road.

At nine o'clock Callaghan went into the tube station at Green Park, found an empty telephone box. He lit a cigarette, dialled a number. He waited, leaning against the side of the booth, the cigarette suspended from the corner of his mouth. His expression was placid.

Juliette de Longues' voice came over the line. It was soft, almost caressing, Callaghan thought.

He said: 'Good evening, Miss de Longues, I am sorry to worry you at such short notice but I think you and I ought to have a little talk. Would you like that?'

There was a pause. She said: 'Is it very important? I *was* going out to dinner.'

Callaghan said: 'You can dine out *every* night, but you can't always talk to me! If I were you I'd cancel the dinner appointment. I take it you were dining with Mr Denys?'

He heard her laugh softly. She said: 'But how did you know? But I forgot – Mr Callaghan knows everything, doesn't he?'

Callaghan said: 'Not quite everything. Really I doubt whether I *know* anything at all. Let's say I'm a good guesser.'

She said: 'Perhaps it's better to be a good guesser than to *know* anything at all. Will you come round?'

Callaghan said: 'I'm on my way.'

He hung up. He went out of the subway; picked up a cab. He sat back in the corner thinking. He was wondering what the reactions of Juliette would be to this or that. He thought wondering didn't get you anywhere. The thing was to find out.

Miss de Longues awaited him at her Lowndes Square flat in a toilette that was quite ravishing. She wore a long amethyst velvet housecoat, caught down the front with one or two antique silver clasps. The coat was matched by her velvet sandals. She looked very attractive, Callaghan thought.

She said: 'First of all, I think you should have a whisky and soda, Mr Callaghan. You like that, don't you?'

Callaghan grinned. He said: 'Yes, it helps me to think.'

She poured out the drink. She smiled at him. She said: 'Or do you mean it helps you to guess!'

He shrugged his shoulders. 'Does it matter?' he asked. 'So long as the guess comes off?'

'And Mr Callaghan's guesses usually do come off?' she queried. She handed him the glass.

Callaghan said: 'You'd be surprised. Anyhow, I won't waste any words. I'm very sorry about having to ask you to cancel your dinner appointment, but I thought this was urgent. I hope you'll agree.'

She said: 'I wonder what could happen to me that would be urgent.' She was smiling.

She sat down on a brocade-covered settee. She was quite relaxed. Callaghan thought it would take a great deal to scare Juliette.

He said: 'There's only one thing that could be urgent. You know what that is. That's this fellow who wrote the anonymous note to Mrs Denys. You remember when I talked to you before, I suggested that he might take this opportunity to try and skewer a little money out of you. He was certain to see something about the Denys Coronet in the newspapers. We agreed he'd be on a good wicket. We agreed that you wouldn't want that. Do you remember?'

She said: 'I remember, Mr Callaghan. I always remember what I do.' She reached out with long, heavily-jewelled fingers; took a cigarette from a box on a nearby table.

Callaghan walked across and lit it for her. He stood looking down at her. He said: 'I wonder how clever a woman you are.'

She smiled up at him, looked at him through half-closed lids. She said: 'I don't know. Perhaps you could tell me. I think *you're* a very clever man.'

Callaghan said: 'We'll see how clever we both are. The point is this: I'm telling you something that perhaps I ought not to tell you. I'm going to tell it to you because I think you're a very clever woman and because I think you know on which side your bread's buttered.'

She said: 'How interesting. Do tell me, Mr Callaghan, on which side my bread *is* buttered.'

Callaghan went back to his chair. He picked up his glass, drank a little whisky. He said: 'You're in love with Denys, aren't you? You've got to be. I don't think he's got an awful lot of money but you've got some, so you're not in love with him for anything you can get. Perhaps, Miss de Longues, wants to stabilize herself. Perhaps she feels she'd like to be mistress of Mayfield Place.' He smiled at her. He went on: 'I don't think it would be a good idea at all.'

She raised her eyebrows. She said: 'No? Would you like to tell me why?'

Callaghan said: 'Certainly. I'm not worrying any more about our boy friend – the one who wrote the anonymous note – making things difficult for you. He won't make things tough for anybody – not any more.'

Her eyes widened. She said: 'Meaning exactly what?'

Callaghan said casually: 'Meaning somebody killed him last night. He's been murdered. I think the police found out something about it late this afternoon.'

She said: 'I see . . .'

There was a long silence. Callaghan said: 'It was quite clever of me to come and see you, wasn't it?'

She said: 'I think it was very clever.' She got up; stood by the fireplace, one hand on the mantelpiece, one slim velvet-shod foot on the fender. She said: 'Does anybody else know about this – death?'

Callaghan said: 'You mean, does Denys know?' He shook his head. 'I haven't told him,' he said. 'I haven't told anybody. I found out myself by accident.'

She said softly: 'I see. How did you find out?'

Callaghan lied glibly. He said: 'I was thinking of you. I thought it would be a good thing to short-circuit this man from doing anything at all. I thought it would be a good thing to give him a warning to lay off you – not to start anything. I went round there knocking at the flat but couldn't get in. I had the door opened. He was dead. He looked as if he'd been dead some time.'

She asked: 'How long is some time?'

Callaghan said: 'I'm not a medical expert. I wouldn't know.' He smiled at her. He said: 'I should think he'd been dead for such a long time that it might be very difficult to work out the exact time of his death. It is sometimes, you know.'

She said: 'I thought they could always tell the exact time.'

Callaghan shook his head. 'Only in detective books,' he said. 'In detective books they can always tell you he died at seven minutes past eleven. In this case I think they'll have to make a guess.'

She looked at him. Callaghan thought that he'd been right in assessing Juliette de Longues as possessing a first-class nerve. She smiled a little. She said:

'I think it's very good of you to take so much trouble about me, Mr Callaghan. I'm very grateful to you.'

Callaghan said: 'With us the customer always comes first.' He grinned. He went on: 'Now shall we be constructive?'

She went back to her seat. She sat down. She folded her hands in her lap, looked at him smilingly. She said:

'Yes. That would be very nice. Let's be constructive.'

Callaghan said: 'The only thing that you've got to be afraid of in this business is a matter of unwanted publicity, isn't it?' He looked at her mischievously. He was grinning. He said: 'Anyway, that's our story. The thing that you've been afraid of is that this man De Sirac, who knew that you were staying at the hotel at Laleham with Denys, might make that fact public. Well, we know now that he won't, but we don't know that he hasn't already done something about it.'

She said quickly: 'Exactly what do you mean by that?'

Callaghan said: 'People who write anonymous notes often continue with the process. He might have written to somebody else and told them. You see, the only thing that's really against you in this business is the fact that you didn't want people to know you stayed at Laleham with Denys. That was natural. You intended to marry him, didn't you? The clever thing for you to do would be this: To admit as publicly as is necessary that you *did* stay at Laleham with him.'

She asked: 'What do you mean by "admitting as publicly as is necessary"?'

Callaghan shrugged his shoulders. 'There's going to be an awful lot of trouble,' he said. 'There's going to be a lot of trouble about this murder. All sorts of things are going to be turned up if somebody – the insurance people or the police, or anybody else – possibly some friend of De Sirac's – thought that you were still afraid of this information being known. They might do something about it, but if they knew you didn't care, you'd be kicking the ground from under their feet, wouldn't you?'

She said: 'Yes, I think that's logical.'

'And,' Callaghan went on, 'there's another thing. I don't want to frighten you, but I don't quite like the idea of this De Sirac business. You see, *if* you wanted that Laleham business kept quiet; if you *really* wanted it kept quiet, you'd have a motive for wanting De Sirac out of the way – wouldn't you? Remember he'd already sent an anonymous note to Paula Denys saying in effect that you'd stayed with Denys at Laleham. You see what I mean . . . ?'

She nodded. She said: 'Of course the idea is quite ridiculous – to me, that is. But it might not be so ridiculous to others. I see what you mean. Well – what can I do?'

Callaghan said: 'Supposing you were to write me a letter; supposing you were to admit in that letter that you were the person who stayed at the hotel at Laleham with Denys; you know perfectly well that the only time I should produce that letter would be on an occasion when it was necessary. It might never be necessary, but it would at least prove to the satisfaction of anyone who was entitled to know that you didn't mind admitting this fact.'

She said: 'I see. And supposing I did that, what's the next step?'

Callaghan said: 'You're not going to like the next step a bit.' He stubbed out his cigarette in the ashtray, lit a fresh one.

She said: 'I think you ought to have another drink. I think you deserve it.' She came over to him, took his glass, refilled it, handed it back to him. She said:

'I wonder why it is that I trust you. You're an extraordinary person, aren't you?'

Callaghan said: 'I've been told that before. As for the reason why you trust me, you're trusting me because you've got to.'

She said: 'Very well. Let's say that I've got to. What's the next thing?'

Callaghan said: 'You write that letter and if you're a wise girl you're going to pack your trunks and take a holiday. Scotland or somewhere like that might be an interesting place at the moment. I think you'd be much happier there.'

She said: 'I see. And what about Arthur?'

Callaghan shrugged his shoulders. 'You could write him a letter too, couldn't you?' he said. 'You could tell him that your rather foolish action in staying with him at Laleham had created one or two situations which you didn't like; that you thought that in the circumstances it would be a good thing to postpone this idea of marriage.'

She said: 'In fact, you're telling me that it would be a good thing to put quite some distance between London and myself?'

Callaghan said: 'I'm telling you just that.'

She poured a little whisky into a glass, squirted in some soda. She came over to him. She said:

'I don't know why I believe in you, but I'm going to do what you say. I'll write that letter. I think I shall leave London tomorrow. I'll write to Arthur before I go.' She held up her glass. 'Mr Callaghan,' she said, 'here's to your very good health.'

Callaghan drank his whisky. They put the glasses down.

She said softly: 'What do you think about me?'

Callaghan said: 'Candidly, I think you're one of the most attractive women I've ever met in my life. The fact that you're not beautiful makes you even more so.'

She said: 'You're very sweet, aren't you? If I knew you a little better I should want to kiss you . . . or would you rather have another drink?'

Callaghan grinned. He said: 'If you don't mind I'll have a little more whisky. And then we'll compose that letter.'

When Callaghan turned into the apartment block in Berkeley Square the clock above the night porter's box told him it was ten-twenty-five. Wilkie, busily engaged in reading the final *Star*, looked up.

Callaghan asked: 'Any news, Wilkie?'

'Yes, Mr Callaghan,' said Wilkie. 'A lady's been to see you. I took her upstairs. She's waiting for you. She said she had an appointment. I hope that's all right.'

Callaghan said: 'That's all right, Wilkie.'

Going up in the lift, he lit a cigarette. He was thinking about his interview with Juliette de Longues. Things were sometimes not very difficult, especially when they suited everyone. Callaghan wondered if the process could be repeated.

He got out of the lift, walked along the passage, opened the door of his apartment. He crossed the hallway, went into the sitting-room.

Irana was lying on the couch. Her fur coat, handbag and hat were on an armchair. She was wearing a dark grey flannel frock with blue collar and cuffs. Her hands were folded behind her head. She looked very beautiful.

Callaghan said: 'I'm glad to see you've made yourself comfortable. Would you like a cigarette?'

She said: 'Thank you. I'd love one.'

Callaghan threw his hat on to a chair, walked to the cigarette box on the mantelpiece.

She got up. As he turned, she stood facing him. She said: 'You know there's an awful lot between you and me, don't you?'

Callaghan said: 'No? Not really! Just what do you mean, Irana?'

She said: 'Besides this business about the Coronet; besides what you've done for me. You know that I'm rather crazy about you, don't you?'

Callaghan cocked one eyebrow. He said: 'You don't say?'

She shrugged her shoulders. She said: 'You're awfully tough, aren't you? You couldn't even believe that a person like myself might be rather attracted to a man like you?'

Callaghan said: 'Sweetie-pie, I can believe anything.'

She put her arms round his neck. She kissed him on the mouth. She said: 'I did that in your office once. That was because I felt rather grateful to you.'

Callaghan said: 'I see. What's this one for?'

She said: 'This one is because I want to.'

Callaghan said: 'Well, I think that's a much better reason. By the way, is that what you wanted to see me about?' He grinned at her.

She said: 'No, it isn't. But I wanted you to know how I felt about you, knowing that you'll probably be inclined to trust me and believe me a little bit more than you did before.'

Callaghan said: 'I have an invariable rule. I always trust and believe everybody. Why not?'

She said: 'Don't you find they sometimes make a fool of you?'

Callaghan shook his head. 'Why should they?' he said. 'They sometimes make fools of themselves. You see I'm not trying to sell anything, except my services. I'm merely a private detective who spends most of his time listening to other people. Sometimes I come to conclusions. Sometimes I don't.'

He gave her a cigarette, lit it for her. She went back to the settee, sat down. She said:

'What conclusion have you come to about me, Slim?'

He said: 'I haven't. After all, you've got to admit that I've believed most of the things you've told me, done most of the things you've wanted me to do. I imagine that you're here tonight because something's happened; because you want something else done.'

She made a little grimace. 'And wouldn't you do something for me?' she asked. 'After I was so nice to you . . . and I could be even nicer. . . .'

'No?' said Callaghan. 'Not really?'

She laughed. She said softly: 'Yes . . . really!'

'All right,' said Callaghan. 'I'll remember that. Now, what's the trouble? It must be something that really matters this time. Mustn't it? Now . . . what *does* matter?'

She said: 'This does . . .' She got up, moved to the armchair on which her fur coat lay. She put her hand underneath it. When it emerged Callaghan saw that it held a square wooden box – one he had seen before.

He said: 'Well, I'll be damned . . . that Coronet again!'

She laughed. She said: 'There's almost a humorous side to it, isn't there?'

'Definitely,' said Callaghan. 'Tell me, how did you get it this time?'

She put the box down on the table. She said: 'Look, you said I was to tell the truth, the whole truth and nothing but the truth. Well, here it is: I didn't take the Coronet back to Mayfield. I've had it all the time.'

Callaghan said: 'That's all right. But why didn't you take it back? Why go to the trouble of telling me that you were going to take it back?'

She said earnestly: 'Truly, at the time I intended to. You'll agree that it seemed the obvious thing to do. But when I considered everything it seemed a stupid thing to do. Quite obviously, De Sirac would have done something about it. If I hadn't asked you to go and tell him that I was putting it back, it would have been all right, but suddenly, after I left you, I felt certain that, knowing it was going back, he'd steal it again.' She shrugged her shoulders. 'It would have been awfully easy for him to do that,' she said. 'He had the key – he knew the combination.'

Callaghan said: 'It looks as if you made fools of both myself and De Sirac.'

'Does it matter about De Sirac?' she said. 'After all, I was afraid of him.'

Callaghan said: 'All right. So you kept the Coronet. What did you intend to do with it?'

She looked serious. 'I didn't know what to do,' she said. 'At first I thought I'd take it back openly. Tell Arthur Denys all about it; make an open confession. Then I thought I'd give it to Paula. Then suddenly I remembered that Arthur had made a claim on the insurance company who were concerned. I became frightened. I didn't know what to do. I don't know what to do now.'

Callaghan said: 'Fine. So you've brought it back to me. Does that mean that I've got to decide what's to be done?'

She got up. She came over to him. She stood close to him, looking at him. She said: 'You think I'm an awful little heel, don't you? Quite candidly, I feel rather a little heel, but the fact that I'm here now; the fact that I've brought the thing back to you; surely that must prove to you what I think of you. I *know* you'll find some way out of this. I know you'll be able to do something about it.'

Callaghan took a cigarette from the box on the mantelpiece. He lit it. He said: 'Irana, my sweetie-pie, somebody ought to smack your tail. And when I say smack I mean *smack*!'

She said seriously: 'I don't think I'd mind – not much – providing *you* did the smacking.'

There was silence. Then Callaghan said: 'So you know I'll be able to do something about it. Do something about what?'

She looked at him hopelessly. She said: 'Well, the fat's in the fire now, isn't it? The insurance company are sure to make an investigation – that is unless Arthur withdraws the claim. If he withdraws the claim it's going to look very odd, isn't it? And why should he? He honestly and sincerely believes the Coronet's been stolen.'

Callaghan said: 'I don't see why you shouldn't take it back to him; why you shouldn't tell him what happened. After all the insurance company aren't going to mind much. They won't have to pay the claim. They're not going to worry about anything else.'

She said: 'I know. But look what a fearful position that puts Paula in.'

Callaghan said: 'I see. So you're thinking about her?'

She said: 'Of course. If I take the Coronet back to Arthur, I've got to explain to him why I had it stolen in the first place, and even *I* can't go back and say that I got De Sirac to steal it for *me*.'

Callaghan nodded. 'That's right. You had it stolen for Paula, didn't you?'

She said: 'Yes, you believe that, don't you?'

He smiled amiably. 'I believe everything you say,' he said. 'I think this time you're telling the truth.'

She said slowly: 'Slim, what are you going to do?'

He looked at her. She was very close to him. A breath of the perfume she was wearing came to his nostrils.

He said: 'This is the first thing I'm going to do.' He put his hand under her chin, tilted it. He kissed her on the mouth. He said: 'You've got something that appeals to me, Irana.'

She sighed. She said: 'I'm *so* glad. That's really the *only* thing that matters to me.'

Callaghan said: 'I think a drink is indicated. Do you ever drink whisky?'

She said: 'Not often. But I'd like to now.'

He went to the sideboard, poured two drinks, gave her one. He said:

'I don't know what I'm going to do about this Coronet. Between you and me and the gatepost this business is becoming a little involved, don't you think? I shall have to think something out, and it'll have to be good.'

She nodded. She said: 'Yes, it'll have to be a good plan.'

Callaghan asked: 'When did you see Paula last?'

She said: 'I haven't seen her. I don't think I want to. I think Paula would be very angry with me.'

He asked: 'Is that why you disappeared? Why was it necessary for you to disappear?'

She said: 'I was miserable and unhappy. When I felt that it wouldn't be right for me to take the Coronet back, I wanted to come and tell you about it. Then I believed that you'd distrust me if I did. You wouldn't believe anything I said. Paula's been angry with me over this business from the first. If Arthur Denys knew the truth about it he'd loathe me. De Sirac has already tried to make all the trouble that he could for me. Don't you see how I felt? I just wanted to get away from everybody.'

Callaghan said: 'Yes, I can understand that. And then suddenly you got tired of that position. You decided that you would like to come back; that you'd got to get yourself into circulation again sometime.'

She said miserably: 'Quite obviously, I couldn't go on keeping the Coronet, could I? That would have been a shocking thing to do.'

Callaghan said: 'Yes, wouldn't it?' He went to the sideboard, poured another whisky and soda. He turned; stood leaning against the sideboard, the glass in his hand, looking at her. He drank the whisky, put the glass down behind him. He said: 'Come here, Irana.'

She came over to him.

Callaghan said: 'You're crazy about me, aren't you? You'd do anything for me.' He put his arm round her.

She said: 'Yes, Slim. I've told you that.' He tilted up her chin and kissed her. She lay against his shoulder, looking up at him with limpid eyes.

Callaghan went on sarcastically: 'So you were miserable and unhappy. You felt it wouldn't be right for you to take the Coronet back. You felt everybody hated you – Paula, for what you'd done; Denys if he knew the truth; and De Sirac because – well, De Sirac didn't like you very much anyway, did he? So you decided you wouldn't take the Coronet back.'

She said softly: 'I've told you that, Slim.'

'You're the most goddam pestiferous little liar I have ever met,' said Callaghan smoothly. 'Go over there and sit down. We'll have a little talk.'

She disengaged herself. Her face was ashen. She went unsteadily to the armchair; sat down. She sat bolt upright, her fingers clutching the edges of the chair.

Callaghan said casually: 'The trouble with you, sweetie-pie, is that one of these fine days you're going to double-cross yourself out of existence. You never intended to take the Coronet back, and you *didn't* take it back. But you thought it would be an awfully good idea if you told me that you were going to. You thought it would be an even better idea if you got me to tell De Sirac that you were going to take it back. You thought De Sirac would believe that. De Sirac would know that I would insist on your taking it back. Or would he? I wonder if De Sirac was a little more clever than you thought.'

She said hoarsely: 'I don't know what you mean. . . . I don't know what you mean. . . .'

'No?' said Callaghan. 'You just don't know anything, do you, Irana? Well, things went rather well for De Sirac, didn't they? Arthur Denys who, according to what you've told me, seldom worries to go and look at the Coronet, suddenly decided to look in the safe and found it had gone. Someone had stolen it! So he did the obvious thing. He put in a claim on the insurance society and the assessors put that notice in *The Times*. Then the fat's in the fire.'

Callaghan helped himself to a cigarette, lit it. He stood, still leaning against the sideboard, blowing smoke rings.

He went on: 'I wonder *what* made Denys decide so suddenly to open the safe and discover that the Coronet was gone. It's almost as if someone had given him the tip-off, isn't it? Don't you think somebody might have given him the tip-off?'

She asked sullenly: 'What do you mean?'

'Isn't it obvious,' said Callaghan. 'There's somebody in this business makes a habit of writing anonymous notes – our friend De Sirac. He wrote an anonymous note to your sister about a blonde woman who was staying at an hotel at Laleham with Arthur Denys. That surprises you, doesn't it? But it's true. Maybe he wrote another note to Arthur Denys suggesting that he might have a look in the safe and see if the Coronet was there. Or perhaps he didn't write a note this time. Perhaps he telephoned. He wouldn't have to give his name. As a matter of fact,' said Callaghan airily, 'that's obviously the thing for De Sirac to have done.'

She said acidly: 'Why? Why should he have done that?'

Callaghan said: 'It's obvious, isn't it? I go to him and tell him that you're going to return the Coronet; that everything's all over; that he's got nothing else that he can blackmail anyone about. Well, he doesn't like that, does he? *You* wouldn't like it if you were De Sirac. So he makes sure of seeing that either the Coronet is returned or somebody gets into trouble, and he does that very easily. He just rings through to Denys and suggests that the Coronet isn't there. And it wasn't! That's what *I* think happened.'

She said: 'What are you going to do?'

He grinned at her maliciously. 'It looks to me,' he said, 'as if you've got yourself into a first-class jam. Maybe I'm going to get you out of it. Maybe I'm not.'

She said passionately: 'Slim, you've *got* to help me. You've *got* to. Surely you feel something for me.'

Callaghan said: 'I don't feel a goddam thing for you. You're very nice to look at, but I don't think you've ever told the truth in your life.' He smiled at her. 'I told you there was something about you that appealed to me. Work that one out for yourself. There are other people as beautiful as you who at least tell a little more truth than you do.'

She said: 'I suppose you mean Paula. I suppose you're for Paula. You *like* her.'

'Since you come to mention it, I do,' Callaghan said. 'I go for Paula in a very big way. She's got everything you've got and a damn sight more.'

She said: 'So you're going to throw me to the dogs. Is that it?'

He shook his head. 'No, I'm not,' he said. 'Maybe I'll still keep you out of this. Maybe I won't. It depends on what happens. But take a tip from me, Irana, behave yourself. You've already started too much. You've started something that you probably can't finish.'

She relaxed a little. Her smile returned. She looked maliciously insolent. She said: 'Aren't you making rather a lot of all this? What have I done? I've been unfortunate, that's all. I did something with a good motive. I had that Coronet stolen because I wanted to help Paula. I wasn't to know that De Sirac would behave like he did.'

'No?' said Callaghan. 'That's another lie. I suppose you're going to suggest to me that you knew De Sirac only casually; that knowing him only casually you asked him, as a matter of course, to commit a little job of burglary for you. I bet you knew De Sirac pretty well. In point of fact you've probably been his mistress. You tried to be clever with him and he won.'

She said: 'That isn't true. . . .'

'Nuts!' said Callaghan. He went on: 'But I wasn't thinking so much about the Coronet.'

She asked: 'What were you thinking of?'

Callaghan said: 'When De Sirac saw that assessors' notice in the paper he knew you hadn't returned the Coronet. He got in touch with you. He was going to make things pretty hot for you. So something had to be done about it. Something *was* done about it.'

She said: 'Meaning exactly what?'

Callaghan shrugged his shoulders. 'Meaning just this,' he said. 'Somebody killed De Sirac. Didn't you know?'

She dropped sideways over the arm of the chair. For a moment Callaghan thought she had fainted. He looked at her closely. He saw one eyelid quiver.

He stood watching her. After a while she moved. She lay back in the armchair, her arms resting on the sides, her eyes closed. Callaghan lit a fresh cigarette. He picked up her glass, poured out a small whisky and soda. He went over to her, gave her the drink. He said: 'You'll feel better after that. You've got to pull yourself together anyway.'

She took the glass. Callaghan went back to the sideboard, stood leaning against it, smoking, watching her. She drank the whisky and soda.

She said: 'So De Sirac's dead.' Her voice was hard. 'Who killed him? When did he die?'

Callaghan said: 'I wouldn't know when he died and I don't know who killed him.' He flicked the ash off his cigarette. He went on: 'There are a lot of people I should think who would have liked to have killed De Sirac. After all he was one of those people, wasn't he? The sort of good-looking young man who haunts the night clubs and makes friends with all sorts and conditions of woman; who does all sorts of odd jobs for anyone who wants an odd job done – such as stealing Coronets.' Callaghan yawned. 'One thing about De Sirac was certain,' he said. 'He was a blackmailer – and blackmailers don't concentrate just on one person, you know. There must have been a lot of people – a lot of women – who hated De Sirac.' He smiled at her. 'You weren't particularly fond of him, were you?'

She said: 'I wasn't particularly fond of him, but I didn't actually hate him. I merely disliked him. I thought he was stupid and crooked.'

Callaghan said casually: 'He wasn't stupid and he wasn't any more crooked than you were. You'd known De Sirac for some time. You were pretty friendly with him. You probably thought you were fond of him. It was only when he got nasty that you found you didn't like him. Anyway, he did you a good turn, didn't he?'

She opened her eyes wide. 'He did *me* a good turn?' she repeated. 'That's very interesting. It would be difficult even for *you* to prove that.'

Callaghan said: 'Now you're beginning to dislike me, aren't you? And that's not clever. You wouldn't know a good turn that De Sirac did for you, would you?'

She said shortly: 'I don't know what you're talking about.'

Callaghan said: 'All right, I'll tell you. Why did you have to re-dye your hair brunette when you wanted to come down to The Crescent & Star to see me – when you wanted to pretend that you were Mrs Paula Denys? The reason's pretty obvious, I think, Irana. You dyed your hair blonde when you went to stay with Arthur Denys at the hotel at Laleham.'

She said hoarsely: 'That's a lie!'

'Nuts!' said Callaghan. He grinned maliciously at her. 'You went down to the hotel at Laleham with Arthur Denys. You stayed with him. De Sirac wrote that note to your sister in order that she should start divorce proceedings. But De Sirac wasn't going to give you away. He knew that Denys, since then, had been getting around with a woman called Juliette de Longues – an attractive but oddly plain woman. So he was careful to state in that note to Paula that Arthur Denys had been staying at the hotel at Laleham with an ugly blonde. That was going to keep her mind off you, wasn't it, Irana? No one could possibly think of you as an ugly blonde.'

She said: 'This is quite ridiculous. Why should De Sirac want to do that? Why should he want to spare me – if this thing were true?'

Callaghan said caustically: 'You wouldn't know, would you? I'll give you a very good reason. Because you arranged with De Sirac to send that note to your sister. It was all part of your little scheme, wasn't it? Do you realize you had a very good motive for killing De Sirac? In point of fact the police might even get the idea that you did kill him. That depends on whether you've got an alibi or not. Quite candidly, I don't think you have.'

She said angrily: 'What do you mean? You're talking the most awful rubbish. You're saying –'

Callaghan said: 'What I'm saying is the truth, and you know it.' He went on: 'If you're a wise woman, Irana, you're going to do just what I tell you. You're not going to argue. You're just going to do what I say and like it. If you do, all right. If you don't I'll throw you to the dogs as sure as my name's Callaghan.'

She said: 'What am I supposed to do?'

Callaghan said: 'You'd better get out of town. Pack your bags and go somewhere for a holiday. Go down to the Chequers Inn at Wilverton in Sussex. It's a nice quiet place. There'll be nothing there to disturb you. You ought to have an interesting time thinking about things. I want you out of London.'

She asked: 'Why?'

Callaghan said: 'Believe it or not, Callaghan Investigations is working for Mrs Paula Denys. She's our client. She knows you – at least she thinks she does. She doesn't know what a little rotter you really are. If she did she'd probably have a fit. And I don't think I particularly want to tell her.'

She said cynically: 'I suppose you want to spare her feelings. You wouldn't do anything that would hurt her, would you?'

Callaghan said: 'Why not? If it was necessary I would.' He smiled. 'How you hate Paula,' he said. 'You've always hated her, haven't you, Irana?'

She said: 'That's not true.'

'Of course it's true,' said Callaghan. 'Would you like me to go into my reasons for saying that? Would you like me to explain fully what's in my mind? Or are you prepared to take my word for it?'

She shrugged her shoulders.

Callaghan went on: 'If I were you I'd be careful, sweetie-pie. The ice is very thin, you know. You could fall through very easily. Well, are you going to do what you're told or not?'

She nodded. She said: 'I don't see there's any choice.'

Callaghan said: 'You don't know how right you are.'

She got up. She said: 'It's not going to be very easy for me to go away.'

Callaghan said: 'No? Why not? A question of money, I suppose?' He grinned again. 'I ought to say that I thought you had a thousand – the thousand you gave me in the first place, that I gave back to you – but of course you haven't got it. I think I know where that thousand is.'

He put his hand in the breast pocket of his coat, brought out a wad of banknotes. He said: 'This ought to look after the holiday.

Incidentally, it ought to look after you until things are more or less straightened out.'

She said abruptly: 'This is very good of you.'

Callaghan said: 'Don't worry. That's not *my* money. Arthur Denys gave me that.'

She said: 'My God! Are you working for him too? You –'

Callaghan said airily: 'I'm just a little busy bee. I'm working for everybody. Now put your coat on, Irana, and get out of here. I'm bored with you. Tomorrow morning I expect you to be out of London. I expect you to stay out of London for at least a month. If you don't you'll find things won't be so good for you.'

He helped her on with her coat. She picked up her handbag, walked towards the door. She stopped suddenly; turned. She said: 'What about the Coronet?'

Callaghan looked at the square box. He said: 'Don't you worry about the Coronet. I'll look after that. Goodnight, Irana.'

She opened the door. She said over her shoulder: 'You may not believe me, but I'm still rather for you. In spite of all the beastly things you've said I still think you've got something.'

Callaghan said nothing. She closed the door softly behind her.

He helped himself to another whisky and soda.

CHAPTER NINE
A MATTER OF TECHNIQUE

CHIEF Detective-Inspector George Henry Gringall, otherwise known as The Jigger, a nickname which he had earned in the remote past for reasons lost in antiquity, sat at his desk in his room at New Scotland Yard. He smoked a short briar pipe; was engaged in his invariable pastime of drawing fruit on the blotter.

He finished an illustration of a melon with meticulous care. He put down his pencil, picked up the telephone receiver. He asked to be put through to Detective-Inspector Marrick. When that worthy came on the line, Gringall said:

'Oh, Marrick, about that De Sirac thing, would you like to have a word with me?'

Marrick said he would. When he came into the room Gringall was standing with his back to the window, biting the stem of his pipe. He asked: 'Has anything turned up?'

Marrick said: 'No, sir. Nothing at all. We're doing the usual check on the dead man – associates – all that sort of thing. I thought possibly there was something in your mind.'

Gringall said glumly: 'There's a hell of a lot in my mind, but at the moment my mind is revolving mainly round Mr Callaghan. By the way, he'll be looking in this afternoon.'

Marrick said: 'You didn't say very much about the circumstances in which De Sirac's body was found, sir. You just gave me a rough idea. I take it Callaghan was concerned in that?'

Gringall said: 'Callaghan told me on the telephone that he had an appointment with De Sirac. That he had to see him about some business; that the business was urgent. So he expected De Sirac to be there. When he got round to the place he knocked but there was no reply. Callaghan didn't like it, so he got the apartment manager to open the door. They went in and found the body. It had been dead some time.'

Marrick nodded. He said: 'I wonder why Callaghan insisted on having the door opened. After all it's not unusual for people to miss appointments.'

Gringall said: 'I know. It's almost as if Callaghan expected to find him dead, isn't it?'

'That's how it looks to me,' said Marrick. 'We shall have to find out what this business was about – this business between De Sirac and Callaghan.'

Gringall said: 'Yes? You won't find it so easy. Callaghan's a clever fellow. Sometimes he's *very* clever. He's very astute.'

'That's as maybe, sir,' said Marrick. 'It doesn't matter how astute he is, he can't very well obstruct a police officer or withhold information.

Gringall smiled. 'Don't think that Callaghan will *obstruct* you, Marrick. Callaghan never *obstructs* anybody. You'll find he'll do his best to help you. Personally *I'd* rather be obstructed by the devil than helped by Callaghan. Another thing,' said Gringall, 'you play him very carefully. He can be quite annoying, especially if he digs his toes in. On the other hand, he *might* help, if he wants to.'

The Detective-Inspector said: 'Well, you know him better than I do, sir.'

Gringall said: 'Yes, I do. The joke is I don't dislike him. He's a peculiar person. He's got his own set of principles and standards. In his way he keeps to them.' He grinned. 'I must say,' he went on, 'they're extraordinarily elastic.'

Marrick asked: 'Can you give me some idea as to how I might handle him, sir?'

Gringall said: 'When he comes here this afternoon I'll see him. I'll have a general sort of talk with him. I'll try and get some idea what he's playing at – if he's playing at anything; that is if this story of his is true. Anyhow he'll probably make it sound true,' said Gringall ruefully. 'Then I'll send him down to see you. If I think he can tell you anything that will help – if I *do* send him down to you – while he is on his way down I'll ring you on the telephone.'

Marrick asked: 'What time is he coming here?'

Gringall said: 'He'll come here about tea-time.' He sighed. 'Whenever I've seen Callaghan at Scotland Yard it's always been round about that time,' he said. 'He likes to come in at tea-time. He thinks the atmosphere is rather more pleasant.'

Marrick said rather acidly: 'He seems to think rather a lot of himself, sir – this Callaghan.'

Gringall said: 'He does. The joke is he's got quite good reason. You know that Vendayne case. He handled that, you remember – a very clever piece of work – one of the most cunning jobs I've ever known in my life. The trouble with Callaghan is,' said Gringall, 'that he's not merely cunning – he's extremely resourceful and sometimes quite brilliant. You wouldn't forget that, Marrick, would you?'

Marrick said: 'No, sir, I won't forget it, but I don't think I'm going to like Mr Callaghan.'

Gringall said: 'You won't. I didn't at first. You'll find he sort of grows on you.'

Marrick went away. Gringall returned to his desk. He picked up his pencil, began to draw a lemon. Half-way through he smiled to himself. He could not help feeling that had Callaghan been present during the conversation with Marrick he would have thoroughly approved the fact that Chief Detective-Inspector Gringall *was* drawing a lemon.

*

Effie Thompson was seated at her typewriter when Nikolls came through the outer office. She folded her hands in her lap and watched his back as it disappeared into Callaghan's office. She heard the lower desk drawer being opened and the bourbon bottle taken out. She heard the subdued gurgle as Nikolls inserted the neck of the bottle into his mouth and took his usual after-lunch swig.

She got up. She moved over to the open doorway, stood watching Nikolls as he sat behind Callaghan's desk extracting a Lucky Strike from his cigarette pack.

He grinned at her. He eased his large bulk back into the chair, sat watching her, running an appreciative eye over her trim suit.

He said: 'What's eatin' you, Effie? You don't look quite so good to me. Clothes O.K. but expression not so hot. You got circles around your eyes. What's the trouble, babe?'

She said: 'I'm beginning to be rather interested in what he's doing. I think even he is going a little beyond himself this time. I don't like this Denys thing. I don't like the way he's handling it. I don't like anything about it.'

Nikolls raised his eyebrows. He leaned over sideways, struck a match on the seat of his trousers, lit his cigarette. He flicked the used match expertly into the wastepaper basket.

'O.K. Why don't you tell him?' he asked. He grinned humorously at her. 'He'd love that. Jeez . . . he'd tell *you* somethin', babe. He'd tear you wide open. . . .' He leaned back, began to blow smoke rings into the air.

She said curtly: 'I know that. But this time he's playing with fire. He's trying to throw the whole onus of this Coronet business on to Mrs Paula Denys. He's going to sacrifice her in order that that Irana piece doesn't get into trouble. He's –'

Nikolls said: 'How do you know?'

'She was here last night,' said Effie coldly. 'Upstairs in his apartment. Wilkie told me.'

'Yeah?' said Nikolls. 'I suppose he just sorta told you. Just like that. Like hell. You prised it outa him, didn't you?'

'Supposing I did,' she said shortly. 'I've already been told to forget that it *wasn't* Paula who came to see us originally about the Coronet. I've practically been told to take it for granted that it was Mrs Denys. That's not the truth. It wasn't. Why should he want to suggest it was?'

Nikolls shrugged. He said: 'You make me laugh, Effie. So you got a big idea that this office oughta start tellin' the truth. You suddenly got around to the fact that the boss is playin' both ends against the middle.' He flicked the ash off his cigarette. 'That's somethin' new in this office, hey? We never told any lies before, did we . . . oh no . . . hear me laugh! You're tying to sell me –'

She interrupted hotly: 'I'm trying to sell you nothing. I'm stating facts.'

'Nuts,' said Nikolls amiably. 'You're takin' yourself for a ride. You don't like this Irana baby; you don't like her because she's got plenty of what it takes an' because the boss is goin' for her plenty. You don't like her because she was around her last night maybe havin' fun an' games with Callaghan Investigations himself. You're goddam jealous, Effie, that's your trouble.'

She said angrily: 'You're talking the most unutterable rubbish, Mr Nikolls. Why should I be jealous? Why should I care what Mr Callaghan does? Why –'

Nikolls yawned noisily. 'You set it to music, Effie,' he said with a grin, 'an' I'll play it on my old guitar. You got the heebie-jeebies. You got hot pants for the boss an' you think he's playin' Irana. You don't like it, that's all.'

'I loathe your expressions,' she said. She was almost hoarse with rage. 'Hot pants indeed! How appalling. I'm merely Mr Callaghan's secretary. I work for him. Personally he doesn't interest me. I wouldn't touch him with a barge pole!'

Nikolls flicked his cigarette stub into the fireplace. 'Don't tell me he's been askin' you to touch him with a barge pole,' he said cheerfully. 'I just couldn't believe it.' He yawned again and stretched. 'Maybe you're right,' he said. 'Maybe he's playin' Irana along good an' plenty. Maybe he's playin' Paula along too. I wouldn't put anythin' above or beyond that guy. He works his own way an' believe me his own way is just nobody's business. Maybe you're right. Me . . . I think it's sorta dangerous playin' around with two dames in the same family. An' when they're as good-lookin' as those two, then it's liable to be dynamite.' He sighed.

'I remember when I was in Wisconsin one time,' said Nikolls reminiscently. 'I was workin' for the Garbkin Agency an' they sent me down to some little place on a job. There was two babies there.

Twins – you couldn't tell 'em apart. Boy, was those babies easy on the eyeballs, or was they? Yes, sir! Well, one night I was talkin' to one of 'em on the back porch. She was lookin' at me sorta soft an' relentin' – if you get me. So I sorta gathered her up an' started givin' her a line that woulda made Casanova look like a cold frankfurter in a snow-drift, an' did she react?'

Nikolls sighed heavily and reached for his cigarette pack.

'She looks up at me,' he went on, 'an' she says: "Windy, you're terrific. You're the cats's earpads." An' I say: "Babe," I say, "d'you remember last night . . . remember all them lovely things I said . . . remember?" She says: "Yeah . . . but tell me again, Windy. Tell me all the things you said last night." '

Nikolls lit his cigarette and shook his head sadly.

'So I told her,' he said. 'An' then she went inta the house an' came back an' hit me over the head with an electric iron she'd got under her jumper.'

Effie Thompson said: 'Why did she do that?'

'It was her sister,' said Nikolls. 'See? A case of mistaken identity. There oughta be some sorta law against twins.'

He got up; stood in front of the fireplace. He said: 'Don't you worry about the boss. It won't do you any good anyway. If he's playin' it off the cuff, that's how it is. An' if you feel in need of comfortin', look me over, Effie. I got a brand of comfort talk that would grow hair on an orange.'

She said coldly: 'I don't need comforting, thank you, Mr Nikolls.'

He grinned at her. 'That's what I thought,' he said. 'I remember some dame in Flatbush –'

He stopped talking as she slammed the door behind her. He scratched his head and stood considering some matter of import. He came to a conclusion. He went back to the desk, opened the drawer, took out the bourbon bottle and took another long swig.

He lay back in the chair, folded his hands across his stomach and went to sleep.

The detective-constable who had brought Gringall's tea-tray into the office was going out of the door when Callaghan came in.

Gringall looked up and smiled: 'Good afternoon, Slim. We've noticed you always come in time for tea.'

Callaghan put his black soft hat on the corner of Gringall's desk. He sat down in a leather armchair, lit a cigarette.

He said: 'Why not? I think New Scotland Yard is a nice place, especially at tea-time. Everybody relaxes, if you know what I mean.'

Gringall said: 'I don't. And I'll tell you somebody who isn't particularly relaxed. His name's Detective-Inspector Marrick, and he's in charge of this De Sirac affair. He'll probably want to have a talk with you sometime, but I thought you might like to have a few words with me first.'

Callaghan said: 'That's what I thought. You know, Gringall, I'd like to help.'

Gringall began to pour the tea. He said: 'I know. That's what I was afraid of.'

Callaghan cocked one eyebrow. He said: 'Now, is that fair?'

Gringall came over with the tea-cup, gave it to Callaghan. He said: 'You've helped us a hell of a lot. You helped us with the Vendayne case. You helped us with the Riverton case. The thing that amazes me about those two jobs is how you managed to keep out of gaol yourself.'

Callaghan said: 'If you're suggesting that I've ever done anything to merit being incarcerated in one of His Majesty's prisons, I'll consider issuing a writ for criminal libel.' He smiled amiably at Gringall, who had gone back to his seat behind the desk.

Callaghan went on: 'The trouble with you fellows is you don't like private detectives. We get around a little more; we're not hide-bound by all sorts of rules and regulations; we can even ask people funny questions sometimes without being called to account.' He sipped his tea. 'I'm awfully glad I'm not a policeman,' he said.

Gringall said solemnly: 'So am I! All we need is *you* on the staff here and we'd be all set for a revolution.'

Callaghan said: 'I think it's tough. I come here in my own time and at my own expense, and in the best frame of mind, to try and give you a hand, and I get nothing but insults. Incidentally, if there's any more sugar, I'd like another piece. Just throw a knob over.'

Gringall did so. He said: 'Look, Slim, I'm putting my cards down with you. Marrick's in a jam over this De Sirac thing. That body had been there for some time. There was no heating on in the flat. It was like an ice-house. That didn't do the Divisional Surgeon any good. He can only give you a very approximate time of death. Another thing, you know how it is in these apartment blocks these days. There's no regular staff, no hall porters, no regular cleaning staff. It's very difficult for us to find who went out and who went in. You know all that just as well as I do.'

Callaghan nodded.

Gringall went on: 'So anything you can tell Marrick about De Sirac will be very useful information.' He went on: 'Marrick thought it was rather funny that you had the flat door opened. He had the idea in his head that you might almost have expected to find De Sirac dead.'

Callaghan said casually: 'To tell you the truth, Gringall, I wasn't surprised. De Sirac wasn't a very nice fellow, you know. A lot of people disliked him. I think he did a little blackmailing on the side.'

'I see,' said Gringall. 'So it was like that. Marrick didn't think his background was very good.'

Callaghan said: 'Marrick's right. His background was lousy.'

Gringall finished his tea; put the cup back on the tray. He produced his pipe, began to fill it. He said:

'I suppose it would be asking you too much to tell me what you were seeing De Sirac about?'

Callaghan said: 'Not at all. You know my methods. I always put all my cards on the table.'

Gringall said: 'Like hell you do. You put *some* cards on the table; most of them you keep up your sleeve.'

Callaghan said: 'Not in this case. It's quite simple. De Sirac was beginning to annoy a client of mine. He tried to skewer a little money out of this client. The client didn't like it, see?'

Gringall nodded. 'I see. So the client came to you and asked you to deal with De Sirac?'

'Right,' said Callaghan. 'Well, I had an appointment with De Sirac. I met him at a club. I talked pretty straight with him. I told him unless he laid off my client I would have to consider going to the police.'

Gringall said: 'I wonder why your client didn't think of that in the first place.'

Callaghan shrugged his shoulders. 'It was just one of those things,' he said. 'Maybe she liked my face more than she would have liked a policeman's. Anyway, she wanted to come to us, so she came.' He grinned. 'We thought we could do just as good a job, if not better, than the police would have done. In fact,' said Callaghan, 'I doubt if the police could have done a job at all.'

'I see,' said Gringall. 'So it was like that, was it?'

'More or less,' said Callaghan. 'Anyhow I had a very straight talk with De Sirac, as I said. I told him he could make up his mind exactly what he was going to do. I told him I'd see him at his place yesterday afternoon, and he'd be there and we'd settle this thing one way or another. Well, I told you what happened. I went round there and I couldn't get in. I knew De Sirac wouldn't have taken a chance of not being there. He knew I meant business.

'I was just going away when I thought it would be a very good idea to have a look round that flat. I won't say there wasn't a vague idea in my head that something might not have happened to De Sirac, because I believe he was a man whom a lot of people didn't like particularly, but I wasn't at all certain about it. I thought it would be interesting to have a look round the flat.'

Gringall said: 'I see. So you had the door opened and you found De Sirac?'

'That's right,' said Callaghan. 'And then I did my duty as a citizen. I informed the police promptly.'

Gringall said: 'I suppose I'd be out of order if I asked you the name of your client?'

Callaghan asked: 'Why would it be out of order?'

Gringall said airily: 'Oh, I don't know. You might get the idea in your head that if this De Sirac was trying to blackmail your client, the client might have had some motive for removing De Sirac. You *might* think something like that.'

Callaghan said: 'Not a hope. My client couldn't have had anything to do with De Sirac's death. She hasn't been anywhere near that apartment for days. I doubt if she's ever been there in her life. I'm not afraid of that.'

Gringall said: 'So it's a woman. It's funny the number of charming women who go to Callaghan Investigations. I can't make it out.' He grinned at Callaghan.

Callaghan said: 'It must be my fatal beauty.'

Gringall lit his pipe. He said: 'It might be a good thing, you know, Slim – and I'm looking at this from your point of view – if you told us who your client was. You know our methods. We don't drag anybody's name into a case unless it's absolutely necessary, but it's better for us to know.'

'I agree,' said Callaghan airily. 'That's all right. My client is a lady called Mrs Paula Denys – a very charming and responsible person. I'm quite satisfied with her *bona fides*, which I checked up carefully, as I always do before I take on a case. She had a very justifiable grouse against De Sirac. She's entirely innocent of any sort of wrong-doing. I really shouldn't have told you her name, but I always try to be helpful.'

Gringall said nothing. He puffed silently at his pipe for a few moments; then he said:

'Mrs Paula Denys – would she be related to the Arthur Denys – the owner of the Denys Coronet?'

'That's right,' said Callaghan. 'She's his wife. She's not living with him. She instituted divorce proceedings against him, but she's his wife all right.'

Gringall said: 'That's rather odd. We've been asked by the Globe and Consolidated to investigate the theft of that Coronet. That's being done by Detective-Inspector Lamming.' He looked at Callaghan. 'That's rather a coincidence, isn't it?'

Callaghan nodded. He said: 'Yes, life is full of coincidences, isn't it, Gringall?' He got up. He said: 'Well, I don't think there's anything else I can tell you. If I can be of any help at any time let me know.'

Gringall said: 'You wouldn't like to go down and have a word with Marrick, would you?'

Callaghan shrugged his shoulders. He said: 'If you like, but I don't see why you can't tell him what I've said.' He grinned at Gringall. 'My time's very valuable just now.'

'I bet it is,' said Gringall. 'All right, Slim. Thank you very much. If I want you again I'll give you a ring. I know you'll do your best for us.'

Callaghan said: 'Of course. So long, Gringall.' He picked up his hat, went out.

When the door closed behind him, Gringall took off the telephone receiver. He spoke to Detective-Inspector Marrick.

He said: 'You'd better come up. Callaghan's just gone. He's told me his story and I don't like it a bit.'

Marrick said: 'Is he being funny? Is he digging his toes in?'

Gringall said: 'No, he's told me a story that sounds so much like the truth that I'm rather worried. Callaghan's being *too* helpful, and I don't like it a bit.'

Callaghan and Nikolls sat on high stools against the bar of The Yellow Anchor Club, off Berkeley Square. Callaghan ordered more whisky.

Nikolls said: 'Look, there's a little thing that maybe you oughta know about – I don't think Effie's quite so pleased with you.'

Callaghan lit a cigarette. He said: 'What the hell do you mean – Effie not pleased with what?'

'Well,' said Nikolls, 'she sorta beefed off this afternoon. She's got an idea you're givin' this Irana dame a sweet run-around. She thinks you're playin' it on to Paula, see – makin' her the stooge. I think it's worryin' her.'

'Yes?' said Callaghan. 'Worry's good for people sometimes. They tell me it produces energy.'

'Maybe,' said Nikolls. 'I think she was a bit steamed up over you tellin' her to sorta forget that Irana came to us in the first place, an' suggestin' that we played this thing as if it was Mrs Denys who came to us. I don't think she sorta likes that.'

Callaghan said: 'That's too bad!'

'O.K.,' said Nikolls. 'So long as you know.'

Callaghan finished his whisky; signalled to the bartender. He said: 'Listen, Windy, tomorrow morning you get through to the Globe and Consolidated. You speak to the manager. Tell him that we're vaguely interested in this missing Coronet. Tell him that one or two little points came our way and we've been sort of free-lancing on the job. Point out that I saw that assessors' notice in *The Times*, and that maybe, if somebody likes to pay me that thousand pounds, I could do something about the Coronet. You got that?'

'I've got it,' said Nikolls. 'But can they play it that way? This thing's been passed to the police. Even if the insurance company was prepared to pay up to get the Coronet back, the cops aren't gonna lay off, are they?'

Callaghan said: 'Why should you worry your head about that? Get through tomorrow, and if you get a good reaction from the manager, tell him I'll look down some time tomorrow afternoon and see him.'

'O.K.' said Nikolls.

There was a silence; then Callaghan said: 'The night you were hanging around De Sirac's place, when you found his body, you were there quite some time, weren't you, watching the entrance, before you went in.'

'Yep,' said Nikolls. 'It seemed like years to me.'

Callaghan said: 'Did you see anybody coming in or going out?'

Nikolls shook his head. 'Nope! I didn't see anybody, but it's not too easy, you know. The entrance is dark. If you're only standin' a few yards away anybody walkin' in the shadow could get in an' outa that dump an' you'd never see 'em – not in a thousand years.'

Callaghan nodded. He said: 'That's what I thought.'

Nikolls swallowed his whisky. He said: 'You had an idea little Irana might be around that dump when I got there? You said perhaps I'd find her there.'

Callaghan said: 'Well, you didn't find her, did you?'

'That's right,' said Nikolls. 'It wasn't my lucky day.'

Callaghan lit a cigarette. He said: 'There's another thing you can do tomorrow. Ring through to the Savoy and see if Denys has left there. If he has, find out if he's gone to Mayfield Place. And get around to Miss Juliette de Longues' flat. You'll find the address in the book in the office. Find out whether she's left town or not. When you've done that ring up Vale or Matthews and get one of them to go to the Chequers Hotel at Wilverton in Sussex; find out if Irana's arrived there.'

'What d'you know?' said Nikolls. 'It looks as if everybody's leavin' town. Maybe they're scared of somethin'. I wonder what it is – air-raids?' He grinned at Callaghan. He went on: 'Look, I don't wanta be curious, but what are the cops gonna do about De Sirac? Those boys are gonna sorta wonder, aren't they, about us? Maybe they'll want you to come clean over that.'

Callaghan said casually: 'I've done all that. I've told them all about it.' He smiled at Nikolls.

Nikolls said: 'I bet you have – like hell! But I'd like to know who killed that guy. I'm sorta curious. Maybe if they can't find anybody else they'll say I did it. I think that would be very funny.'

Callaghan said: 'No one would ever think that you could kill anybody. Besides, if you wanted to kill De Sirac, you wouldn't have had to do it with a fireiron.'

'No,' said Nikolls. 'I'd have just hit him once. I don't think I liked that guy.'

Chief Detective-Inspector Gringall finished writing a letter, locked the drawers of his desk, looked at his watch, walked to the hat-stand. He was just putting on his overcoat when the telephone bell rang. It was Marrick.

He said: 'Mr Gringall, there's a rather odd thing turned up. I think you ought to know about it. I've got Lamming here. I think he'd like to have a word with you.'

Gringall said: 'All right. Send him up.'

'Would you mind if I came too?' asked Marrick.

Gringall raised his eyebrows. He said: 'So it's like that, is it, Marrick?'

'Yes, Mr Gringall. It's like that.'

Gringall said: 'All right. Come up – both of you.'

He went back to his desk. Two minutes later the two detective-inspectors came into Gringall's office.

Lamming said: 'Here's rather an odd thing, Mr Gringall, in connection with the Denys Coronet. It looks to me as if there's a tie-up between that and the De Sirac murder.'

Gringall said: 'You don't say? Life is full of surprises, Lamming, isn't it? What's happened?'

'The Globe and Consolidated Insurance Company received an anonymous letter,' said Lamming. 'Here it is, sir.' He laid the note on the table in front of Gringall. He went on: 'The writer of this typewritten letter advises the company not to pay the claim on the Denys Coronet. Naturally, I was very interested. If you'll hold that sheet of paper up to the light you'll find it's got a most extraordinary watermark.'

Gringall looked at the paper. He held it up, examined it closely. He said: 'That watermark must have been very helpful to you, Lamming.'

Lamming smiled. 'It was, sir. There's only one firm who make that paper – Vayne and Howling in Conduit Street – and the joke is they only make that paper in foolscap size usually. But on this particular occasion they cut a few thousand sheets in quarto – they had an odd lot or something. Well, the lot was bought by one purchaser.'

Gringall asked: 'Have you discovered who the purchaser was?'

Lamming nodded. 'Callaghan Investigations of Berkeley Square bought the lot.'

Gringall said: 'This becomes more interesting every moment, doesn't it?'

'I don't know about that, sir,' said Lamming. 'But that letter was written in Callaghan's office. I went down to the Globe and Consolidated and checked through their correspondence files. Callaghan represented them five months ago in a case where they wanted an investigation made. This same paper was being used as follow-on sheets to his headed notepaper. One of the typewriters in his office is the machine that wrote that letter.'

Gringall said: 'I see.' He began to fill his pipe.

Marrick said: 'Having regard to what you told me, Mr Gringall, about your interview with Callaghan, it looks to me as if here is the time where we've got Mr Callaghan where we want him – just for once. I remember what you told me about him. You said he was a very clever fellow. I don't think this is so clever.' He pointed to the letter. 'The least he could have done was to have got himself another sheet of notepaper.'

Gringall shook his head sadly. He said: 'Marrick, you don't know Callaghan. Callaghan wrote that letter, and he selected that piece of paper in order that it should be traced back to his office. He knew perfectly well that when that claim was put in for the Coronet, even if the owner didn't come to us about it, the insurance company would. Callaghan wrote that letter to protect himself. He knew the Coronet had been stolen and, whilst he wasn't going to write an official letter to the insurance company and tell them not to pay the claim, he was clever enough to write an anonymous letter which he knew damn well we could trace back to his office.'

Marrick looked at Lamming. He said: 'Well, I'm damned! So he's as good as that, is he?'

Gringall said: 'Yes, sometimes he's very good.'

'All right, sir,' said Lamming. 'What do I do?'

'That goes for me too,' said Marrick. 'This is one of those things where I think a little direction is indicated, sir.'

Gringall said: 'I'll bet you any money you like that Callaghan knows that we're having a discussion about this letter. He probably thinks we've had it before. Well, what can we do about it? We can get him round here. We can tell him we've traced that letter back to his office. What's he going to say? If he wants to he'll say he doesn't know anything about it, and although it may be a piece of circumstantial evidence, the evidence doesn't prove anything. It only proves that some anonymous individual was doing what he considered to be his duty as a good citizen and getting the insurance company to stall paying that claim. Well?'

Gringall looked from one to the other of his subordinates. I don't see how you can put the screw on Callaghan for that.'

'I'm not suggesting that, sir,' said Marrick. 'But we might ask for an explanation.'

Gringall smiled. He said: 'You ask for one and see what you'll get. You'll get an explanation that sounds so true that you'll probably guess it's lies. My advice is this: When in doubt, don't do anything. And, believe it or not, I'm very much in doubt. Marrick, you carry on with your investigations about De Sirac – his background and associates. And if I were you, Lamming, I'd just sit around and smoke for a bit.'

'Do you really mean that, sir?' asked Lamming.

Gringall said: 'I mean it. This letter is a tip-off from Messrs Callaghan Investigations to us. The only thing we can do is to see what Callaghan's going to do, because he's going to do something. He didn't write that letter because he wanted to practise typewriting.'

CHAPTER TEN
MIDNIGHT DIALOGUE

CALLAGHAN came out of The Yellow Anchor Club at eleven o'clock. He stood undecided on the corner of the street. He wondered if he were drunk or sober. He allowed his mind solemnly to dwell on this subject for some moments, concluded that in any event it really did not matter. He began to walk towards Charles Street.

Ten minutes later he descended an area not very far from Park Lane; rapped on the door. He waited. After a few minutes the door opened slightly.

Callaghan said: 'This is Callaghan.'

A wheezy voice answered: 'Good evening, Mr Callaghan. Come in. It's a long time since you've been here.'

Callaghan said: 'That's my misfortune.' He went inside.

The long passage had originally been one from which had led the kitchens, store-rooms and sculleries of a large house. Now the place had been converted into one of those illegal night clubs which abound in London, sufficiently quiet and unimportant not to attract the attention of an overworked police force, but sufficiently important to cause quite a lot of trouble for those people for whom trouble always waits in the long run.

At the end of the passage, in what had originally been a large coal cellar, but which was now panelled in imitation oak, and lit by cleverly shaded lights, was a bar. Callaghan ordered himself a double whisky and soda. In the next room someone was playing a piano softly – a tune called 'In Days Gone By.' Callaghan vaguely thought it was rather a nice tune. For some unknown reason it brought the Vendayne case to his mind – and Audrey Vendayne. He began to make comparisons in his mind between Audrey Vendayne and Paula Denys. He found the process amusing but concluded it wouldn't get him anywhere. He wondered how much more whisky he could drink without becoming too optimistic about anything. He finished the whisky and soda; ordered another one.

The wheezy individual who had opened the door said: 'What about having one on the house, Mr Callaghan? We miss you. You used to be here a lot in the old days.'

Callaghan said: 'I used to do a lot of things in the old days that I don't do now. Didn't somebody tell you there was a war on?'

The wheezy one said: 'Yes, I heard about that.'

Callaghan lit a cigarette. He said: 'What about having a drink, Jimmie – on me?'

Jimmie said: 'I'd like to, but we'll have one on the house first.' He ordered the drinks. He grinned at Callaghan. He said: 'What is it, Mr Callaghan? You know I'd do anything for you.'

Callaghan said: 'Like hell you would, and what is what?'

Jimmie shrugged his shoulders. He said: 'You never come here unless you want something.'

Callaghan nodded. He said: 'Maybe you're right. Did you ever hear of a man called De Sirac?'

'Yes,' said Jimmie. 'I've heard plenty about him. He used to get around – that one. They tell me somebody's caught up with him. They tell me somebody fogged him. Were you interested in the boy?'

'Not particularly,' said Callaghan. 'Not particularly in the fact that somebody rubbed him out. Did you ever hear of a woman called Irana Faveley in connection with De Sirac?'

Jimmie nodded. 'Plenty,' he said. 'She was one of those babies who went for him in a big way. Why, I don't know. She was good-looking. She had money. She was a classy one – that one. What she saw in De Sirac I don't know, but they used to get around together plenty until –'

'Until what?' asked Callaghan; then he went on: 'Wait a minute. Supposing I make a guess, Jimmie. Until some other woman turned up. Is that right?'

The other nodded. He said: 'That's right.'

Callaghan said: 'And this other woman would be a rather odd sort of woman – a woman with a fairly nice figure, legs and ankles, good hair, a good carriage – a personality – but a rather plain face that didn't matter because all the other stuff was so good. A woman named de Longues. Is that right?'

Jimmie said: 'You're ahead of me. What do you want to ask me questions for? You know all the answers.'

Callaghan said: 'I didn't. I was only guessing.'

He finished his drink; said: 'Now you'll have one with me.'

Jimmie said: 'I've never seen anybody drink whisky like you do. I think you got hollow legs. Do you ever get high?'

Callaghan said: 'You'd be surprised! I think I'm a little cockeyed now. I'm not certain.'

Jimmie nodded. He said: 'I know. Maybe you're one of those guys who's a bit better when he's a little cut.'

Callaghan said: 'Who knows?'

When the bartender brought the drinks he picked up the glass; swallowed the double whisky at one gulp. He said: 'I'll be seeing you, Jimmie.' He went out.

Outside, the night air was cold. Callaghan thought you always felt the night air more when you had a lot of whisky inside you. He wondered what he was going to do. He began to walk towards Park Lane.

Callaghan supposed that most people spent quite a lot of their lives pondering on what they were going to do. He imagined that De Sirac and Irana Faveley must have spent a lot of time in consideration of the same problem. Life was like that. You were either a person who had not to be concerned particularly with anything, or you were one of those people who were always slightly worried about something, wondering what was going to happen; what the next move in the game was going to be; how you were going to play it.

Callaghan sighed. He crossed the road at St George's Hospital, began to walk towards Knightsbridge. Vaguely he found himself wondering why he was walking in that direction. Then he smiled to himself. He thought he knew the answer to that one.

A clock struck midnight as Callaghan rang the bell at the flat in Palmeira Court. He stood there ringing it for a considerable time; then the door opened. Inside, framed in the doorway, stood Paula Denys.

She was wearing a wine-coloured housecoat tied with a powder-blue sash; velvet mules to match the housecoat. Her hair was tied with a blue watered silk ribbon.

Callaghan leaned against the doorpost. He said: 'Has anyone ever told you that you're really *quite* lovely?'

She said with an odd little smile: 'Mr Callaghan, have you come here at twelve o'clock at night to tell me that?'

Callaghan shook his head. He said: 'No, if I told you really what I'd come here for you wouldn't believe me.'

'I shan't know until you tell me what you *have* come here for,' she said.

Callaghan grinned mischievously. He said: 'You know how difficult it is to get a drink at this time of night in London. I wondered if I could have a whisky and soda.'

She said: 'Why not? I suppose that would be included in the two hundred and fifty pounds?'

Callaghan cocked one eyebrow. He said: 'You mean my retainer? I hadn't thought about that, but then I very seldom think about money.'

She said pleasantly: 'Really? It seems at the moment you're thinking in terms of whisky. Will you come in?'

'I think that's very nice of you,' said Callaghan.

He hung his hat up in the hall, followed her into the large sitting-room. She went to a side table, poured out a whisky and soda. She brought it to him.

She said: 'In a minute I shall probably find out what you've really come here for. You're an odd person, aren't you, Mr Callaghan?'

'I wouldn't know,' said Callaghan. 'Maybe I'm a direct person. Possibly that's why you think I'm odd. But then you don't like me very much, do you?'

She said: 'I've never really thought a great deal about that.'

Callaghan said: 'No . . . I'm certain you haven't!'

She brought a box of cigarettes and a table-lighter; lit his cigarette. She said:

'Do you know anything about Irana?' Her face was serious.

Callaghan said: 'Has anyone ever told you about your voice? A long time ago when I used to read books of poetry – don't laugh – but I *used* to read books of poetry – I read something about a lady with a grave caressing voice. I think you've got a grave caressing voice.'

She said: 'Have I? I don't think there's very much difference between my voice and Irana's. Haven't you noticed the same thing about her?'

Callaghan said: 'I've noticed a hell of a lot about her, but believe it or not, it doesn't interest me. *You* do.'

She said caustically: 'That's very nice of you, Mr Callaghan.'

Callaghan said: 'You just don't know how nice of me that is.' He smiled at her. 'But one of these days you will.'

She raised her eyebrows. She said: 'Yes? Why?'

Callaghan said: 'You think a lot of Irana, don't you? You think she's a rather more headstrong edition of yourself. You think she's just like you but with a little more vitality, a little more sense of adventure. You probably consider yourself the quiet sister. Isn't that right? You probably have a vague sort of admiration for Irana.'

Callaghan moved to the fireplace, stood in front of the fire. She went to an armchair and sat down. She crossed her legs, arranged her robe. She sat there looking at him.

After a while she said: 'Yes, you're quite right. I've always thought that Irana has a vital spark that I lack.'

'You don't need any vital spark,' said Callaghan. 'And she could do with a few less.'

She shrugged her shoulders. She said coolly: 'Do you think so? I believe you know where Irana is. I believe you've known for some time. I've an idea that you're playing some game of your own, Mr Callaghan. I wish I knew.'

Callaghan said: 'What game should I be playing? What game *is* there to play?'

'I don't know,' she said. 'I think you're rather attracted to Irana. Most people are. But it doesn't matter as regards *most* people. It might with you.'

Callaghan grinned happily. He drank some whisky. He said: 'Marvellous! So it might matter with me. You think that Irana might actually be interested in Mr Callaghan of Callaghan Investigations?'

'She might,' she said. 'You're quite a forceful character, aren't you, and if she were in a difficult situation – if she were frightened . . .'

'Nonsense,' said Callaghan abruptly. 'I wouldn't touch Irana with a barge-pole. If I'm attracted to anybody in the Faveley family it's you. I like everything about you. I told you that once before.'

She made a little bow. She said: 'So you did, but I didn't believe it.'

Callaghan said: 'You can believe it now. You can believe one or two other things that I'm going to tell you too. It's about time you began to believe me. It might be good for you.'

She put her hands behind her head. She said: 'You're not drinking that whisky you wanted so badly.'

Callaghan picked up the glass, drank some more whisky. He said: 'I really didn't need the whisky that much.'

She said: 'I know. It was the most annoying thing you could think of at the time, wasn't it, Mr Callaghan – to ask for a whisky; to pretend that you were treating this flat as a night club or something like that, but I'm beginning to know you. I didn't take that seriously.'

Callaghan grinned. He said: 'A case of mutual unattraction.' He drew on his cigarette. There was a silence.

She said eventually: 'I'm intrigued in what I am to believe.'

'I'll tell you,' said Callaghan. 'And you might remember what I say. It's important. You remember what your instructions were to me. They were to look after Irana and to keep her out of any trouble if I could. A pretty tough assignment I must say.' His tone was sarcastic. 'Well, strangely enough, Callaghan Investigations often try to carry out their client's instructions – if we like the client.'

She nodded. She said: 'I understand so far.'

Callaghan said: 'This is the story and you've got to hold it up. When Arthur Denys refused to give you a divorce, you decided to go off for a week-end to think things over. During that period you wrote a letter to your sister Irana, in which you told her that it would be a good thing if you decided to leave Denys, that you took the Denys Coronet with you; that it might give you some sort of lever to effect a settlement and get some of your own money back.'

She looked at him with startled eyes. She said: 'How do you know all that?'

Callaghan said: 'You'd be surprised. I've seen that letter – well, some of it – the second page anyway.' He went on:

'Then you decided to take the Coronet. You weren't awfully keen on doing it yourself but you got in touch with a man you'd known casually – a man who's been murdered within the last day or two – called De Sirac. You gave him a key to get into Mayfield Place and you gave him the combination of the safe. He took the Coronet for you and he handed it over to you. Well, you stuck to it, but when you saw the assessors' notice in *The Times* saying that it had been stolen, you got a little worried. You didn't know what to do. You hated the idea of returning it to your husband and making yourself look small. You couldn't very well return it any other how, so you employed me to return it.'

She said: 'But I never had it. I –'

Callaghan said: 'You should worry. *I've* got it. And that's the story. That *has* to be the story.'

She said: 'I see, and why does that *have* to be the story?'

Callaghan grinned. He said: 'Irana stole that Coronet from Mayfield Place. She stole it – or rather she had it stolen by an accomplice. *She didn't steal it because she intended to give it to you.* She had it stolen for her own ends – because she wanted to be revenged on Arthur Denys. She can be sent to prison for that.'

Her hands gripped the arms of her chair. She said: 'Is that true?'

Callaghan drank some more whisky. He nodded. 'That's true enough,' he said. 'But it's not the worst. At the present moment she stands a very good chance of finding herself an accessory to a murder charge. You wouldn't like that, would you?'

She said: 'My God!' She looked at him. Her face was white, her eyes wide.

Callaghan walked to the table, helped himself to a cigarette. He said: 'It isn't so good, is it?'

She said: 'It can't be true. *How* could that be true? I must know everything about this. I'm terribly worried about Irana.'

Callaghan said casually: 'I'm not worrying about Irana.'

She asked: 'Then what are you worrying about?'

He said: 'I'm worrying about you.' He grinned. 'I'm trying to carry out my instructions. Believe it or not, I've got a bet with myself that I'm going to earn that two hundred and fifty pounds.'

She said: 'You're a strange person, aren't you? You're trying to earn that two hundred and fifty pounds but you returned the *thousand* pounds that Irana gave you.'

Callaghan said: 'That's different. I'm rather particular about my customers. You'd be surprised what I'd do for a client – sometimes.'

'I'm beginning to believe that,' she said. Her voice was soft. 'Tell me about this murder,' she went on. 'How does it affect Irana? What could she possibly have to do with such a thing? It isn't possible!'

'No?' said Callaghan. He began to grin. 'It's funny how little sisters know about each other. I suppose you think you know all about Irana. I imagine you consider her to be a charming, beautiful, rather headstrong and impulsive girl. Instead of which she's an extremely tough woman with damn few scruples and her eye on the main chance most of the time. When I've talked to you I don't think you're going to like Irana very much.'

She said miserably: 'I've got to grow up, haven't I? Possibly it would be good for me to hear what I should hear.'

Callaghan said: 'All right.' He held his empty glass towards her. She took it, mixed another drink, brought it back to him. She handed him the drink. She was quite close to him. A breath of the perfume she was wearing came to Callaghan's nostrils.

Callaghan put the glass behind him on the mantelpiece. He turned towards her, took her face between his hands, kissed her on the mouth. She did not move. She stood there, perfectly still, her hands hanging straight down by her sides. Callaghan felt that she was entirely relaxed, almost at ease.

She said: 'I wonder what was responsible for that? Was that part of the Callaghan technique or was it the whisky?'

He smiled at her. He said: 'Does it matter? Just at that moment it was indicated. *I* liked it very much. And it wasn't included in the two hundred and fifty pounds.'

She sighed. She looked at him for a long time. Then she said: 'I wonder why I ever allowed myself to be persuaded into doing *anything* by you. I wish I could answer that question. I wish I knew *why* you are here at this moment. Why I allow you to kiss me. Why I'm not terribly rude to you and tell you to go at once.'

Callaghan grinned. He looked like a mischievous schoolboy. He said: 'I don't know that I can answer those questions – well not all of them. The answer may be that I'm a delightful person – but I don't think so. I think it would be more truthful to say that I'm here because I've got to be here, and the fact that I am here is very good for you. Believe it or not.'

She asked: 'Why, Mr Callaghan?'

He said: 'Go to your armchair and sit down and I'll tell you. But it isn't going to be particularly good hearing.'

'I've gathered that,' she answered. She went back to her armchair.

Callaghan picked up his glass from the mantelpiece. He drank the whisky slowly. Then he put the glass down, stood looking at her.

She lay back in the chair, her hands folded in her lap.

Callaghan said: 'You've got a good nerve. You're frightened about as much as you ever will be and you're making a damned good attempt not to show it. I like that. I hope you keep it up.'

She asked: 'Where is Irana? I'm certain you know where she is.'

He nodded. 'She's all right,' he said. 'At the moment she's staying at a quiet hotel in the country. A place I sent her to. She'll stay there until I think it's right for her to leave. At the moment she's better out of London.'

She smiled. She said: 'I'm glad she's safe, anyhow. I'm afraid she won't like the country hotel very much. Irana doesn't like quiet hotels.'

'No?' said Callaghan. 'Well, she liked the quiet hotel at Laleham – when she stayed there with your husband.'

She sat upright. Her face was tense. She said: 'That's not true. That is *not* true. That woman wasn't Irana. It couldn't be!'

'It could be, and it was,' said Callaghan. 'She dyed her hair blonde specially for the occasion.' His grin was cynical.

'But the letter,' she said. 'The anonymous letter said that the woman was an *ugly* blonde. No one could describe Irana as ugly.'

'Listen to me,' said Callaghan. 'Most of my ideas are based on guesses – but I'm a good guesser, and there are a lot of facts to back the guesses up. Consider the position in the first place. You ask your husband for a divorce and he won't give you one. His reasons don't matter. Well . . . I bet you talked that over with Irana, didn't you? I bet you told her all about it and asked her advice.'

She said slowly: 'Yes . . . I did. She was staying with us at Mayfield. I told her *all* about it. She said she'd speak to Arthur. She said she might be able to persuade him. She –'

Callaghan interrupted. 'All right,' he said. 'So Irana was going to persuade him. And she suggested that it might be a good thing if you went off for a week. So that she could talk to Arthur without his being annoyed with your presence. Right?'

'Yes . . . that is absolutely right,' she said. 'I went away. I thought it would be a good idea.'

Callaghan threw his cigarette stub in the fire behind him. He said: 'It wasn't a bad idea. And it was a damn good one from Irana's point of view. Well . . . whilst you were away you wrote a letter to Irana. You told her that you'd made up your mind to leave Denys. You thought it would be difficult to get any satisfactory financial settlement out of him. He'd had most of your money and you were angry about that. So much so that you lost your point of view for a little while. You suggested in that letter that it might be a good idea for you to take the Coronet with you when you left. But in the meantime Irana had got an idea or so too. She gets some very nice ideas, that young woman. . . .'

'What idea did she get?' she asked. Her eyes, large and intense, were concentrated on his face.

Callaghan grinned. 'She got the big idea that she would marry Denys,' he said. 'She suddenly saw herself as his wife. Denys is a tough proposition, and she needed someone tough to look after her. There were one or two people in London who weren't particularly pleased with her. There might be more than one or two. . . .'

She said: 'How terrible. So she did that. She knew that before she could marry Arthur there must be a divorce. She knew that –'

Callaghan interrupted again. 'She knew that if she could persuade Denys to go off with her to a hotel, that would provide the necessary evidence. Denys trusted her. He certainly did not think that *she* would arrange that you found out about it.'

She said: 'This is quite terrible. Would you give me a cigarette, please?'

He gave her a cigarette. He went on: 'Having spent her fortnight with Denys at Laleham, the next thing is to let you know about it. Then you're going to start your divorce action. That's where De Sirac came in. Irana knew De Sirac pretty well – too well I should think. She arranged with him that he should send you that anonymous note. But her identity was to be concealed. She didn't intend that you should know that *she* had been the woman in the case. So she dyed her hair blonde and De Sirac described the unknown woman as a blonde who was not particularly good-looking. Never in a million years would you, or anyone else, associate Irana with that description.'

Callaghan lit a fresh cigarette. Somewhere in the flat a clock chimed one o'clock.

'Then your lawyers sent the usual private detectives to Laleham,' Callaghan went on. 'They carried out the usual procedure. They took one of your photographs with them and asked the hotel people if you were the woman who had stayed with Denys. Of course the answer was no. So the woman is just another unknown woman co-respondent. Irana knew that in no circumstances could Denys defend the action. He couldn't do that for her sake. So it's going to be an undefended suit and when it's all over she's going to marry him. That's what *she* thought . . . well . . . it didn't come off.'

She asked: 'What do you think happened?'

Callaghan said: 'Denys changed his mind. In the meantime he'd met another girl friend – a woman named Juliette de Longues who, oddly enough, was a blonde and plain in a very attractive sort of way. De Longues had money. And Denys wanted money. She was prepared to pay to be the mistress of Mayfield Place, and the proposition appealed to Denys. So that was that. He told Irana just where she got off. He told her that there was nothing doing.'

Callaghan drew on his cigarette.

'I bet she went off the deep end,' he said. 'Can't you visualize that scene? I can. Irana must have been as mad as hell. She probably threatened Denys with everything she could think of. But what could she do? And he held a trump card. He probably told her that if she tried to make any trouble for him he'd tell you about the Laleham incident and about her little plot. Even Irana couldn't bear the thought of that, so she had to stand for it and like it. Only' – Callaghan smiled cynically – 'she *didn't* like it. So she thought up another little scheme.'

She moved a little in her chair. She said: 'So it's going to be even worse. . . .'

Callaghan saw the tears in her eyes. 'I'm afraid it is,' he said. 'The story certainly doesn't improve as it goes on. But it's got to be faced, and the sooner we get it over the better for everyone – including Irana.'

She said: 'I feel that I'm beginning to hate her. I'm beginning to think of her almost as a stranger – a rather hateful stranger. . . .'

'That's a good idea,' said Callaghan cheerfully. 'It'll probably make things easier for you.'

She nodded miserably. She said: 'Please go on. I'd like to hear the worst.'

'She wanted to get her own back on Denys,' said Callaghan. 'But even more than that she wanted money – a lot of money. I rather fancy she contemplated going off somewhere. So she decided to steal the Coronet. She knew the combination of the safe and somehow or other she'd got a key to Mayfield. So she fixed with her boy friend De Sirac to do the job. She promised to pay him two hundred and fifty pounds down and a like sum when she had the Coronet. But she reckoned without one thing. She reckoned without De Sirac.'

Callaghan inhaled tobacco smoke deep into his lungs and exhaled slowly. He went on:

'De Sirac took the first two hundred and fifty pounds, went down to Mayfield, stole the Coronet and came back with it. He knew he wasn't taking very much of a chance. If anything had gone wrong the story was going to be that he was doing it for *you* on Irana's instructions. After all she had the letter from you saying you contemplated doing it. But when De Sirac had the Coronet safely back in his room he proceeded to double-cross Irana. He told her he didn't intend to part with it unless he got a very large sum of money.

'That puts her in a spot. But not for long. She conceived the quite clever idea of dyeing her hair back to its original colour, coming to me, saying she was Mrs Paula Denys and getting me to retrieve the Coronet. I should think that the thousand she gave me was just about her last.

'Her idea really was good,' said Callaghan, 'because if my astute secretary hadn't noticed that her hair was dyed back to brunette, I should never have checked on her and she stood a chance of getting away with it. Although it wasn't very much of a chance.'

'Why not?' she asked. 'Why wasn't it much of a chance?'

'De Sirac,' said Callaghan. He flicked his cigarette stub into the fireplace. 'I got the Coronet from De Sirac and I was a little rough in the process. Now he was really angry. He was even more angry when, after I'd seen Irana and she'd made her pretty little confession, I went back and told him that she intended to return the Coronet.'

'You mean De Sirac didn't believe that?' she said. 'He knew she was trying to bluff him?'

'Precisely,' said Callaghan. 'Personally, I think that Irana and De Sirac were a pair of first-class double-crossers. If they'd only played straight with each other they might have had a chance. But it just wasn't in their nature.'

'What did De Sirac do?' she asked.

'It was a perfectly simple matter for him,' said Callaghan. 'All he had to do was to get in touch with Denys and ask him if the Coronet was back at Mayfield. Denys discovered that it had gone. Now De Sirac knew that Irana still had the Coronet, and he would probably have turned his attentions to her and tried a little further blackmail, but something else happened. He got another idea. A big idea. Can't you guess?'

She nodded slowly. She said: 'I think so. I think I see what you mean.'

'De Sirac saw the assessors' notice in *The Times*,' said Callaghan. 'He knew that Denys had claimed on the insurance company. He knew that Denys didn't give a damn about the Coronet being stolen. It was over-insured and he wanted the money. I also imagine that Denys had a pretty good idea as to who was really behind stealing the Coronet; but he *wanted* to think it was you, and I've always been careful to let him think that it was you, and that anyway that was going to be my story and that I'd stick to it. In fact,' Callaghan continued, 'he gave me a thousand just to continue thinking along those lines. He doesn't like you very much, does he?'

She looked at him. She seemed faintly amused. She said: 'There's just one little point we seem to have overlooked. It seems that all along you've been helping everyone, including my husband, to prove that *I* took the Coronet. Do you think I might know why? I feel it would be awfully unfair if I were arrested quite wrongfully at the instigation of my own private detective – Mr Callaghan, of Callaghan Investigations!'

Callaghan grinned at her. He said: 'Please take my word that you needn't worry about that. You'll know all the answers to that one probably sooner than you expect. Tomorrow I should think. But I'd like to go on with my story. We haven't come to the crux yet.'

She said: 'So it's going to be even more terrible.'

He nodded. 'Things began to happen now,' he said. 'First of all Irana saw that notice in *The Times*, or, if she didn't, De Sirac let her know all about it. She was afraid of De Sirac. He was a nasty piece of work, and she knew he'd stop at nothing when he got going. Also she was furious at the idea that Denys – who had given her such a raw deal – should be going to collect the insurance money.'

'What did she do?' asked Paula Denys.

'She joined forces again with De Sirac,' said Callaghan. 'I'm pretty certain that she suggested to him that, having regard to the fact that Denys believed – or wanted to believe – that the Coronet had been taken by his wife, it might be a good idea to suggest to him that unless he handed over some of the insurance money – when it was paid – he, De Sirac, might suggest to the insurance company that the theft had been a put-up job between you and Denys. After all, that letter of yours to Irana might support such a theory.'

'This is quite awful,' she said. 'I can hardly believe that Irana could do things like this. It seems incredible.'

'Well, it isn't incredible,' said Callaghan. 'It's just plain, honest fact, and the proof of all that was that Irana intended to return the Coronet to someone who would be prepared to hold up the story that it had been originally stolen at your instigation. She returned it to me,' he went on. 'I've got it. And after that, I think I ought to have a whisky and soda. I haven't talked so much for years!'

She got up; poured him a fresh drink. Callaghan watched her.

He said: 'Really I didn't want the drink so much as to see you move. You're a very graceful person, aren't you?'

She brought him the whisky and soda. She said: 'You're the most amazing person, Mr Callaghan. You come to my flat in the early hours of the morning. You tell me the most extraordinary stories which, unfortunately, I believe to be true. And then you tell me that you like to see me move.'

Callaghan said: 'Why not? Why shouldn't a private detective have a sense of beauty?'

She said: 'A sense of beauty won't help you very much in this case, will it? So Irana brought back the Coronet to you? Why did she do that?'

Callaghan said: 'There's the snag. I'm not quite certain as to whether Irana really intended to return that Coronet. I'm not quite certain that she didn't think that she might even once again try to double-cross De Sirac. But she *had* to return it.'

She asked: 'Why?'

Callaghan said: 'She saw De Sirac on the night he was murdered. So she decided to return the Coronet to me the next day.'

She said hoarsely: 'You mean –'

Callaghan said: 'I mean anything you like. If you're asking me whether Irana killed De Sirac, I say it's quite possible. In point of fact she had every motive for doing so. There was something else too,' said Callaghan – 'something that's not at all nice.'

She looked at him. She said: 'I've heard so much that's terrible tonight, I don't think there is anything else that I couldn't hear.'

'I'm going to tell you something,' said Callaghan. 'My assistant – Windemere Nikolls – discovered the De Sirac murder quite a time before we let the police know. I had my own reasons for wanting that time lag. I went round and I saw the body. I was there in the small hours of the morning. De Sirac hadn't been dead for very long. Stuck under the blotter where the police would have found it when they searched, was the second page of your letter to Irana – the original letter you wrote saying that you contemplated taking the Coronet.'

She said: 'My God! Are you suggesting that she left that there, and if she did that –'

Callaghan said: 'I'm suggesting just that. Somebody left that letter there and they left only the second page. Do you know why?'

She said: 'No. Tell me why.'

'The first page,' said Callaghan, 'would bear the name of the person to whom the letter was addressed. The second page merely says "my dear" in the text. Don't you see you're the person who was supposed to have employed De Sirac to steal the Denys Coronet. The suggestion being that you knew him. That page of letter might have been written by you to him. The words "my dear" would simply indicate that possibly you were another of his lady friends.'

She looked at him, not moving. She seemed unable to speak. She said: 'And you think Irana did that? She must be the most terrible woman in the world.'

Callaghan said: 'She may not have done it. If she didn't, there's only one way she's going to save herself.'

She said: 'What is it?'

Callaghan said: 'I don't think I want to discuss that with you at the moment. We've talked enough for tonight. I think you've got a pretty good idea of the position.'

She said: 'Yes, I think I have. And what about my own position? It doesn't seem awfully secure, does it – after what you've said?'

Callaghan grinned at her. He said: 'I told you I was looking after your interests. If you don't think you're safe, maybe you'd like to employ somebody else.'

The expression on his face brought a smile to her lips. She said: 'Up to the moment I cannot say I'm quite dissatisfied. Even if I don't like you very much, you certainly seem to know your business, Mr Callaghan.'

Callaghan said: 'Thank you very much. To be serious for a moment – I think possibly tomorrow I shall ask you to come down to my office. There might be some other people there. If I do ask you to come, leave the talking to me; agree with what I say. Our story is this: You originally wrote that letter to Irana. You were angry with your husband. You intended to take the Coronet when you left Mayfield Place. You were put on to De Sirac who agreed to do the job for you. You supplied him with the combination of the safe which you knew, and a key to Mayfield Place. De Sirac took the Coronet, but when he had it he wouldn't give it to you. He tried to blackmail you, so you came to me. I got the Coronet back. I've had it ever since. You understand that?'

She said: 'Yes, I understand.' She looked at him. Her expression was quizzical. She said: 'I must trust you rather a lot to agree to all this, mustn't I? I don't know what's in your mind, but somehow inside me I've got an idea that you're being perfectly straight with me; that you're doing the best you can for me. Perhaps the idea's wrong, but I hope it isn't. I'm trusting you because I've got to trust you. I've got to lean on somebody.'

Callaghan said: 'That's all right. If you've got to lean on somebody you'd better lean on me. There's no reason why you shouldn't start now, Mrs Denys.' He smiled at her.

She said: 'Even at a dramatic time like this your sense of humour is rather infectious. What exactly did you mean by that, Mr Callaghan?'

He said: 'I would much rather demonstrate than explain. Let me show you. . . .'

CHAPTER ELEVEN
ANYTHING BUT THE TRUTH

DETECTIVE-Inspector Marrick, who had been too busy to eat lunch, but who was not worrying too much about the fact, walked slowly down the corridor towards Lamming's room. Marrick was in a thoughtful mood; at the same time there was a look of near-complacency on his face.

He pushed open the door of his colleague's room, went inside. Lamming was sitting at his desk, smoking a cigarette. Marrick thought he looked bored.

Lamming said: 'Well . . . and how is it with you?'

Marrick put his hat down on a table. He said: 'I'm beginning to be really rather interested in this De Sirac thing. Nothing adds up. And when nothing adds up something is likely to emerge.'

Lamming shrugged his shoulders. 'I'm glad you feel so good about it,' he said. 'I wish I felt the same way – about the Coronet.'

'So it's like that!' said Marrick. He sat down in the chair opposite Lamming's desk. He went on: 'So you don't feel you're doing so well?'

Lamming said: 'I'm not doing *anything*. After our talk with The Jigger what can I do? All I do is hang around and twiddle my thumbs until something happens.'

The other nodded. He said: 'Well, believe it or not, I think something has happened.' He lit a cigarette. 'I've been digging into this De Sirac's past – a nasty sort of bloke. But one interesting fact emerges. He used to get around a great deal with a certain Irana Faveley. She used to go and see him a lot. I think they were pretty thick.'

Lamming nodded. He said: 'So what?'

'Don't be impatient.' Marrick flicked the ash off his cigarette. 'Irana Faveley is the sister of Mrs Paula Denys. How do you like that one?'

Lamming whistled. He said: 'Now that *is* interesting. What do we do about that?'

Marrick said: 'I'm not doing anything at the moment. But it's funny, isn't it?'

'Very funny,' Lamming replied. 'I –' He stopped speaking as the telephone jangled. He took off the receiver; said who he was. He listened.

First his face showed surprise; then a certain joy. Still listening carefully, he raised his eyebrows at Marrick. Eventually he hung up the receiver. He said:

'I think this is my lucky day.'

Marrick said: 'What's the story?'

Lamming said: 'Not at the moment. Just now you push off. You smoke a couple of cigarettes and let me get at a typewriter. When I've finished, I've rather got an idea that even The Jigger is going to tell us to stop hanging around and get a move on. Incidentally' – he grinned joyfully – 'I think we might even have Callaghan where we want him.'

'That,' said Marrick, 'would please me a great deal. I've been hearing a lot about Mr Callaghan. He's a clever one – that one. He's sailed so near the wind on half a dozen occasions that I'm surprised he hasn't gone overboard.'

Lamming said: 'Don't worry. This is the time when I think he goes overboard. Just leave me in peace, will you?'

Marrick said: 'All right. But I'm curious. I'll be back in half an hour.'

'That'll be long enough,' said Lamming.

He went over to the typewriter table and sat down at the machine. He began to type:

19th September, 1943.
Criminal Investigation Department,
New Scotland Yard.

INTER-OFFICE MEMO.
From: Detective-Inspector H. G. Lamming.
To: Chief Detective-Inspector G. H. Gringall.

Having regard to our last conversation on the Denys Coronet matter, I feel I should call your immediate attention to these facts which have been reported to me at three o'clock this afternoon by Mr Richard Gervase, General Manager of the Globe and Consolidated Insurance Co.

(1) It appears that at ten-thirty this morning Windemere Nikolls, who appears to be Chief Assistant to Mr Callaghan of Callaghan Investigations, telephoned Mr Gervase and suggested that Mr Callaghan might like to interview him. He also asked if the thousand pound reward advertised by the Assessors in the original Times *advertisement was still payable in respect of any new or fresh information as to the whereabouts of the Denys Coronet.*

Mr Gervase, who, as you know, has already been in touch with this Department with reference to the Coronet, considered it advantageous to receive any further information that might be forthcoming, and therefore, whilst not exactly promising anything, he allowed himself to suggest that in certain circumstances the Insurance Company might still be prepared to make an ex gratia *payment in respect of any definite information which would enable the Coronet to be recovered.*

(2) Mr Nikolls then suggested that Mr Callaghan himself would call and see Mr Gervase, and at 12.30 today Callaghan went down to the Insurance Co.'s office in Gracechurch Street and saw Mr Gervase.

(3) Callaghan was careful to suggest to Mr Gervase that any conversation between them must be absolutely confidential and, whilst not promising this, Mr Gervase indicated that there could be no possible reason for his making public any discussion, as naturally the Insurance Co. were only interested in:

(a) *the return of the Coronet to its rightful owner,*

or

(b) *the payment of the claim.*

Callaghan then asked why the claim had not already been paid, to which Mr Gervase replied that in the first place the Company did not consider that sufficient time had elapsed for the police to have a chance to investigate thoroughly and, secondly, that an anonymous letter had been sent to the Company suggesting that they would be very foolish to pay the claim until further investigation had been made. (We of course know that this anonymous letter was written on special paper supplied to Callaghan Investigations and on a typewriter used in that organization. This information, however, has not, as you know, been made known to Mr Gervase.)

(4) Callaghan then suggested that 'all things being equal' – (Mr Gervase says this was the actual expression used by Callaghan, and it obviously suggested to him that Callaghan meant if the thousand pounds reward was still payable) – he (Callaghan) might be in a position within a short time to arrange that the Coronet should be handed over to the Insurance Company for return to its rightful owner.

(5) Mr Gervase was of course curious as to how Callaghan was in a position to make such a statement, to which Callaghan replied that he was making no definite promise but, having regard to certain information which had come into his possession he thought that there was a very good chance, within a matter of days, of the Coronet being available for return.

Mr Gervase then suggested that if this were so, he had no doubt his Company would behave in the proper manner.

This seemed to satisfy Mr Callaghan, who took his leave after saying that he hoped to communicate with Mr Gervase within a few days.

As soon as possible Mr Gervase communicated this information to me.

I shall be glad, having regard to the above, of your further advice and/or instructions.

H. G. Lamming,
Detective-Inspector.

Having completed this work Lamming lit a cigarette and smoked peacefully for a few minutes whilst he re-read the copy he had just typed.

Life, he thought, was not so bad after all.

At a quarter to four, in response to a telephone message from Chief Detective-Inspector Gringall, Marrick and Lamming went up to his office.

They found The Jigger smoking his short briar pipe, busily engaged in drawing a bunch of grapes on his blotter.

He said: 'Sit down and let's talk this thing over. I've read your report, Lamming, and I think it's very interesting. What are your ideas about it?'

Lamming said: 'I haven't any ideas really, Mr Gringall, except that everything seems to point in the same direction. Incidentally, Marrick here has a little information which, although it may not matter a great deal, might constitute a sort of tie-up between the Coronet case and the murder of De Sirac.'

Gringall raised his eyebrows. He said: 'Yes? What is it, Marrick?'

Marrick said: 'I told Lamming earlier this afternoon I had traced a connection with De Sirac and a Miss Irana Faveley. Miss Faveley is Mrs Paula Denys' sister.'

Gringall drew on his pipe. He said: 'Fancy that now! That does look as if it might be something, doesn't it? Except that it doesn't exactly *prove* anything – does it? What do you want to do, Lamming?'

Lamming shrugged his shoulders. He said: 'Well, sir, with all respect to you, I think it's about time we got after this Callaghan. I think that he's being a little bit *too* clever. You've read my report. You saw what the general manager of the Globe and Consolidated says. It's my considered opinion that Callaghan knows where that Coronet is. That being so, he's been withholding information – well, there are three or four things we could get him on. You know that as well as I do.'

Gringall said: 'You mean it might be a good thing to put the screw on Callaghan; that he might be inclined to talk, having regard to the fact that we know he's gone to the insurance company and suggested that they give him some money?'

Lamming said: 'That's what I mean, sir.'

Gringall examined the bowl of his pipe. He tapped down the tobacco with his thumb, re-lit it. He said:

'Listen, you're handling this case, Lamming, and I don't want to stop you doing anything you want to do. But it looks to me as if all this business is a little too obvious. Do you see what I mean?' He looked at the two officers.

Marrick shook his head. 'Candidly, sir,' he said, 'I don't. I don't quite know what you mean by too obvious. But it looks to me as if from *our* point of view it's obvious enough. As I see it Callaghan knows where the Coronet is, and as I see it there's some tie-up between the Coronet robbery and De Sirac. Callaghan had an appointment with De Sirac on the day that he was murdered. Irana Faveley is sister to the wife of the owner of the Coronet and *she* was friendly with De Sirac. We know Callaghan sent that anonymous letter to the Globe and Consolidated suggesting that they shouldn't pay the claim. Well, why does he do that? He does it because he doesn't want the claim paid because if it's paid he's not going to get his thousand pounds reward. Possibly he didn't know where the Coronet was at that time, but he had an idea that he might know. He wanted to stall for time.'

Gringall nodded. 'I follow,' he said. 'Go on.'

'The next move in the game is,' Marrick continued, 'that Callaghan actually finds out where the Coronet is, or at least he gets a pretty good idea, but he's not quite certain as to what the situation is with regard to the insurance company. Now he must have known that the company would have come to us. He's uncertain as to whether they're still going to pay him the reward, and there's only one thing he can do. He's got to try and find out, so he goes down and sees Gervase, who handles the interview very tactfully.'

Gringall nodded. 'That's pretty good reasoning, Marrick,' he said. 'And I suppose the idea is now that Lamming sees Callaghan and tells him that he either talks or there might be a charge of "withholding information" on the Coronet thing?'

Marrick said: 'We might even bluff a little, sir, and suggest there might be a "withholding information" charge on the De Sirac murder. I wouldn't be surprised if Mr Callaghan didn't know a little bit more about that than he's let on.'

Gringall said: 'Neither would I.' He got up, walked to the window. He stood looking out, his hands clasped behind his back. After a minute he turned, came back to the desk, sat on the edge of it. He said:

'There's just one thing we're forgetting. We're forgetting that Callaghan's not such a fool as that.' He took his pipe out of his mouth, looked at it for a moment, put it back again. He said: 'Once on a time – in that Riverton murder thing – you remember that, Lamming, some years ago – I thought I had Callaghan sewed up. I thought I had him in the bag, but I hadn't. He'd left a little hole to wriggle out of.' He held up his hand as Lamming began to speak. He said: 'You listen to me. I'm perfectly certain that Callaghan knew that anonymous letter would be traced back to his office. I'm perfectly certain that he intended it should be, and I'm perfectly certain of something else too.'

Lamming said: 'You mean, sir, that this interview with the general manager of the insurance company is also phoney.'

Gringall nodded. 'That's what I mean. I'm perfectly certain that Callaghan knew that Gervase was going to get through to you and tell you all about it as soon as he could. Callaghan *wanted* you to know.'

Lamming said: 'All right, sir, he wanted us to know. Well, what the devil's he playing at?'

Gringall said: 'Don't ask me, because I don't know. But he's play-ing at something. Callaghan's a man who prepares the ground very well. When he creates a situation he creates a good one. And most of the things he does are usually intended to create situations at some time or other. That's his technique. Callaghan seldom wastes a lot of time making enquiries, doing all the routine jobs that we have to do. He does all the things that we can't do. He threatens people.' Gringall grinned. 'Just imagine what would happen to us if we did that. He tells them half truth and half lies. He talks to them. He creates situ-ations into which they walk and from which they find difficulty in escaping without giving *something* away.'

Gringall sat down in his chair, picked up his pencil and began to draw a banana. He said: 'I still believe he's preparing the ground for something, but he's got to move pretty quickly, hasn't he? He's got to do something fairly soon. Don't you agree, Lamming?'

Lamming asked: 'Why, sir?'

Gringall said: 'He's practically suggested that he knows where the Coronet is. If my idea is right he was certain when he told Gervase, that Gervase would come through and tell us. If Callaghan doesn't do something within a matter of a day or two he knows we've got to move, and I don't think he'd like that. You know, believe it or not, that gentleman has a very great respect for the police.'

Marrick said gloomily: 'I'm glad to hear it.'

The telephone bell on Gringall's desk jangled. Gringall took off the receiver. He said: 'Hello!' Then he looked at Marrick and Lamming. He grinned. He said into the telephone: 'Good afternoon, Slim. I wondered when you were going to ring up!'

Effie Thompson came into Callaghan's office. She said: 'Two police officers – Mr Gringall and Mr Lamming – are here, Mr Callaghan.'

Callaghan said cheerfully: 'Show them in, Effie.' He got up, walked towards the door. He was freshly shaved, wearing a neat blue suit, a blue silk shirt, a black tie with a small pearl in it.

Gringall and Lamming came in. Callaghan said: 'I'm very glad to see you, gentlemen. In fact, I don't think I've ever been more glad to see police officers.' He smiled at them. His expression was frank and sincere.

Gringall said: 'Well . . . I'm glad to hear that, Slim. I must say I've been a bit worried about you – and so has Lamming.'

'Sit down,' said Callaghan, 'and smoke.' He produced cigarettes. He went on: 'I'm expecting Mrs Denys here any minute now. When I fixed this appointment with you I asked her to come because I wanted her to hear everything I've got to say. It concerns her and it might save her a lot of bother some other time.'

Lamming settled back in his chair. He took a long look at Callaghan. He thought: You look just as clever as they say you are. I wonder what you're going to try and pull on us now. How you're going to try and get out of that anonymous letter and the interview with Gervase. It's going to be *very* interesting.

He said: 'I can do with all the help I can get, Mr Callaghan. This thing hasn't been easy. And there's a new point arisen, too, which Mr Gringall said I might discuss with you if I wanted to. My colleague Marrick, who's working on the De Sirac murder, thinks there may be some sort of tie-up between that and this Coronet job.'

Callaghan shrugged his shoulders. 'That might be so,' he said, 'but at the moment I'm only concerned with the Coronet.'

Lamming said casually: 'You know something about that?'

Callaghan grinned. 'I know a lot about it,' he said. 'I've got it. It's in the safe over there.'

Lamming said nothing. He looked very surprised.

Callaghan lit a cigarette. He went on: 'You know I've been in rather a spot since this case started. Life can be very difficult for a private detective. There are times when he doesn't quite know what to do. He's got to think of his client's interests and he's also got to be careful of getting entangled with the law. You can understand that?' He looked at Gringall and then at Lamming. He was smiling pleasantly.

Gringall said: 'For a private detective who doesn't want to get entangled with the law you're looking very happy, Slim. Maybe that's because you've got a nice happy conscience?' He grinned at Callaghan.

'That's probably the reason,' said Callaghan. 'Anyhow, I haven't got anything on my conscience in this affair.'

Gringall sighed. He said: 'That must be a nice change for you.'

There was a knock at the door. Effie Thompson came in. She said: 'Mrs Denys is here, Mr Callaghan.'

Callaghan said: 'Ask her to come in.'

Paula Denys came into the office. She was wearing a black Persian lamb coat over a grey coat and skirt. Gringall looked at her quickly. He was thinking that it was a long time since he'd seen such a beautiful woman.

Callaghan said: 'Mrs Denys, this is Chief Detective-Inspector Gringall – an old friend of mine, even if he isn't always aware of the fact – and Detective-Inspector Lamming, who is the officer in charge of the Denys Coronet business. Gentlemen, this is my client, Mrs Paula Denys.' He pulled forward an armchair for her. He went on:

'Sit down, Mrs Denys. Smoke a cigarette and relax. I wanted you to come here because I wanted you to hear what I've got to say to these officers.'

Lamming said amiably: 'I expect this business has been a worry to you, Mrs Denys.'

She said: 'Much too much of a worry. I shall be very glad when it's all over.'

Callaghan said cheerfully: 'It's all over now I think.' He went on: 'I think I'd better start at the beginning; give you the whole story as I know it. If you want to ask any questions you can ask them.'

Gringall said: 'I think that'd be a good idea.'

Paula Denys looked at Callaghan. He sat in the big chair behind his desk, his hands lying on the desk in front of him. He was poised, smiling, immaculate. She began to feel a certain admiration for Callaghan. She thought: I wonder what you're going to do about all this mess. Whether you are clever enough to deal with it. She felt a strange confidence that he *would* deal with it. She felt her heart beating a little faster.

Lamming sat bolt upright in his chair. His mind was working easily and well. He thought: You're going to slip up somewhere, Callaghan, and when you do I'll have you. You've *got* to slip up. You'll never get out of that Gervase business, and when you admit that, I've got you where I want you.

Gringall wished he was smoking his pipe. He looked at Callaghan casually. He thought: It's going to be interesting to see how you play this. But you've got *something* up your sleeve. We'll see . . .

Callaghan said: 'All right. Well, I first came in contact with Mrs Denys because she asked me to investigate the fact that her husband was supposed to have stayed at a hotel at Laleham with a woman. She was considering a divorce, you see.' He stubbed out his cigarette end; took a fresh one from the box on the desk, lit it. He took a lot of time.

Gringall said easily: 'I thought you didn't handle divorce cases, Slim?'

Callaghan said: 'We don't. In fact we didn't *handle* this one. Mrs Denys had already employed some other firm of private detectives to do that. But she wanted some outside advice. The actual investigation down at the hotel was made by the other people.'

Lamming said: 'I see . . .' He drew on his cigarette. He went on: 'It's a small point, and I don't know that it's got anything to do with this business – except possibly from one small angle – but were they able to establish the identity of the woman who stayed down there with Mr Denys – the co-respondent?'

Callaghan shook his head. 'No,' he said. 'They weren't very lucky about that. Perhaps they weren't a very good firm of detectives.' He smiled at Paula Denys.

Gringall said: 'So the co-respondent was the usual "unknown woman." I suppose you advised Mrs Denys that the Court aren't usually very pleased with that sort of petition. They like to know who the co-respondent is – don't they?'

Callaghan said: 'That's right. I told Mrs Denys that.'

Lamming said: 'So nobody knows who that woman was?'

'Oh yes,' said Callaghan, '*I* know. I was interested so I made it my business to find out. It was a woman called Juliette de Longues. When this trouble started about the Coronet she got a little bit frightened of things. She thought she might be mixed up in an unpleasant case. I told her that the best thing she could do would be to admit that she was the woman who stayed at the hotel with Denys; that anyway he was certain not to defend the divorce petition that his wife was bringing against him, so she wouldn't have to appear in court.'

Gringall nodded. 'That was wise of you,' he said. 'So the woman was Miss de Longues, who didn't mind being cited so long as she hadn't to appear in a defended action.'

'Right,' said Callaghan. 'I was very glad to fix all that for Mrs Denys. Miss de Longues was good enough to write me a letter stating the facts of the case. I've sent the letter to Mrs Denys' lawyers. And that's that.'

He blew a smoke ring carefully, watched it as it rose in the air.

He said: 'Although what that's got to do with the Coronet business I don't know.' He looked at Lamming.

Lamming said quickly: 'But it might have to do with something else. It might –'

Callaghan interrupted. 'Just a minute,' he said with a grin. 'What *else* are we talking about? I thought you came here to listen to me?'

Gringall said: 'Mr Callaghan's quite right, Lamming. Let's keep to the Coronet affair.'

Callaghan said: 'Well . . . that was that. But unfortunately some more trouble started. A situation arose which wasn't very good – in fact it was a very nasty situation for Mrs Denys. You see,' he went on casually, '*she* was responsible for the Coronet disappearing originally.'

Lamming said: 'What!' He looked from Callaghan to Gringall and back again. He presented a picture of complete and utter amazement.

Callaghan shrugged his shoulders. 'Gentlemen,' he said suavely, 'it is not for me to question what my clients do or do not do. It is my business, to the best of my poor ability, and of course *within* the laws of the country, to look after their interests. It is not for me – or for you – to sit in judgment on Mrs Denys. But the fact of the matter is that, when considering this divorce, Mrs Denys was concerned with the possibilities of a future financial settlement. I regret to tell you that her husband had played ducks and drakes with her money. She was terribly upset at the time and she wished to take some step – no matter how drastic – to safeguard her future interests.'

Gringall nodded. 'I understand,' he said. 'So Mrs Denys took the Coronet when she left her husband.'

'Not quite like that,' said Callaghan. 'It seems that Mrs Denys had made the acquaintance of a young man named De Sirac – you know the name, gentlemen. She met him casually at a dance club. I believe she was introduced to him by her sister, Miss Faveley. Mrs Denys decided to go away for a few days, and before she went she arranged with De Sirac that he should go to Mayfield Place and take the Coronet, after which he would hand it over to her. She gave him a key to get into the house and she gave him the combination of the safe. De Sirac carried out this part of the business, for which Mrs Denys gave him a small sum of money. He got the Coronet and handed it over to her.'

Callaghan stopped talking. He stubbed out his cigarette, helped himself to another, lit it. He said: 'I'll have to cut these cigarettes down. I'm getting a fearful cough.' He smiled. His smile embraced everyone in the office.

Gringall said: 'So far so good. And then I think you said some trouble started . . .'

'Naturally,' said Callaghan. 'With a man like De Sirac, what could you expect? De Sirac was nothing more or less than a cheap blackmailer. You can imagine what his next move was. Having handed over the Coronet to Mrs Denys, he then proceeded to inform her that unless she paid him a further sum of money he would tell her husband the whole story.'

Callaghan paused and blew another smoke ring. 'I leave it to you, gentlemen,' he said, 'to imagine the state of mind which this threat brought to Mrs Denys. She was very worried anyhow. She was furious with her husband. She had just instructed her lawyers to bring divorce proceedings against him, and here was De Sirac threatening to do something which would have given her husband the very lever he wanted. So she came to me and I gave her some very good advice.'

Gringall smiled. There was a world of experience in that smile. He said quietly: 'I bet the advice was good advice, Slim.'

Callaghan nodded. 'It was,' he said. 'I told her that she need not worry about De Sirac; that I would deal with him and that if I had any trouble I'd go to the police. But I told her first of all that the Coronet *must* be returned. I said that whatever happened she must return the Coronet at once, and she agreed. But she couldn't do it.'

Lamming said: 'Why not? Why couldn't she do it?'

Callaghan's face was serious. He said evenly: 'She couldn't do it because she'd mislaid the damned thing. You see, she was in process of moving from a hotel to her flat in Palmeira Court. She had all sorts of luggage all over the place. When De Sirac gave her the Coronet she put it away in one of her trunks.' He smiled benevolently. 'The sort of thing that could happen to any harassed woman,' he said. 'But anyhow, it didn't matter. Two days ago she remembered where she'd put it, and telephoned me. Then all was well . . .'

Lamming said: 'It seems an amazing thing that you didn't inform someone about this. After all –'

Callaghan raised his eyebrows. 'Inform someone!' he said. His voice held a note of extreme surprise. 'Why should I inform anyone? What legal onus was there either on Mrs Denys or myself to inform anyone?'

Lamming's jaw dropped. He said: 'But . . . But . . .'

Gringall interrupted. 'Just a moment, Lamming,' he said. 'I think that possibly Mr Callaghan is right. I think he is going to say that at the time the Coronet was removed Mrs Denys was the wife of Arthur Denys and domiciled with her husband –'

'That's as may be,' said Lamming, 'but –'

Gringall went on: 'I think Mr Callaghan is going to say that the law of our country says it is not illegal for a wife to remove from his custody the property of her husband while she is domiciled with him. In any event, he couldn't bring a charge against her.'

He smiled, almost paternally, at Lamming.

Callaghan said: 'That's the point. I didn't *have* to inform anybody, and I didn't *want* to inform anybody. All I wanted was for Mrs Denys to find that Coronet as soon as she could so that it could be returned. You see?'

'Not quite,' said Lamming. 'I understand the position up to that, but what about the insurance claim! When Mr Denys put in that claim on the Globe and Consolidated surely you must have realized that it was necessary for *them* to know where the Coronet was. They might have *paid* the claim.'

Callaghan nodded. 'I know,' he said. 'That was troubling me. I was in a devil of a position. Either I had to disclose business which I regarded as confidential between my client and myself, or I might have to stand by and see the company pay that claim. I had to do something about that. I definitely did . . .'

The shadow of a grin began to appear about the mouth of Chief Detective-Inspector Gringall. He said: 'And eventually you thought of something – eh?'

'Yes,' said Callaghan. 'I wrote an anonymous letter to the Globe and Consolidated. I advised them not to pay the claim. I knew they'd stall payment after getting that letter. Well . . . they did, didn't they? They didn't pay, and they went to Scotland Yard.'

Callaghan looked at the two police officers. His smile was almost infectious.

Paula Denys thought: You're rather a wonderful man, Mr Callaghan. You really are. You are quite unscrupulous, the most expert liar, extremely clever and rather fascinating. I think I like you a great deal.

Gringall looked at Lamming. Lamming sighed heavily. He said nothing at all.

Callaghan said: 'Well . . . everything was all right so far as it went. The insurance company were holding up the claim. The matter had been put into the hands of Scotland Yard.' Callaghan grinned. 'I began to feel almost happy,' he went on. 'And then we had some luck. Mrs Denys found the Coronet and telephoned me. But I was still in a bad spot. I couldn't very well run down and tell the insurance company the story. That would have created a most difficult situation.'

Gringall said amiably: 'So you thought up something else?'

'Yes,' said Callaghan. 'I thought up something else. I got my assistant, Windemere Nikolls, to telephone the insurance company. Then I went down and saw them. Of course I knew that there wasn't any chance of getting a reward out of the company, but I had to put on an act to that effect. I saw Gervase, the general manager. I told him that I had an idea I'd be able to get my hands on the Coronet within a day or so. Then I felt quite happy.'

'Did you?' asked Lamming. 'Why?'

Callaghan smiled at him benignly. 'Well,' he said. 'I knew that directly I'd left the office Gervase would telephone through to you at Scotland Yard and tell you the whole bag of tricks. Then *you'd* be happy. You'd know that if I'd said I was going to return the Coronet I'd return it. After all' – Callaghan's face took on a saintlike expression – 'after all this organization has a reputation to live up to.'

Gringall began to cough. He seemed to have difficulty in breathing. Lamming looked at the floor. He was thinking that he would give a year's pay to cut Mr Callaghan's throat.

There was silence. Eventually Paula Denys' soft voice said: 'I'm terribly grateful to Mr Callaghan. He has been very kind. And I was so worried in case he got into any sort of trouble over this.'

Gringall said dryly: 'I shouldn't worry about that, Mrs Denys. I think Mr Callaghan can take very good care of himself.'

Callaghan stubbed out his cigarette. He said: 'There was one thing that worried me a great deal, gentlemen. It's worried me more than anything else.'

'I expect you mean De Sirac,' said Lamming. 'After all, the fact that our law allows a wife to have use and custody of her husband's goods doesn't allow a third party to commit the offence of breaking and entering. It doesn't allow a third party to remove goods, the property of a husband –'

Callaghan sighed heavily. He said: 'I'm sorry to contradict, but De Sirac always acted as Mrs Denys' agent. He did what he did on her instructions. And he didn't break and enter. He was supplied by her with a key and the safe combination. But that wasn't the point I was trying to make. Of course, I never did like De Sirac. He was a nasty piece of work, and I should have dealt adequately with him if someone hadn't killed him first. Not that he didn't deserve being killed. It's a good end for a blackmailer.'

He lit a fresh cigarette slowly, inhaled deeply. 'The point is, Lamming,' he said easily, 'that in no circumstances can Mrs Denys be blamed. In no circumstances at all. It's no good talking to me about the claim being put in on the insurance company, or the fact that Scotland Yard have wasted time and trouble over this thing. First of all the claim shouldn't have been put in, and even if it had been it *ought* to have been withdrawn.'

'Why?' asked Lamming. 'Mr Arthur Denys was entitled to put in the claim. His Coronet had been removed. He was entitled to think that it was stolen. Why should *he* have withdrawn the claim?'

Callaghan shrugged his shoulders.

'It's not for me to make accusations,' he said. 'But I don't think that Mr Denys really thought the Coronet had been stolen all along. He might have thought so in the first place. But I'm certain that you will agree with me that if he had any idea that it was in his wife's possession it was – to say the least of it – a very misguided thing for him to allow the insurance company even to *consider* paying the claim; and if he became certain that the Coronet was in his wife's possession he should immediately have informed the company of that fact.'

Lamming shifted in his chair. He said: 'I don't quite understand this, and I'd like to. Are you suggesting that Mr Denys knew – at any time – before or after the claim was put in, that his wife had the Coronet? Are you really suggesting that?'

Callaghan grinned at Lamming. 'It's no use getting annoyed with me, Lamming,' he said. 'That isn't going to help. And I'm not *suggesting* anything. I'm *telling* you that Denys knew his wife had the Coronet.'

'How do you know that?' Lamming asked shortly. 'How do you know he knew?'

'Because *I* told him,' said Callaghan. 'And it might interest you to know he gave me a thousand pounds to keep my mouth shut!'

Detective-Inspector Lamming sat back in the corner of the taxi-cab. He was breathing heavily. In the other corner, Chief Detective-Inspector Gringall smoked his pipe.

He said: 'I told you Callaghan had something on the ice. It was sticking out a foot that he meant that anonymous letter to be traced back to his office. That was his get-out if anything went wrong. And he knew that Gervase would come through and tell us about the other business. Callaghan's no fool. He's got a hell of a good story and he's going to stick to it.'

Lamming said: 'So you don't really believe it, sir?'

'No,' said Gringall. 'Not all of it. Callaghan's got enough truth in it to carry the lies. He's the most expert liar I know. He's very good indeed.' He drew on his pipe with pleasure.

Lamming said hotly: 'Well . . . are you going to let him get away with it? After all –'

Gringall interrupted. 'You try and pick a hole in his story. You'll find you can't do it. It's watertight. You can't do a damned thing about it. Facts matter. And the fact that matters most is that, at the present moment, you've got that damned Coronet under your arm and Callaghan has a perfectly good receipt for it, signed by you. You can't do a thing. And there's no reason why you should want to.'

'I'm sorry, sir, but I don't agree,' said Lamming.

Gringall grinned. 'You don't agree because you don't particularly like Callaghan,' he said. 'But you will – one of these fine days. He sort of grows on you. Incidentally, he's done us rather a good turn.'

'Has he?' demanded Lamming. 'Did I miss something? I didn't notice any good turn!'

Gringall said: 'A good police officer doesn't allow his feelings to get the better of his judgment. Possibly you were so keen on picking a hole in that nice story of Callaghan's that you didn't notice the implication – the thing that really mattered. It wasn't what he said; it was what he didn't say . . .'

Lamming fumbled for his cigarette case. 'I don't get it, sir,' he said.

Gringall said slowly: 'You will. Callaghan told us that Arthur Denys knew that his wife had the Coronet. Callaghan told us that he told Denys. I believe him. Well . . . there was someone else who knew that Mrs Denys had the Coronet. Callaghan told us who. And there was someone else who must have known that Denys had claimed from the insurance company. And that somebody was a blackmailer. Callaghan told us *that*. D'you see what I mean, Lamming?'

'My God!' said Lamming. 'De Sirac! De Sirac knew that Mrs Denys had the Coronet. Of course he knew. And if Denys claimed on the insurance company *knowing* his wife had it, De Sirac had him where he wanted him. De Sirac would go out for Denys like hell. He'd blackmail him till the cows came home. And then –'

'Precisely,' said Gringall. 'And then Denys killed him. That was what Callaghan was telling us, wasn't it? Just that.'

Lamming said: 'By jove, he's a clever basket. I don't like the goddamned man, but he's got brains. I wonder if he can prove that too. I wonder if he can.'

As the cab turned into New Scotland Yard, Gringall said: 'There isn't any need to worry. If I know anything of Mister Callaghan he's not going to leave things where they are. We'll be hearing from him again.'

CHAPTER TWELVE
BLUFF FOR THREE

CALLAGHAN turned the car into the driveway that led to the Chequers Inn, looked at his wrist-watch, saw that it was nearly ten o'clock. The September night was chilly and the cold moonlight, flooding the driveway, was almost as bright as daylight. Callaghan liked the scene. He thought it attractive; that he would like to spend a month at the Chequers, with all telephones disconnected. The idea of a month's quiet drinking in rural surroundings appealed to him. He thought maybe he was tired. He parked the car in the deserted garage behind the inn, went in by the side entrance. He said to the woman in the reception desk: 'My name's Callaghan. I've an appointment with Miss Faveley.'

She said: 'Oh yes, Mr Callaghan. Number ten on the first floor is her sitting-room. Do you think you could find your way up? We're rather short of staff.'

He grinned at her. He said: 'I know where number ten is.' He went up the stairway, walked along the passage, tapped at a door. A voice told him to come in.

Callaghan went in. The room was large, comfortably furnished. A fire was burning in the grate. The atmosphere was restful. Irana Faveley was standing in front of the fire. She smiled at him.

Callaghan looked at her for a long time. She looked very attractive. She was wearing an apple green corduroy frock with long sleeves, rust coloured court shoes, beige silk stockings. She wore a single diamond brooch at her throat. Definitely a woman, thought Callaghan.

She said: 'I expect you want a drink, Slim. You must be tired. Can I give you one?'

Callaghan said: 'I'd like a whisky and soda. Incidentally, whether you realize it or not, you're a most pleasing sight.'

'I put this frock on for you,' she said. 'When you telephoned I made up my mind I'd be as attractive as possible.' She made a moue. 'I've an idea that I'm not terribly popular at the moment. I've got to do everything I can to try and make a come-back.'

She went to a side table, began to mix the drinks. Callaghan put his hat, coat and driving gloves on a chair in the corner. He went over to her, took the glass from her, swallowed the whisky. He put the glass on the table.

He said: 'You're dead right, about not being terribly popular at the moment. And you've certainly got to do everything to make a come-back. Only, whatever you did, the come-back wouldn't really be so good.' He stood in the centre of the room, smiling at her.

She went back to the fire. She looked at him for quite a while. She said: 'You were pretty beastly to me the last time I saw you. *Fearfully* beastly. I don't think anyone's ever talked to me like that in my life before. The joke is that for some strange reason you attract me. I suppose it's because you're tough and forcible . . . Anyhow, you'll admit I've done what you asked me to. I've stayed down here as quiet as a small mouse and waited for you to come and release me. Life is a little *too* restful down here, I'm afraid.'

'You didn't do what I *asked* you to. You did what I *told* you,' said Callaghan shortly. 'After all, you hadn't a hell of a choice, had you?'

'Hadn't I?' she replied. There was a touch of the old insolence in her voice.

'No, you hadn't,' said Callaghan. 'But there isn't any need for us to begin an argument. That won't get us anywhere. And there's other business to be discussed. Serious business.'

She raised her eyebrows. 'So!' she said softly. 'Serious business! Serious for whom?'

Callaghan thought: I know just how I'm going to play it with you, my dear. Anyhow, I think you'll fall for the line. So here goes.

He began to lie. He talked in the easy casual voice that he used for lying. Its tone was almost soothing. He said:

'Serious for Paula. You wouldn't like anything *really* bad to happen to her, would you?'

'That depends on what it is,' she said. 'After all, nobody has any sympathy for me. Why should I have sympathy for Paula? Anyhow, what's the trouble . . . and why is it so serious?'

'When Paula first of all began to think about taking the Coronet,' said Callaghan, 'she wrote a letter to somebody or other about it. She said in that letter that she considered taking the Coronet because it might give her a lever to get a better financial settlement with Denys. That letter was in her handwriting, and it was on two separate sheets of notepaper. The second sheet was found by the police under the blotter in De Sirac's room – but *only* the second sheet. That piece of notepaper *might* have been a complete note on its own. It *might* have been written by Paula to De Sirac – that is if she had known him – and being found there, in those circumstances, it isn't very good for Paula. The police might think all sorts of things, mightn't they?'

She nodded. 'Of course they might,' she said. She smiled maliciously. 'And what am *I* supposed to do about that?' she asked.

Callaghan said: 'I've an idea that that second sheet was part of a letter she wrote to you when she first had the idea about the Coronet. I thought *you* might have the first page, addressed to you, *obviously* written to you. If you had it – or even if you remember the letter, that would make things better for Paula. Otherwise the police may begin to make all sorts of unpleasant enquiries. They might come to an entirely wrong conclusion.'

'They might even think that Paula killed De Sirac, mightn't they?' said Irana. 'And that would be too bad!'

'Do you remember the letter?' asked Callaghan. 'Have you still got the first page?'

She shook her head. 'Sorry, my dear Slim,' she said. 'But I don't know anything about any letter. I don't know what you're talking about.'

Callaghan smiled at her. 'That's too bad,' he said. 'It's really *too* bad.'

'I agree,' said Irana pertly. 'It might be very, very inconvenient for Paula.'

'Oh no, it won't,' said Callaghan. He came close to her. 'It's only going to be bad for one person – and that's you. You lying, traitorous little bitch! It's going to be very bad for you!' His voice, almost caressing, made the threat even more effective.

She said: 'What do you mean – you damned trickster? What do you mean?' She was frightened.

Callaghan said easily: 'The police didn't find *any* second page of *any* letter in De Sirac's room. *I* found it. I got there first. Would you like to see it?'

He produced the sheet of notepaper; held it so that she could recognize it.

He said: 'You know what that means, don't you? It means that you're in a hell of a spot. It means that unless you're a very good girl and do exactly what you're told to do, you stand a remarkably fine chance of having that pretty neck stretched. Of being hanged by the neck until you are dead. And you wouldn't like that, Irana, would you?'

She said nothing. She stood, swaying a little, looking at Callaghan with eyes that burned in an ashen white face.

He went on: 'That's scared you, hasn't it, Sweet. And you know exactly why . . . don't you?'

He walked to the side table, poured another drink. He said: 'You'd better sit down and relax. You and I are going to do a little talking. At least I'm going to do the talking and you're going to listen.'

She moved slowly to an armchair by the side of the fire. She sat down. Her eyes never left Callaghan's face. She said in a low voice: 'The trouble about you is that I never know when you're lying and when you're telling the truth. If I did . . .'

Callaghan said: 'That's as maybe. But it's certainly true that I've got that sheet of notepaper and the police haven't – although somebody intended them to have it. That sheet of notepaper was the second sheet in a letter written to you by your sister. She wrote it on the weekend she was away from Mayfield – the weekend she left you down there with Arthur Denys.'

Callaghan took out his cigarette case, lit a cigarette.

'You liked that, didn't you?' he continued. 'That was fine. You'd already arranged with Denys to go off to Laleham with him, and here was a chance of getting close to him. Of showing him how much you loved him and how lucky he would be to be free from Paula. So you gave him her letter. *You gave it to him.*'

She said: 'That's a lie. There never was a letter sent to *me*. I never gave it to Arthur.'

Callaghan said: 'I see. Well, that's going to be very bad for you. It's going to be very bad for you if you *didn't* give that letter to Arthur Denys.'

Her voice was more composed. She said: 'Really . . . why?'

Callaghan lied glibly. He grinned at her. He said: 'I've not only got the second page of that letter. *I've also got the first. It's addressed to you by name.* It was written to you by Paula and you got it. So – if you didn't give it to Denys – *then you killed De Sirac.* Because the person who killed De Sirac left that letter under the blotter for the police to find. The person who left that letter there *must* be the one who killed De Sirac.'

She said hoarsely: 'Where did you get the first page from . . . where did you get it from?'

Callaghan said casually: 'Where I got it from and how I got it is my business. The fact that matters is that I *have* got it. And as you say you didn't give it to Denys, that letter is going to hang you, Sweet!'

She sat looking at the carpet in front of her. Her face seemed drained of blood. She shrugged her shoulders. She said: 'You win, damn you . . . Yes . . . the letter was written to me . . . and I gave it to Arthur . . . I couldn't resist doing that . . .'

Callaghan said: 'Well . . . that's that. So Denys killed De Sirac . . . You knew that anyway. You must have guessed that it was Denys. After all, it was you who *found* De Sirac's body first. You were there even before I was!'

She looked at him dully. 'How did you know that?' she asked. Her voice was trembling.

Callaghan said: 'On the night De Sirac was murdered you went to see him. I guessed you were going to see him. You *had* to see him. I had an assistant watching the place. De Sirac hadn't fallen for the story that I told him about your having returned the Coronet. So he got in touch with Denys – and Denys discovered that the Coronet was gone. Then he put in a claim on the insurance company. De Sirac must have seen the notice in the paper.' Callaghan grinned. 'I bet that burned him up,' he said. 'Here was Arthur Denys going to get a large sum of money from the insurance people and here were you – who had outsmarted De Sirac with my assistance, walking around with the Coronet under your arm. De Sirac must have been very, very annoyed with you. So he got in touch with you too. He told you that unless you handed over that Coronet he would fix you – didn't he?'

Callaghan threw his cigarette stub into the grate.

'So you went to return the Coronet. You let yourself in with a key – because I imagine you've visited that flat many times before – and you found De Sirac dead. You were pretty frightened I should think. You got out of that place as quickly as you could and you went into the nearest telephone call box and rang me. You telephoned me about twelve-fifteen because you *had* to see me the next day. You'd got to get rid of that goddam Coronet somehow. So you thought up another cock-and-bull story for my benefit and handed it over.'

She looked into the fire. 'Why did Arthur have to kill De Sirac?' she said. '*Why* did the damned fool have to do that?'

Callaghan said: 'That one's easy. De Sirac had telephoned Denys after he spoke to you. After you'd said you'd return the Coronet to him. He told Denys that he was going to take the Coronet down to the insurance company and get the thousand pounds the assessors were offering. Well . . . Denys wasn't going to stand for that. He couldn't very well, could he? So he came up to town and saw De Sirac. I bet there was a hell of a scene. I can see those two telling each other all about it. Well . . . one thing led to another and then Denys got really mad and slugged De Sirac with one of the firedogs. Exit one black-mailer. Then you arrived and found the body, while Denys goes off with his girl-friend Juliette de Longues to The Chemin de Luxe Club and does a little gambling. He left the second page of that letter behind because it was going to look as if it was written by Paula. She was going to be the number one suspect for De Sirac's murder. Well . . . ?'

She said nothing. She shrugged her shoulders, looked into the fire.

Callaghan went on: 'You three – Denys, De Sirac and yourself – were a really first-class trio of double-crossers. But Denys was the worst. Denys was a really first-class swine. Listen to this! Leaving that note behind was a swell piece of work. He knew that you were probably going to see De Sirac, and he knew that when the murder was discovered the police might have thought Paula had been to see him too. If Paula got out of that jam then he knew suspicion would fall on *you*. If the police didn't suspect Paula they *had* to suspect you. If she didn't write that letter to De Sirac there was only one other person she would have written it to. Can't you see that – you little mug!'

She muttered: 'My God . . . the cur . . .'

Callaghan said: 'And what about you? The pot calling the kettle black.'

She said: 'What's going to happen to me?'

'I don't know,' said Callaghan. 'With luck I'll get you out of this. Not because I want to, but because of your sister. But there's something you're going to do first.'

'What do I have to do?' she asked. She looked at him suspiciously.

Callaghan said: 'I want a complete statement from you and I'm going to have it. You're going to sit down and write it now. And it's going to be the truth, the whole truth and nothing but the truth. You're going to tell the whole goddam story from the start *in full* – about that letter, about Laleham, about you and De Sirac and you and Denys. It's going to be one hell of a statement, and you'll do it because there's nothing else you can do if you want to save your skin. I've got to *have* it. When I have that I've got *you* – you won't be able to wriggle out or try any more of your lousy tricks.'

She said viciously: 'I'd like to kill you. You . . .'

'I'm sure you would,' said Callaghan. He lit a cigarette.

She got up and went to the side table, poured a drink. She drank the whisky in one gulp.

She said: 'Very well . . . let's do your damned statement . . .'

Callaghan awoke, yawned, looked at the ceiling, stretched, reached for the telephone, spoke to his office on the floor below. He said to Effie Thompson: 'What's the time, Effie?'

'Four o'clock, Mr Callaghan,' she said brightly. 'I wouldn't have you disturbed earlier. Wilkie told me that you didn't get in until six o'clock this morning.'

'Good girl, Effie,' said Callaghan. 'Tell them to send me up some strong tea; then call through to Mr Gringall at Scotland Yard. Tell him I want to see him particularly. It's urgent. Tell him I'll be along in an hour.'

She said: 'Very good, Mr Callaghan.'

Callaghan got up, walked into the sitting-room. He opened the drawer of the writing desk. Inside was Irana Faveley's statement. He took it out of the drawer, glanced through it, grinned, threw it back, locked the drawer.

He switched on the radio. An orchestra was playing a soft, carefully syncopated number. Callaghan listened for a moment, went to

the sideboard, took out a bottle of whisky, drank a little, lit a cigarette, went into the bathroom.

He lay in the bath with the taps running, smoking, looking at
the ceiling.

The first bluff had come off. He began to think about the second
. . . and if that came off . . . the third.

Gringall sat behind his desk, smoking his pipe, looking at
Callaghan. His expression was amiable. Detective-Inspector Marrick,
looking rather grim, leaned against the fireplace, his hands in his
trouser pockets. Callaghan, wearing an expression of deep humility,
sat opposite Gringall. For once he was not smoking.

He said: 'You know damned well, Gringall, that I'm not quite a fool.
But I've very nearly been one. Maybe I've tried to be a bit *too* clever.
I don't know. Anyhow, it looked as if there ought to be a show-down.
Well . . . you know the story. Now it's up to you.'

Marrick said: 'If you wouldn't mind, Mr Gringall, I'd like to hear
what Callaghan told us about the night of the murder. I'd like to hear
that bit again.'

Callaghan said: 'I'll go through the whole goddam thing again.
It's simple enough.'

He thought: It's all right. I'm getting away with it. It's going to
be all right.

He lit a cigarette. He said: 'I've told you I was worried about my
client, Mrs Paula Denys. I'd investigated De Sirac's background and
I'd come to the conclusion that he was just poison. He'd got my client
where he wanted her. He could make a lot of trouble for her. The
main thing I *didn't* want him to do was to go and tell Denys the story
of how she'd employed him to take the Coronet from Mayfield. That
would have made a lot of trouble for Mrs Denys. It might have affected
her divorce. It would certainly have put Denys into a position where
he could make things pretty tough for her. And she's a damned nice
woman. She's not used to dealing with crooks like De Sirac – or even
worse crooks like her husband. You can understand just how I felt?'

Marrick nodded. 'I get all that,' he said.

Callaghan went on: 'I made up my mind I'd keep De Sirac under
observation. On the night he was murdered I had Nikolls watching
the place to see if De Sirac came out. I thought the time was ripe

for him to try something. Well – nothing happened and Nikolls got impatient. He thought he'd see if De Sirac had slipped out. So he walked over the road, went into the apartment and let himself into De Sirac's place with a skeleton key.' Callaghan grinned. 'Nikolls always carries a bunch,' he said. 'When he got inside he found De Sirac dead. You can imagine he got out quickly!'

Marrick said: 'I bet he did.'

'Nikolls didn't know what to do until he'd seen me,' Callaghan went on. 'And I was out on another job. I didn't get back until some time afterwards. When I got to my apartment I found him waiting for me. He told me all about it. So I decided to go there myself and have a look.'

Gringall said: 'You know, Slim, one of these fine days you're going to get yourself in a jam that you can't get out of. You take too many chances – or else you think we're too good-natured.'

'I hope you're going to be good-natured over this,' said Callaghan. He smiled at Gringall. He went on:

'I took a look round and I found the note under the blotter. I recognized it as being in Mrs Denys' handwriting. I thought at first that it was a note she'd written to De Sirac. And then I realized that this was the idea that the person who'd left that note wanted to plant in the hands of the police. I asked myself who else could have received such a letter from Mrs Denys. Well – there was only one person she'd write to like that – her sister Irana. You see Irana knew how unhappy Paula Denys was with her husband. Irana's always disliked him. It was quite obvious to me that Mrs Denys had written that letter to *her*.'

Gringall said: 'I think that's fairly obvious.'

Callaghan nodded. 'I went to see Miss Faveley,' he said, 'and asked her if she received such a letter. She remembered it at once. She remembered it particularly because she'd received it whilst she was actually at Mayfield and because she'd lost it the day after she received it.

'Then I knew. I knew that Denys had it. I realized that he'd recognized the handwriting on the envelope when it arrived at Mayfield, and he'd been waiting a chance to get a look at it. *I realized that Denys had that letter.* That told me a lot.'

Callaghan looked from Gringall to Marrick.

'It told me that if I was right in my guess then Denys knew his wife had the Coronet; that he was playing some game on his own. So I took a chance. I saw Denys and I told him straight out that his wife had the Coronet. He wasn't at all surprised. Of course he wasn't. And it suited him perfectly. He was going to get the insurance money! He gave me a thousand just to remember to forget, and he suggested that when the insurance company paid up there'd be some more. That's fairly clear, isn't it?'

Marrick said: 'It's not only clear. It's obviously the truth. But you were taking a lot of chances, Callaghan.'

Callaghan nodded. 'I know,' he said. 'But what the hell was *I* to do? Well . . . when I saw the note on De Sirac's desk I knew who'd killed him. And I knew *why*. De Sirac knew that Mrs Denys had the Coronet, and he also knew that Denys had claimed from the insurance company. He was blackmailing Denys, who didn't want the Coronet and who did want the money. Denys probably told De Sirac to go to hell, and then I imagine De Sirac said he'd walk along to the insurance company, tell them the story and draw the assessor's reward of a thousand pounds.'

Callaghan shrugged his shoulders.

'That was a bit too much for Denys,' he said. 'He went along to see De Sirac. They had one hell of a row and Denys killed him. He left the second page of the letter he'd stolen from Miss Faveley because that letter was going to plant the whole thing on his wife, and that suited him too. He'd been waiting for a chance to get back at her. Here it was, and he took it.'

An expression of sorrow crossed Callaghan's face.

'I was a damned fool to take that note,' he said. 'I realize that now. I ought to have informed you of the murder at once, instead of waiting until next day. But I was worried. I wanted time to think. You see, I'd been a bit foolish myself. I'd taken that thousand from Denys. That wasn't so good.'

Marrick said: 'I wonder where the first page of that letter is.'

'Denys would have destroyed that,' said Gringall. 'He'd have to do that.'

Marrick said: 'Of course. Well . . . what's the next step, sir?'

Gringall knocked out his pipe. He looked at Callaghan. He said: 'Listen, Slim, I've known you a long time, and I don't dislike you.

Rather the other way. But you've got to take a pull at yourself. You can't go on running that damn detective business of yours on these lines. One of these fine days you're going to get yourself into something that you can't get out of. This isn't the first time, you know. However . . .'

Callaghan got up. 'You're being damned decent,' he said. 'But you always have been, Gringall. And I shan't forget it. Maybe some other time I shall be able to give you a hand . . .'

Gringall said: 'You've got your damned nerve all right. You get out of here and think yourself lucky I'm not doing something serious about you. And you be on tap. Marrick may want you. This thing isn't over yet.'

Callaghan said: 'Well . . . you know where you can get me. I'll be around in case Marrick needs me. Anyhow, my motives have always been good.' He smiled at Gringall. 'Callaghan Investigations always does its best for one and all,' he concluded cheerfully.

Gringall looked at him darkly. 'You get out of here,' he said, 'before I begin to tell you what I really think of you!'

Callaghan grinned. He said: 'You don't have to tell me. I know! So long . . . I'll be around if you want me.'

He went out.

Marrick looked at Gringall. He said: 'Well . . . it all fits in . . .'

Gringall said: 'Denys left Mayfield early on the day that De Sirac was killed. He went to a hotel that night. If he can't alibi himself up to eleven o'clock we've got him. And he can't. The evidence is circumstantial, but it's damned good circumstantial evidence.'

Marrick said: 'Shall I . . . ?'

Gringall nodded. 'Get a warrant and pick him up,' he said. 'And don't waste any time. You can get down there in two hours.'

Callaghan picked up a cab in Whitehall, told the driver to go to Berkeley Square. He paid off the cab on the Bruton Street side of the Square, walked slowly in the direction of his office.

Arrived there, he took the lift up to his apartment. He threw his hat on a chair, lit a cigarette. He walked into the bedroom, went to the private telephone, dialled 'Trunks'. He asked for a Chessingford number. He sat down on the side of the bed smoking. A few minutes passed. Then the bell jangled. Callaghan picked up the receiver. He said: 'Hello . . . Denys? This is Callaghan.'

Denys said: 'Yes . . . What is it?'

Callaghan said: 'You listen to me. They've caught up with you. It's all over bar the shouting.'

'Meaning what?' Denys' voice was almost disinterested.

'Meaning this:' said Callaghan. 'I've just left Scotland Yard. They've grilled hell out of me. They gave me the biggest spring-cleaning I've ever had in my life. They know the whole book. They know you killed De Sirac.'

'Yes?' said Denys. 'That's very interesting. I wonder how they know that?'

'It's not very difficult to guess,' said Callaghan. 'Irana Faveley shot the whole goddam works. She's made a statement. They read it over to me. Believe me, that girl ought to be in the literary business. I've never heard such a story in my life. It's dynamite.'

Denys said: 'Really?'

'Yes,' said Callaghan, 'really. She's disclosed that she gave you that letter she had from your wife. The letter saying that Mrs Denys intended to take the Coronet. Well, apparently, when the police discovered De Sirac's body they found the second page of that letter under the blotter. And it's got *your* fingerprints on it. They showed me the pictures. Well . . . it's not so good. I had to tell them about that thousand you gave me. Naturally, I was in a jam. It looks pretty bad for you.'

Denys did not say anything.

Callaghan went on: 'They've got you just where they want you, Denys. I wouldn't like to be you.'

Denys said: 'So it seems. It was nice of you to telephone. Why?'

Callaghan said: 'I don't like the idea of a man like you being hanged. It's undignified. It's not good, is it? There's a warrant out for you by now, and if I'm not very much mistaken Detective-Inspector Marrick is on his way to Mayfield Place to collect you. It's too bad . . .'

'I'm sorry you feel like that,' said Denys. 'I ought to have known better than to have anything to do with a bastard like you.'

'You're dead right,' said Callaghan. 'You ought to have known a *lot* better. But don't let anything worry you. They treat you awfully well when they're going to hang you in this country. And there's only about three weeks between the sentence and the execution. Besides, the trial ought to be *very* interesting. Even in war-time. All the little tricks you played. All that stuff about Irana and you down at Laleham. What a nice fellow you are, aren't you?'

Denys said: 'So she told them about that too?'

'She had to,' said Callaghan. 'She just opened her pretty little mouth and let it stay open. The words came out on their own. You see, she got the idea in her head that if the police thought *she'd* left that piece of letter there they might even get around to thinking that she'd killed De Sirac. Well . . . she didn't want them to think that. So she talked. They tell me she was down there at Scotland Yard for nearly six hours.'

'She's a nice little thing,' said Denys. 'I'd give a lot to wring her neck.'

'It's a pity you can't,' said Callaghan. 'After all, they can only hang you once, and it's a hell of a shame that De Sirac, she and you can't *all* be put out of your misery. Some *trio!*'

Denys said:

'So you think they're going to hang me?'

'Of course,' said Callaghan. 'They'll hang you because you haven't got the decency to stop 'em. You haven't got enough guts to do anything to stop them hanging you. You'd rather stand for what you'll have to go through at the trial. Just to get yourself a few weeks more life.' Callaghan sighed. 'You make me feel sick,' he said.

'Sorry about that,' said Denys. 'You can imagine how I feel about you, can't you?'

'Yes,' said Callaghan, 'I can. Well . . . so long, Denys. See you on the scaffold.'

'I don't think so,' said Denys. 'Goodbye – and damn your eyes!'

Callaghan hung up the receiver. He stubbed out the cigarette, lay down on the bed. He closed his eyes.

It was seven o'clock when the telephone rang. Callaghan opened his eyes, rubbed them with the backs of his hands, reached for the telephone.

It was Gringall. He said: 'Hello, Slim . . . ? I was a bit worried about you this afternoon. I felt we'd have to take some sort of action about your playing around in this De Sirac business the way you have. But it's all right. This time!'

Callaghan said: 'Yes . . . Why?'

Gringall said: 'Denys shot himself. He left a note. When Marrick got down there this evening he was just a little too late.'

'It just shows you, doesn't it?' said Callaghan. 'Well . . . I think you've been very kind, Gringall. Thanks a lot.'

'Don't thank me,' said Gringall. 'It's just your luck. If Denys hadn't finished himself off you'd have been for it.'

Callaghan sighed. 'I'm so glad he did,' he said cheerfully. 'You can't think . . .'

He hung up the receiver, yawned, went into the sitting-room. He took the bottle of whisky out of the sideboard cupboard, put the neck in his mouth and took a very long swig. He put the bottle down, went to the desk, opened the drawer, took out Irana Faveley's statement, put it in the fire.

He sat down in the armchair and watched it burn.

The triple bluff had worked.

Chapter Thirteen
Unlucky for Nobody

The late September sun was dying behind the trees. The early evening wind stirred the dead leaves that lay on the gravel path that bisected the lawn behind The Crescent & Star.

Callaghan sat on the top step of the wooden flight that led from the back verandah on to the lawn. He had a large whisky and soda in his hand. The fat frog, denizen of the lily pond on the lawn, stuck out his head and watched Callaghan with a bleary eye.

Suzanne Melander came round the verandah from the front of the house. She said: 'Mr Callaghan, there's a lady to see you. She's in the back sitting-room.'

Callaghan asked: 'What sort of lady?'

'*Chic,*' said Suzanne. 'But definitely! And beautiful, it's the one who came before. I personally go for her in a very big way. I wish *I* looked like that. If I did I might get some place. Well . . . are you going to see her, or shall I say you're not at home?'

He finished the whisky. He said: 'I'll go. Just to save you the trouble.'

Paula Denys was standing near the fire in the small sitting-room behind the office. When Callaghan went in he said:

'I think that every time I see you you're a little more beautiful. But I expect you know all about that.'

She smiled. She said: 'That's your opening gambit, isn't it? Just part of the Callaghan technique. Does it make the clients feel important – and happy?'

Callaghan said: 'I wouldn't know. I've never been a client. What can I do for you? And won't you sit down?'

He stood looking at her. His eyes were mischievous.

She sat down. She said: 'I'm staying over at Chievley – only seven miles away – with friends. I thought I'd like to come over and see you. I wanted to say thank you. You've done an awful lot for me. I'm very grateful.'

'Not at all,' said Callaghan. 'After all, we were paid, and between you and me, I rather enjoyed it. I think it was a *nice* case.'

She said: 'It might not have been so nice. And you took an awful lot of chances. If things hadn't turned out the way they did . . .'

'But they did,' said Callaghan. 'By the way, how's Irana?'

'She's on her way to Australia,' she said. 'She's going to make a fresh start. She –'

'God help Australia,' said Callaghan devoutly.

'The Coronet's been sold,' said Paula Denys. 'I'm glad. I should hate to have it.'

Callaghan smiled at her. 'That's fine,' he said. 'So everybody's happy – except Irana. I hope the Australians fall for her line. If they don't she'll probably start a revolution.'

She looked at the carpet. She said: 'I thought, at one time, that you were rather keen on Irana. I thought . . .'

'No, you didn't,' said Callaghan. 'You didn't think anything of the sort. The remark was merely *your* opening gambit. It was my cue to say "No . . . I never liked Irana" – after which you ask me why, and I tell you.' He looked at her and smiled. 'And I don't intend to tell you,' he concluded.

She said: 'You can be very difficult. You're an extraordinary person, aren't you? At one time I thought you were very unscrupulous, very slick, very dangerous.'

'Yes?' said Callaghan. 'And what do you think now?'

She got up. 'I'm not going to answer any questions, Mr Callaghan,' she said. She opened her handbag. 'I've bought you a cigarette case,' she went on. '*I* think it's rather a nice one. I expect lots of other people have given you cigarette cases, but perhaps you wouldn't mind adding this one to the collection.'

She gave him the case. Callaghan looked at it.

'A marvellous case,' he said. 'I shall keep this for special occasions.'

She held out her hand.

'Goodbye, Mr Callaghan,' she said. She smiled at him. Her eyes were misty. 'And bless you, Mr Callaghan!'

She moved towards the door. Callaghan snapped open the cigarette case. He saw what was inscribed inside.

He said: 'Just *one* minute, Mrs Denys!'

Suzanne Melander sat on the top step of the verandah and threw little stones at the frog in the lily pond.

Nikolls – a bottle of lager beer in one hand, a glass in the other – came across the lawn. He said:

'Hello, babe. How's things? Where's the boss?'

She said: 'If you mean Mr Callaghan, he's in the back sitting-room with a client. *I* think she's a very important client. I just looked through the verandah window and I think *he* thinks so too. Also . . . take a tip from me and don't interrupt him.'

'Why not?' asked Nikolls. He began to pour out a glass of lager beer.

'Because, at the moment, Mr Callaghan has his hands full,' said Suzanne darkly. 'And not only his hands. His arms as well.' She made a little hissing noise. 'I'm furious,' she went on. 'He's never kissed *me* like that.'

Nikolls drank the beer. He smacked his lips. 'You ain't ever been a client, babe,' he said. 'With Callaghan Investigations the client is always right.' He poured some more beer.

'When Callaghan Investigations kisses a client,' said Nikolls, 'believe it or not, honey, the client stays kissed – and likes it.'

Suzanne said: 'Pah!'

Nikolls went on: 'I remember some dame in Oshkosh. Was she a honey, or was she? I remember one night I was sittin' on the back porch with this dame . . .'

He stopped talking. She was gone.

'Ah . . . the hell!' said Nikolls. 'One of these days somebody is gonna listen to that story and like it!'

He finished the beer.

THE END

CPSIA information can be obtained
at www.ICGtesting.com
Printed in the USA
LVHW010154010222
709870LV00009B/659